THE JOURNEYS OF McGILL FEIGHAN com-
bine the epic sweep of *The Lord of the Rings* and
the tight suspense of the *Dune* trilogy with the wry
humor and techno-fantastic imagination of *Stranger
in a Strange Land* . . .

Book IV: CLIFFS

Welcome to a world of unlimited possibilities,
in a universe of no escape!

Fourth in the series by
KEVIN O'DONNELL, Jr.

Berkley books by Kevin O'Donnell, Jr.

ORA:CLE

THE JOURNEYS OF McGILL FEIGHAN

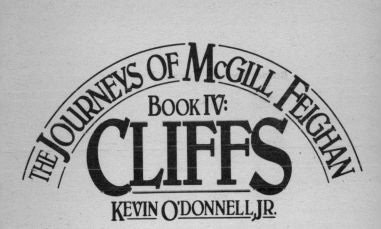

THE JOURNEYS OF McGILL FEIGHAN
BOOK IV:
CLIFFS

KEVIN O'DONNELL, JR.

BERKLEY BOOKS, NEW YORK

CLIFFS

A Berkley Book / published by arrangement with
the author

PRINTING HISTORY
Berkley edition / February 1986

ISBN: 0-425-08387-X

I owe thanks to Mary Kittredge, Mark J. McGarry, and Joel Rosenberg for their helpful comments on earlier drafts of this book; to Melissa Ann Singer and Beth Fleisher for editing it so well; to Howard Morhaim for handling all the business details with his customary skill; to Janet Aulisio for four marvelous McGill Feighan cover paintings; and of course, to my wife Kim Tchang, for her love and her understanding.

To Mark J. McGarry,
for years of friendship,
for moral support and insightful criticism,
and for his dreams of EMPIRE, too,
I dedicate this book with affection and gratitude.

▪ **Chapter 1** ▪

**Tuesday, 22 September 2105
—Thursday, 24 September 2105**

Autumn had officially, if just barely, come to New York. Already the morning wind down Park Avenue drove a hint of winter before it. The day would surely warm up, but at the moment McGill Feighan needed to indulge in a small shiver.

A high, thin voice said, "If you're cold, just think how *I* feel!"

Feighan looked down from his one hundred ninety centimeters at Sam, his three-year-old ward. "A good brisk walk will warm you up."

"I'm not a mammal, McGill, and this is not a brisk walk." Sam lashed his long tail from side to side in irritation; the knife-blade fins that marched the length of his backbone had shriveled in their attempt to conserve his body heat. Eight a.m. light glinted dully off his mottled green scales. "My legs are shorter than yours, even if I do have four of them, so I hafta run to keep up with you and it's just too cold to run. This is a dumb idea, McGill."

"It's only four blocks. And we do need the exercise, kid."

"*You* need the exercise. *I* don't eat half a bag of cookies every night."

"Only 'cause I've got them on a shelf you can't reach."

"*Why* I'm not getting fat isn't the point, McGill." They stopped at a corner for the light to change. A crowd of pedestrians clumped up around them, apparently ignoring Sam's alienness, but keeping an extra centimeter between themselves and him nonetheless. "The point is, you're getting fat, and I'm getting cold because of it." He yawned; his magenta tongue curled out from his sharp-toothed mouth. "Besides, I'm sleepy."

The light blinked to green; the swarm crossed the street. Feighan pointed to the time/temperature sign above a bank entrance. "It's ten degrees Cee, Sam. That's not cold."

"It is if you're a Rhanghan. Why can't you Fling us? It's quicker, it's warmer, and nobody steps on my tail."

"All right, all right." He truly liked the young Rhanghan, and found it hard to deny him anything. Pitching his voice above the roar of an oncoming truck, he said, "If it's chilly tomorrow morning, I'll Fling you."

"Thank you." He drawled the words with enormous dignity.

Feighan laughed.

"McGill!"

"Sorry, kid." He patted Sam on the shoulder. "Listen, do you want me to pick you up this afternoon, or can you make it back to the hotel on your own?"

"I get out at two. Where are you going to be?"

"I'm not sure. I'm on from nine to one and five to nine today. I thought I might go househunting after lunch."

"Are you doing that again?"

"We can't stay at the hotel forever."

"Why don't we just go home?"

"Sam, I—" He caught the rebuke before it broke loose. "I don't want to talk about it, okay?"

"Okay." His tone made clear that he thought Feighan's attitude was silly. "Can you be here at two o'clock?"

"I can."

"Okay. Pick me up, please." They had reached the steps to All Saints School; Sam put a hand on Feighan's belt. "You don't have to walk me to the door, McGill. This is far enough."

"Okay." He remembered, dimly, how it felt when his overly solicitous parents had escorted him inside. Embarrassing, as he recalled it, even if subtly reassuring at the same time. "I'll see you at two, then."

"But please don't be late, okay? I hate to wait out here for you."

McGill Feighan could understand that, too. The probing stares of strangers could prickle like a rash. The energy tunic he wore—the swirling bands of multi-colored light generated by his Flinger implant—drew the eyes of the curious and the comments of the rude, and standing around vulnerable to both discomforted him enormously. He could well imagine the intensity of interest his ward drew, even in ostensibly blasé New York. He smiled gently. "I'll be here. Promise."

"Thanks, McGill." Sam waved as he went up the steps. "See you at two."

Feighan waved back, waited till Sam had disappeared through one of the revolving doors, and closed his eyes. Then he opened them again. After making Sam walk, it would hardly be fair to teleport himself back to the hotel. . . .

Turning, he headed upstream. No longer enveloped in the protective space his ward's rough hide and many sharp teeth had created, he ran into shoulders and elbows and parcels and umbrellas; now and then a misplaced foot thwacked him sharply in the shins.

Sam was right. Flinging did make more sense.

But then, nothing he was doing that autumn seemed to make a whole lot of sense. The hotel, for example. A thousand dollars a night for a two-bedroom suite with a kitchenette. Granted, he could afford it, if not from his salary, then at least from the income generated by his ten million dollar trust fund, but still, why was he paying three hundred sixty-five thousand dollars a year for the roof over their heads? He already owned a penthouse apartment twice the suite's size, and it sat empty.

That is to say, no one currently lived there.

Rather, no one alive lived there.

But Greystein would be there. Marion Jefferson Greystein, McGill Feighan's roommate at the Flinger Academy and best friend ever since. He had helped Feighan scour the city for a suitable residence, had hand-wired all the electronic controls—including Oscar, the apartment computer—had argued with Feighan about carpet piles and furniture styles and the colors of the hangings on the walls. He had livened the place with his laughter and saddened it with his sorrows. His spirit had soaked so deeply into the very fabric of the apartment that the place still trembled with an echo of his essence.

Greystein had gone bad, though. Something had snapped inside him. He took to drink and degeneracy and Feighan himself had had to put him down like a mad dog.

Surely Greystein's ghost stalked the penthouse.

How could Feighan return to that?

By now thoroughly dismal, he reached their hotel. With a shuffling half-step he adjusted his pace to the twirl of its revolving door. The security apparatus built into the entrance arch measured him from forty different angles and compared its findings with data stored at the time he registered. Identifying him, it trained its tranquilizer guns on the next person in line and permitted him to pass unscathed.

Glitterati from a hundred worlds mingled in the lobby; he moved through them like a knife through shadow. No one acknowledged him, though a bell captain stepped out of his way as he walked up to the elevators.

Eighty-eight stories later, he moped down the corridor to their suite. The door stood open.

It should not have.

He tensed: For too many of his twenty-two years a crime syndicate called The Organization had stalked him, hoping to wring from him the truth of his relationship to the Far Being Retzglaran. Though it was a mystery he himself had been trying to solve all his life, The Organization had never believed him. McGill Feighan had learned never to leave a house or a home or even an overpriced hotel suite without locking its doors thoroughly.

He flattened himself against the wall. His hand rested on his jewel-studded leather belt; his mind bubbled with the powers of his Talent.

Gryll, a sub-chieftain in The Organization, had called a truce after their encounter on Actu. If someone from The Organization had violated that truce by invading Feighan's privacy, that someone would regret it for a long time to come. Slowly he peered around the edge of the doorframe, ready to strike.

And then he reddened. No one had broken into his room. A squat, wheeled maid clad in sheet mirrors was dusting the coffee table, first wiping it with a wax-impregnated cloth and then bathing it in ultraviolet light before buffing it to a sheen. The soft scent of lemon hung in the air.

The hotel promised security, and delivered security. It guarded its guests against danger from the macroscopic to the microscopic. If in the process of keeping its promise it had to sterilize the environment, obliterating all traces of occupancy and restoring the room to its original state of anonymity, well, better that than a neurotic billionaire disgusted by a stray hair in the sink.

Feighan did not know if he could take it much longer. He stepped inside. "Are you about done here?"

The maid's cleaning attachments continued to whir, but the middle segment of its three-tier turret spun around to train a camera lens on him. Behind the mirrored panels that cloaked its chips and gears, something clicked. "Mr. Feighan." The voice evoked images of humanity, but was not itself human. "I will be done in fifteen minutes and thirty-seven seconds. Or I could return later. Please specify your choice."

"Come back later." He crossed the room and dropped

into an easy chair. "What did you do with the morning paper?"

"It is on the desk in the right-hand bedroom. At what time will it be convenient for me to return?"

"Any time after nine."

"A.m. or p.m., Mr. Feighan?"

"A.m." He checked his watch. "Forty-five minutes from now."

"Will you be out all day, or will you be returning early, Mr. Feighan?"

"I'll probably be back about one in the afternoon."

"Very good, Mr. Feighan. Your room will be ready for you." It gave the table one last whisk with the buffing cloth, then retracted its attachments and rolled to the door. "Please be certain to attach the chain lock after I leave, Mr. Feighan."

"Sure thing." And when he had, he retrieved the paper and carried it into the bathroom.

At two minutes to nine he dropped the paper on the floor, stood, and stretched. The phone rang.

At a snap of his fingers, an unseen microphone clicked on. He could activate the video display later, if he needed it. "Yes?"

A cool, nearly-but-not-quite feminine voice said, "Director Walking Mule's office here, Mr. Feighan. The director would appreciate your stopping in to see him before you report to work. May I tell him you will be here soon?"

"I'm on my way."

"Very good, Mr. Feighan."

He closed his eyes, the more carefully to visualize his destination: a spacious, well-proportioned reception room, with a soft grey carpet and friendly orange walls and wall-holos of the American southwest. While a portion of his mind held that image steady, another portion built up a picture of himself: a tall young man, broad-shouldered, sporting a Roman nose and tousled black hair. As he overlaid the first vision with the second, he *knew,* though he would never be able to verbalize his manner of knowing, how to place the second picture into the first.

Not difficult, child's play in fact, since the two were so close and their differences so minor, just a tug here and a twist there and—

*PI—

It began: the Fling: the teleporting: in a blackness deeper than blindness, a blackness that wrapped him ineluctably though he grew faster than thought till he curled fetally on the edge of infinity while simultaneously he shrank below the electronic scale and entered the worlds of charm and color and magic—

—and for one instant not of time because it was all of time, he was the entire universe yet none of it—

—and, as always, the contradiction rent him, sparking pain brighter than the greatest of supernovae as half of him went large while the other half went small and the pain would not end because it had never begun—

—and his growing met his shrinking and the two became one, puffing out the fiery candle and—

—NG*

The Fling ended.

Cheery orange walls surrounded him; a soft grey rug supported him. In the holo before him a notocactus tracked the sun's path with dishes of blazing yellow blossoms.

Teleporting directly into Walking Mule's office would have been quicker, but courtesy required him to materialize in the reception area.

Not that he honored all the rules of protocol. Brushing past the simulacrum at the desk, he closed the door on its perturbed squawkings. "Hi, Walking Mule, I got your message. Something up?"

A thousand pillows of a thousand colors and sizes carpeted the floor, rising into mounds where previous visitors had built themselves backrests. In the corner, cross-legged behind a Japanese-style table, sat a middle-aged Amer-

Indian. He lifted his head. Long black braids framed a dark face full of warm brown eyes. "Nothing you don't want to hear, McGill. Have a seat. But keep your shoes off the silk, will you?"

"Sorry." As it was impossible to take another step without treading on at least one of the pillows, he tugged off his shoes and left them by the doorway. Sprawling on a stack of cushions, he laced his hands behind his head. "I am due at my booth in a minute or so, though."

Walking Mule waved a hand. "It looks to be a slow day today, so don't fret about falling behind. Got some good news for you: The final paperwork came back from the Hub, and you are officially cleared. All sanctions against you have been lifted—"

"I thought you lifted them three months ago, when I got back from Actu."

The Director flashed him a glance of annoyance. "Well, *I* did, but you know as well as I do that those paper-pushing desk jockeys back at the Hub have their own ways of doing things. It's taken us this long to get the paperwork cleared up." He narrowed his eyes. "Course, I could have wrapped things up a sight quicker if you hadn't had this strange aversion to being recertified by PsychSection."

Feighan squirmed. Alone of all living Flingers, he—thanks to the electronic wizardry Marion Jefferson Greystein had deployed at the Academy—had successfully escaped a program of mental indoctrination that would, he felt, have deprived him of free will. If PsychSection ever got him on their couches, they would discover this. He refused to give them a second shot at his head. "I appreciate that, Walking Mule," he said softly.

"Well, I sure as hell hope you do, McGill, 'cause I had to do a song-and-dance the likes of which hasn't been performed in this office at any time in recorded history."

The corners of Feighan's mouth curved into a smile. "Did it rain?"

Walking Mule raised his eyebrows.

"Sorry." Feighan spread his hands. "I couldn't resist."

"Next time try harder." But his own lips twitched. "The upshot of it all is, those reprimands my predecessor filled your file with have been removed. You are officially restored to Active Status, which means Personnel now carries you as an employee instead of as an independent contractor, and you are no longer forbidden to leave Earth." He cocked his head. "You have stuck close to home since we got back, haven't you?"

"Actually, yes." He had obeyed, not to conform with the restrictions imposed by Flinger Network Control, but because he could travel almost nowhere in the Network without being reminded of one dead friend or another. "The farthest I've gone was to Gettysburg with Sam, last month."

"You don't know how good that is to hear, 'cause if you had violated the terms of your parole—"

"C'mon, Walking Mule, you know me better than that."

"Yeah, I suppose I do . . ." He fussed with a pile of papers on his table, squaring their edges and placing them to one side. "Now, about this here quest of yours for the Far Being Retzglaran—"

"Since I don't have a clue as to where I should look next—" Feighan shrugged. "And what with tutoring Sam after school and seeing Gina at night, I don't have quite the time to dig clues up that I used to."

Walking Mule nodded. "I can appreciate that. But what I wanted to say was, now that you are officially back in the good graces of the papermongers of the FNC, I've got no problem with your questing. That's as long as you do it on your own time, hear? In fact, I've got a few sources of my own, and once in a while I hear stories that would probably be of more'n passing interest to you. If you like, I'd be happy to repeat them for you."

Feighan sat up straight. "Repeat away."

"I said 'once in a while,' McGill. Truth is, I haven't heard anything since we got back from Actu. But I will keep my ears open, and that's a promise."

"Thank you." He glanced down at his wristwatch. "Uh—"

"I know, you're due at your Booth, and I won't keep you but a few seconds longer." He sighed. "Let me tell you something, McGill. Getting promoted has its good points, and its bad points. Used to be the two of us bumped into each other half a dozen times a day, and I truly got a kick out of jawing with you. Now they've got me cooped up in this office—"

"But you're the best Director we've ever had!"

Walking Mule smiled appreciatively. "Even the best Director's still a boss, McGill, and it seems folks around these parts just don't enjoy dropping in on the boss to pass the time of day. I used to think that line about it's being lonely at the top was a crock. I was wrong."

Feighan had the grace to blush.

"I'm not trying to make you feel like the low-life skunk you undoubtedly are, McGill—" He grinned at his protégé. "—but I don't want you thinking that just 'cause I'm Numero Uno around here I aim to avoid my old friends. I still care about you. Maybe even more'n I did when I saw you six times a day."

"Thank you." A sudden odd congestion in his throat made it difficult to say anything more.

"You're welcome. And now that that's settled, when are you going to have me over? Been a long time since I had any of Oscar's alleged home cooking."

Feighan squirmed. "Well, Walking Mule, I'm not in the penthouse any more—"

"You sold it?"

"Well, no, it's, ah . . ." He could not meet his old friend's steady gaze. "What it is, Walking Mule, is I'm not quite ready to go back."

"Greystein?"

Rolling back on the pillows, Feighan closed his eyes. "Yeah." All Greystein's stuff was still in his room. He knew he should have cleaned it out right away, but that had proved impossible. He had gone in once, intending to get it over with, but just could not touch a thing. He had turned around, closed the door, and walked out—and had not been back since. But how could he explain that to Walking Mule?

The director steepled his fingers and looked over their tips. "You wouldn't be punishing yourself, would you?"

"No, of course not."

"Then I reckon you're depriving yourself of a lot of happy memories on the grounds you might get stung by the melancholy ones."

He shook his head. "No." Happy memories? *The storm wracked the beach, flailing him with winds and cold rain. His crazed friend loomed above him demonic, deadly. Blood ran down Feighan's arm, and still he held off, hoping—* "No, but I do feel guilty—still—because if I hadn't—"

"Somebody else would have, and not with love, either." Walking Mule sighed. "McGill, what I'm trying to say here is that all the wishing and moping in the world won't change the past a bit. If you'd stayed out of the whole thing, you'd still be torturing yourself, only you'd be saying, 'If I'd just gone after him myself, things would have been different.' Well, they wouldn't have been. They'd have been just the same, no matter what. The difference is, the way things are, you know Greystein got every human consideration possible, and then some."

Ball bearings bulleted across the sand. Greystein folded. Rain drained through the hole in his chest and gushed out the other side pink. "Did he?" he said quietly.

"McGill, you figure ol' Greystein would have wanted you to behave like this? I recollect he did a few things he wasn't proud of, but he just went ahead and made the best of what came next. Now, I ain't recommending that you model your behavior after his, but I do think maybe you could learn a little something from it."

There was nothing he could say in reply. "I suppose you're right."

"I am right, and you know it."

"All right, Walking Mule, you're right, and I know it."

"You move back into that penthouse. It's gonna feel mighty strange the first hour you're there, and you might even have to indulge in a little manly weeping when you clean Greystein's things out of his room, but I promise you, it'll wear off, and before you know it—"

"It'll be like Greystein never lived there?" he said bitterly.

"Oh, no." Walking Mule's voice went soft, now. "Oh, not that, not ever. What's going to happen is, um, your perspective will shift. Right now, you hurt because of what you don't have any more. Someday, you're gonna be happy because of what you did have, even if you only had it a while."

He tried a laugh. It did not work very well. "And when will 'someday' be?"

Walking Mule opened his hands. "I don't know. Sometime after you've stopped dodging your past, and started facing up to it."

"Thanks." He stood. "You and Sam have said some things today that . . . Apparently I was doing stuff I didn't realize I was doing. I guess sometimes it takes ah, an impartial observer—"

"Sam and I ain't what you might call 'impartial,' McGill."

"And thanks for that, too." He smiled. "Okay, an outside observer, then. But I'm inside myself, lost in the maze of my own feelings, and sometimes I need you guys to let me know that there is a way out. I do appreciate it."

"Ain't nothing." He tapped his watch. "And unless you got something more pressing, you probably ought to get yourself on down to your Booth, huh?"

"Right." He winked. "Later."

He stepped well away from Walking Mule's desk (because Flinging created the equivalent of a vacuum that tugged at any Flingers left behind, awakening in them a wistful, melancholy, irrational longing to follow in the departing Flinger's wake, and it was rude to so upset another's equilibrium), grabbed his shoes, thought, concentrated, visualized, felt, knew, and—

PING

—materialized inside the control cubicle of Flinger Booth Twelve. He groaned. And got to work.

For all the power of his Talent, McGill Feighan earned his pay like a bus or truck driver did: he transported people and cargo from one place to another. The difference was that he stayed put.

He sat at the console and looked down through the picture window, into a large room with white walls and scuff-marked tile floors. Two pallets, six crates, and four humans—no, three humans and a dark-furred something else—cluttered the mathematical center of the room. He checked the console's screen. Under DESTINATION it read "Hub." Under WEIGHT glowed the numerals "916.9".

He touched the microphone controls. "Hi, folks, sorry I'm late." Now that he was here, in the driver's seat so to speak, he was ready to work. He needed to work. The Talent built up tension, tension that would not dissipate except through exertion of the Talent. "The scale says you have one-point-one extra kilos, if you want them."

The alien in the group swung its cylindrical head from side to side. One of the humans said, "No, we're fine. Thanks anyway."

"Okay. Hold tight." He closed his eyes, visualized the Flop Booth at the Hub, imagined the trillions of girders and panels surrounding it, the long metal corridors, the emptiness that lay outside the artificial world-city . . . Good, good, he had it, it was right; he froze the feeling and parted his eyes to let the image of his freight seep in and overlay the first and as he held the two in juxtaposition, he *felt* how the one belonged around the other, and *knew* how to make it so, and—

PING

Emptiness surged through the huge white room. With frantic precision he held the two images firm in his mind, reached for additional angular momentum into the Energy

Dimension, a hazy, tumultuous non-place that existed everywhere just beyond the bounds of perception, and carefully added the increment to the momentum his freight already possessed. Gently now, easily, expertly, he set the pallets and crates and beings down on a white-tiled floor thirty light-years away, and he knew (though he could never say how) that they had not even bumped.

He let his breath out and made ready to do it again.

So the morning went.

Fling.

And Fling again.

Twelve times an hour. All morning long. Never once leaving his chair.

The digits shifted on the clock built into his console. One p.m. The readout informed him that no one waited in line for transport elsewhere. He could break, now; he had four hours to himself. He had to pick Sam up at two, but until then he had plenty of time for lunch, or a nap, or... *or for a quick run to the penthouse just to make sure everything's in order ...*

A warm, happy voice broke into his thoughts. "Hi, McGill."

He straightened up. "Gina!"

Gina Maccari, the NAC Staff Telepath, swept swiftly, gracefully, across the room and dropped a kiss on his upturned lips. Stocky, and a full head shorter than he, she had silken black hair and a smile that delighted him all the way to his toes. Today she wore a black suit and an ivory blouse, and wore them very well indeed. "Lunch?"

"Sure." *Plenty of time for the penthouse later ...* "I do have to pick Sam up at two, though."

"The three of us can have lunch together, then."

"You don't mind?"

"Having Sam along?" Her brown eyes widened. "Don't be silly. Do you?"

"Ah, no ..." It was not that he minded taking Sam along; it was that afterward Sam, still very much the child, would indubitably tease him. And it was not that he wanted to deny having a girlfriend. It was that he could tolerate the squeaky sing-song "Muh-Gi-ill has a girlfriend, nyaah nyaah nyaah nyaah nyaah" only so many times before he would begin to fantasize about how much fun he would have wrapping an entire roll of adhesive tape around his ward's snout. "No, it sounds good to me."

Hands on his shoulders, she peered over the top of his head to his console clock. "One-oh-five... I have some paperwork to clear up; why don't you come by my office about tive to two and pick me up?" She kissed him again, hugged him, and headed out the door.

Feighan felt adventurous. When he and Maccari materialized outside Sam's school, he said, "What'll it be? Chinese, Italian, Mexican—"

Maccari raised a hand. "Mexican."

"Are we going to lunch?" said Sam.

"You got it."

"But I *ate* lunch already. In the barfateria."

To Maccari, Feighan said, "Mexican it is."

PING

Even as they materialized outside the cantina in Acapulco, Feighan frowned down at his ward. "Sam."

"I know, McGill, you don't like me to call it that, but the food is *awful!* You know the fat old lady who dumps the stuff on our plates?"

"How could I forget her?" Sam had been talking about "the fat old lady" since the first day of school. Apparently she was convinced that someone as far from his native world as Sam would starve to death on Earth unless someone else made sure he got enough to eat. He claimed she not only filled his plate beyond its capacity, but slipped him candy bars on the side. "What'd she do today?" Feighan led them into the restaurant.

"Well, usually she puts a spoonful on your plate and says, 'More?' Today she says, 'I'm sorry,' puts *half* a spoon-

ful on the plate, and then says, 'You can have more if you
want it, but I don't remo—'" Magenta tongue flicking in
frustration, he tried again. "'—recommend it.'"

A translucent simulacrum in a serape that swirled just
on the edge of visibility escorted them to a booth. Gina
said, "Was she right?"

Sam rolled his eyes. "I was the only kid at my table who
took a second bite."

"And a third and a fourth too, huh, kid?" said Feighan
teasingly.

The Rhanghan child shrugged. "I was hungry."

"So after you finished yours, how many other plates did
you clean, my hollow-legged little ward?"

"Well, *somebody* had to! There's this mean old man who
stands by the place where you leave your trays? And if you
haven't eaten your lunch, he makes you sit down where he
can watch you and finish it all. You can't go out and play
until you do."

"All of which is to say, Gina, that young Sam here had—
what, eight servings? Nine?"

"There were only six kids at my table, McGill."

"Six servings." He shook his head and clucked solemnly.
"I'll bet the poor boy doesn't even have room for chocolate
cake."

Sam slapped Feighan's shin with the tip of his tail. "I
always have room for chocolate cake!"

He smiled at his ward. "Ready to order, Gina?"

She nodded, told her menu what she wanted, and slipped
it into its slot in the table. Feighan followed suit, then looked
from Sam to Maccari. "I, uh, have an announcement to
make."

They looked at him expectantly.

He found it difficult to meet Maccari's eyes: She had
always had a special soft spot in her heart for Greystein,
and he was not sure how she would take the news. "Unless
there are major objections, I figure Sam and I ought to move
back into the penthouse—"

Sam whooped in delight, drawing the stares of a dozen nearby diners. Embarrassed, he slipped down in his chair. "Sorry, McGill."

"Apology accepted—this time. Don't do it again."

"All right."

"As I was saying, we need a place to live, I haven't found anything suitable anywhere, and the penthouse is empty. So-o-o. . . ." He took a breath, glanced at Maccari, and to his great relief found a sympathetic smile on her face. "We missed check-out time at the hotel today, so we might as well stay there one more night—but tomorrow we move back home."

Maccari reached across the table and took his hand. "Congratulations," she said softly.

"Congratulations?" It seemed an odd thing to say.

"On making a *very* tough decision. I know what you've been going through, and—and congratulations."

"Thanks."

"You're welcome." She leaned back in her chair with a thoughtful expression. "We'll have to have a celebration. How long will it take to get Oscar back in harness?"

"I don't know. A couple of minutes? I don't see why it would take much longer than that."

"Okay! Friday night, then." Before he could say a word, she held up a finger. *"After* you get off shift." She turned to Sam and stroked his skullplate gently. "You going to be free nine-thirty Friday night, kiddo?"

The nictitating membranes of Sam's eyeballs slid up and down as he pushed his head against Gina's fingers. "As long as we have lotsa cake, I'll be there."

Wednesday afternoon, Feighan picked Sam up at school. "Got everything?"

"You bet, McGill. Are we—"

PING

They materialized on the marble-topped Flop Table in the corner of the living room. The apartment was spotless, with every piece of furniture in its proper position and not a speck of dust visible anywhere. The air tasted pure but exhausted, as though the cleaning machines had stolen a bit of its vigor on every cycle.

Sam hopped down off the table and raced around the living room, scrambling up over the onyx force couch and crowing with joy.

Feighan stood still for a long moment, afraid to move. Only three months had passed since he had last stood on that tabletop, but they seemed like years.

Sam dashed into the kitchen. Chairlegs scraped on the floor and cupboard doors slammed. "Hey, McGill, there's no food!"

An involuntary smile broke the set of his lips. He stepped down. "Be grateful for that, Sam. Think what the place would smell like if Oscar hadn't cleaned everything out."

The kitchen door swung outward and Sam appeared. "Well, are you going to order more? Huh?"

"Didn't the fat old lady feed you today?"

Sam scuffed all four of his feet on the carpet. "Well, yeah, sure, she did, but that was a long time ago, McGill. Can I help it if I'm hungry again?"

"You keep eating this way, your underbelly's going to be scraping the sidewalks, you know that? And you don't have any armor there, either."

"My legs aren't *that* short!"

"Oh, yeah? Let's just see how much clearance you have here." He dropped to his knees by Sam's side and pretended to measure the distance between Sam's stomach and the rug. "A centimeter, tops. Not a millimeter more. You gain one more kilo, kid—"

"McGill! I got lots more room than that. I got more than you do!"

"Only when you suck it in. And you don't do that unless I do this." He threw his right arm over Sam's back and began to tickle the child ferociously. "Hah? What do you say to that?"

"McGill! Please!" The young Rhanghan squealed in delight. "Stop! Help! Police!"

Feighan said, "Oh no—"

"The resident Sam has called for emergency assistance," rang a metallic voice. "This computer will now summon the police."

That was not precisely true: To enable household residents to cancel false alarms before a wave of uniformed cops poured into the living room, Greystein had programmed in a delay loop that prevented Oscar from notifying the police for ten seconds. Hastily, Feighan said, "Tell Oscar to cancel, Sam."

The child laughed. "It would serve you right, McGill!"

Feighan glared at him.

Sam retreated a step. "Okay, okay! Oscar, cancel: Please do not call the police, I am all right, everything's fine; do it now."

"Very well," said the apartment computer. "Mr. Feighan, you were due at the Flinger Building fifteen minutes ago. Do you require medical assistance?"

About to protest, Feighan remembered that Oscar was still programmed with his—and Greystein's—old schedules. "No, I don't need a doctor, Oscar." He turned to Sam. "Why don't you go amuse yourself? I have to update Oscar on our new routines, order some groceries, make sure everything's all as it should be."

"Can I watch the hovee?"

"Sure. But keep the volume down, huh?"

"Okay." He scampered off to the kitchen.

Feighan crossed the room to a closed door. He leaned against its frame. *You can't keep avoiding it,* he told himself. His hand shook as he turned the doorknob. *Aw, jeez.* He stopped. Drawing himself up straight, taking a deep breath, he marched into Greystein's old bedroom.

It hurt. Oscar should either have let the dust accumulate here, or gone all the way and packed up Greystein's books and tools and electronic projects. As it was, the soldering laser lay next to a half-finished circuit board, the glowing CRT displayed an intricate schematic, and the whole place was so damn clean that it seemed Greystein would surely be back in a few minutes.

But he would not.

Ever.

Tears welled up Feighan's eyes. He tried to blink them back, to set his jaw and wait for the emotion to subside, but everything in the room conspired to evoke memories. In the middle of Greystein's desk, a holocube commemorated their graduation from the Academy: They stood in early summer sun, arms around each other's shoulders, mortarboards tilted rakishly and the spinning bands of their energy tunics gleaming through their gowns. On the bookshelf, the souvenir beer mugs: They had taken a week's vacation and partied their way through Munich's *Oktoberfest* together. In the corner, an incubator: Greystein had built it to ensure the successful hatching of the egg a Rhanghan named Sahaang had given Feighan, the egg from which Sam had emerged.

Feighan sat heavily on the edge of Greystein's bed. His lips trembled. He could not hold back any longer. Giving a giant sob, he buried his face in his hands. *It's all my fault. I'm a jinx. My parents, my best friend...Rothono and Nadia and all the rest, all dead...Everybody I touch dies! Oh, God, it's just not fair!* Nor was it true, and he knew it, but as he rocked back and forth, grieving for his lost friend, his lost innocence, he could not make himself believe it.

"Ah, Greystein, I miss you so damn much..."

He slept poorly that night. He lay tense and wakeful for what seemed like hours before he finally dropped off. And when he had, when his eyes finally closed for the last time, he began to dream.

Sheer white cliffs rose on either side of him. Two hundred meters tall, they stretched into infinity fore and aft. Below, a thin ribbon of water sparkled in the spring sun.

His chest muscles ached with fatigue. He wanted to stop, to rest on the cliff top, chew the seeds in the pouch at his waist, and work on his latest carving. He could not. He had to keep moving.

All around him wheeled clouds of oversized birds. He knew them: his father and mother at twelve o'clock high, his nestmates strung out on either side of his wingtips, the rest of the flock enclosing them all in a great feathered shell.

Those he did not know, he recognized, except for one. He could not attach a name to that beak, though it seemed as familiar as the rest. Larger than most, and golden, it banked suddenly, and soared before him. It spoke with a voice from another world. It was a human voice, a voice that once belonged to a man named Greystein. As it tacked back and forth in his path, it moaned, over and over, "Come to Rehma, I need you!"

· Chapter II ·

Thursday, 24 September 2105

Nathaniel Davis, who thought himself a clever man, derived enormous pleasure from the sheet of paper that lay beside the platter of croissants on the force desk of his cabin. The puns delighted him.

OPERATION PLAYGROUND

1) Sub-operation **Draft**	Agent White	COMPLETE
2) Sub-operation **Needle**	Agent Silver	COMPLETE
3) Sub-operation **Haystack**	Agent Tan	RUNNING
4) Sub-operation **SNAFU**	Agent Red	RUNNING
5) Sub-operation **Featherduster**	Agent Lime	READY
6) Sub-operation **Mintmaker**	Agent Gold	READY

He nodded to Green and Red, who sat on the other side of his desk. "Gentlemen, we are off to an excellent start. I remind you: Operation PlayGround's success, and The Organization's very security, depend on you. The penalties for failure are . . . unimaginable." He smiled. Evilly.

· Chapter III ·

Thursday, 24 September 2105
—Saturday, 26 September 2105

Feighan woke up panting. His pectoral muscles hurt, as though he had done a thousand push-ups overnight. Despite Oscar's fine hand on the temperature controls, sweat soaked his twisted sheets. Morning light poured through the unpolarized windows; he groaned.

Oscar said, "Wake-up call number three. It is 7:25 a.m. You must get Sam to school by eight o'clock. Get up, Mr. Feighan. It is nine degrees Celsius in New York City under cloudless skies. It is 7:26 a.m. Time to get out of bed."

Yawning, stretching, gasping at the stiffness that held his upper body in thrall, he lowered his feet to the floor and stood up. Maybe coming back had been a mistake. Three months in the hotel and not once had he writhed through dreams like *that*. Jesus. If he was going to have to put up with that sort of stuff every night, maybe he should find another place to live.

No, he thought. *Give it a few more days.* He had, after all, expected that moving back to the penthouse would detonate a few psychological land mines. While he had hardly anticipated giant golden birds begging with the voice of a dead friend, he had tried to brace himself for something unusual—and traumatic.

The shower sprayed him with chill needles. He shivered. "Oscar, order: Make the water four degrees warmer; do it now."

"Yes, Mr. Feighan."

The water heated instantly. "Ah, yes..."

Sam's scaled green snout parted the shower curtains; his transparent inner eyelids sealed protectively against the mist. "Morning, McGill."

"Morning, Sam."

"Are you going to eat before we leave?"

"I hadn't planned on it. Should I?"

"No! I don't want to get there late." He tugged the curtain closed and walked away.

Gingerly, wary of his sore muscles, Feighan soaped his chest. Jesus, it ached. He had probably been flapping his arms all night long. Weird. Stray images still flickered through his mind—he could still see, from the corner of his eye, the flow of white-spattered cliffs and the wink-blink of sunlight on moving water.

Disturbed, he eased his face into the spray. The dream should have dissipated under the shower's relentless pounding. Could it be more than it seemed?

A thoroughly modern twenty-second century American, he would die of embarrassment before admitting that he sometimes thought his dreams spoke to him. Or rather, he thought that sometimes Somebody spoke to him through his dreams. He suspected it was either the Far Being Retzglaran Itself, or one of the Far Being's emissaries, like the giant gastropod that had so thoroughly complicated his life by kidnapping him at birth. What McGill Feighan could never resolve, even to his temporary satisfaction, was *why* Someone should be speaking to him. Not once had he received an explanation. At most he awoke with a feeling, an impetus, that lingered with him long after he would have forgotten a regular run-of-the-pillow dream.

Of course, he thought, as he reached for a fluffy black

bath towel, early twenty-first century types would have died before conceding that teleportation, telepathy, and telekinesis had any basis in reality. It had taken the arrival of the Flinger Network Control exploratory ship to open that aspect of nature to the world. And even in 2105, years after that first ship had swung into orbit around the planet, years after alien merchants, diplomats, and tourists had begun to roam the Earth, millions of people insisted that it was all a hoax, perpetrated either by Hollywood holo-makers in pursuit of publicity, or by power-mad politicians trying to impose world government on the independent nation-states.

So . . . maybe they were not just-plain-vanilla dreams. Maybe Somebody was sending him messages, instructions. And if so . . .

Maybe I ought to go to Rehma.

He had been there once, three years ago, for perhaps five minutes. He—

"Hey, c'mon, McGill, I'm gonna be late!"

"Just a minute, Sam."

A comb and a brush beat his unruly black hair into relative submission. He dressed quickly, easing into his favorite white pants and his knee-high black boots. He pulled on a cable-knit white sweater because any other color would muddy the bright hues of his energy tunic. Then he hurried into the living room.

Sam waited by the Flop Table, bookbag in his six-fingered hand. "You know, you're pretty slow in the morning, McGill."

"Insulting someone who's twice your size and grouchy to boot is not the sign of a real quick mind itself, Sam."

The Rhanghan child thought that one over for a moment, then gave a sheepish smile. "Sorry, McGill."

"Right." He frowned down at his ward. "You got everything?"

"You bet!"

"Can I ask a question?"

"Sure."

"How come you want me to Fling with you, instead of me just Flinging you to the front door?"

"It feels better."

"What feels better?"

"Flinging." His saurian features scrunched up in thought. "Flinging alone is scary. All the stretching and the lights—it hurts! I mean, I know it's gonna be over soon, and when you're with me it's okay, but when I go alone I'm afraid the monsters are gonna get me."

"The monsters?"

"Yeah! They're just waiting there to gobble you up, and they scare me."

"Sam, there aren't any monsters out there."

Sam cocked his snout and looked Feighan in the eye. "McGill, I know when something wants to hurt me. And you know I know, right?"

He had to admit that that was true. "But—"

"Well, when we Fling, I *know* that there are monsters right around the edge and they want to hurt us. But since you're there, they can't." He twitched his tail from side to side. "And it's getting late, can we go now?"

"Sure, kid." Puzzled, he took Sam's hand into his own, closed his eyes, visualized, felt, knew, and—

*PI—

At the last instant before Flopping he sensed that someone/thing else occupied the spot where he intended to materialize, so he swerved a couple of meters into emptiness and—

—NG*

A little girl with dark blonde pigtails and a faceful of freckles squealed as they appeared at her side. Blue eyes widening, she backed away, pointing, her mouth opening and closing. She bumped into Sister Mary Margaret, the elderly principal of All Saints School. "Help me, S'ter, help!"

The nun glanced sharply in their direction. When she recognized Feighan and Sam, she sighed. "Now,

Winona—" She bent down to speak to the little girl. "—mind your manners. Sam is a very nice young . . . student who just started in our kindergarten. And I'm sure Mr. Feighan, who is a Flinger and Sam's guardian, never meant to frighten you." Lifting her head, she impaled Feighan with her gaze. "Did you, Mr. Feighan?"

He felt like he was seven years old again, and about to be kept after class. "Of course not, Sister." He smiled at the little girl. "Winona, I'm very sorry I startled you by popping up at your side that way. Let me introduce you to Sam."

Winona clung to Sister Mary Margaret's skirt. "Does he bite?"

Sam slapped Feighan's calf with his tail. "McGill! Did you—"

"Hush, Sam."

"He talks!" said Winona in astonishment.

"Of course I talk!"

"His problem," said Feighan dryly, "is *not* talking."

Sister Mary Margaret restrained a laugh. "The bell is about to ring," she said sternly. "And children who are not in their seats when the bell rings will stay in their seats after school."

"Yes, S'ter," they both said in unison. Winona vanished through the doorway. Sam said, "Pick me up at two?"

"Sure."

"Okay. Bye." He followed the little girl into the building.

That left Feighan standing alone with the nun, while hordes of small children streamed past on either side. "You do make a rather dramatic entrance, Mr. Feighan."

"And I am sorry for frightening Winona, Sister." He felt perfectly foolish. "I'm sure you realize it wasn't intentional—"

"Yes, Mr. Feighan, I realize that."

"It's just there's no private place around here for me to Fling to."

"Why do you Fling here, Mr. Feighan? There are other

means of transportation."

"For one thing, it's quick. I'm not a morning person, Sister, and this lets me sleep as long as possible."

"Sam is a remarkably bright young... person, Mr. Feighan. Is it necessary for you to accompany him every day?"

"Necessary?" He squirmed. He *hated* being grilled by nuns. He always felt guilty, even when innocent. "Believe me, Sister, I wouldn't be doing it if I didn't think it was necessary."

She raised her thin eyebrows. "Why is it necessary, then?"

"Because... Well, for one thing, Sam draws a lot of attention here. New Yorkers are pretty cosmopolitan, but they're not really used to Rhanghans. You saw how Winona ran away from him. I mean, he's just a kid. That sort of thing hurts."

"Given that you're raising him as an American, don't you think that is the sort of thing to which he should become accustomed? Please don't misunderstand me, Mr. Feighan. I applaud your concern for his tender feelings—but he'll encounter xenophobia for the rest of his life. Shouldn't he be developing a resistance to it now, when he's still young?"

Feighan shrugged. "Maybe. I'd guess he gets a fair exposure to it from his classmates, but maybe he needs more. I don't know. Do you?"

Somewhere in the depths of the building a school bell rang shrilly. Sister Mary Margaret's eyes swept the street for stragglers. "At recess we let the children on the playground. Inevitably fights break out, especially between the little boys. We intervene, of course—but not immediately. Life poses certain hazards to all of us, Mr. Feighan, and survival demands that we be prepared to deal with those hazards. Do you understand what I'm saying?"

"Yes, Sister." He sighed. "I'll think about it. And now, if you'll excuse me—"

"Of course. I am glad we had this talk."

"Yes, Sister." He nodded—

PING

—and materialized on his living room Flop Table. "Sheesh!"

"Mr. Feighan," said Oscar, "while you were out, Ms. Gina Maccari telephoned. She asked that you return her call at your earliest convenience."

"Thanks, Oscar." He strolled over to the phone and tapped out her number.

She answered on the second ring. "Hello?"

"Hi, beautiful. It's me."

"Hi." Her voice smiled. "I forgot to ask last night, are we doing anything this weekend?"

"Sure." He blinked. "Uh . . . what would you like to do?"

"Oh, I . . ." It was her turn to sound vague. "I was hoping you had a brilliant idea or two up your sleeve."

"Well . . ." He ran through the possibilities in his head— *ballet, symphony, Broadway, ball game* . . . Unexcited, he looked out the window, looked over the rooftops and into the shadow-deep streets, the *white cliffs and tumbling water*—

He jerked away in alarm. Why did the image still haunt him? Then: *Why not?* "Gina, have you ever been to Rehma?"

"The birdworld? No, why?"

"Umm . . ." He would tell her of the dream in person— the message demanded a better medium than the telephone. "I was there once, for just a few minutes, and it seemed pretty nice. I was thinking it might be fun to spend some time there."

"That sounds marvelous! Do we need visas?"

"*I* don't—"

"You Flingers never do."

"—but you and Sam probably do. Do you want to check on it?"

"All right. But I'll have to get back to you this evening, because I won't be in to work today."

"Why not?"

"I had my physical the other day, and they called me

back in for some more scans. They think I might have a tumor."

She might toss it off that nonchalantly, but it rocked him. His stomach felt suddenly hollow; his voice shook. Did all his friends have to die young? "Gina, I didn't—I didn't know."

"Neither did I, silly, so how could you?"

"No, I mean—geez, I feel awful, I—"

"McGill Feighan, you stop that this instant. It's not like I'm dying."

"But tumors are—I mean, they're serious, Gina, and—"

"McGill, if it were large enough to be serious, they would have picked it up on the first scan. The doctor said if there is one, it's no bigger than the point of a needle right now. Which is why I'm going back in; they're going to look for a needle in a Maccari."

"That's not funny."

"Sorry." But she sounded annoyed, not apologetic. "Look, McGill, I'll call you after I get out of the lab and let you know what they found—okay?"

"Sure." He decided to buy a videophone, so he could blow kisses at the screen when he talked to Maccari. "You take good care of yourself, now, you hear?"

"Will do. And you do the same. Bye."

"Bye."

The receiver clicked, then hummed vacantly. He paced the length of the living room, hands behind his back, head bowed, knowing it was futile to worry so early and without definite cause, but also knowing that he could not help but worry. He always worried about people for whom he cared, and he cared a great deal for Gina Maccari. If anything happened to her . . . Through eyes that were suddenly misty he stared into a bleak future. Then shook his head. And sniffed.

"Oscar, query: Brief overview of the planet Rehma, R-E-H-M-A; answer it now."

The apartment computer's speaker snicked briefly in response to a flurry of electronic signals within. "Searching, Mr. Feighan." It emitted a high-pitched, almost inaudible, whine, then said, "Rehma. The fourth planet of a star moderately larger and brighter than our own sun, with surface gravity and illumination levels comparable to Earth's. The dominant life form is a large, intelligent avian. The planet has an oxygen-based atmosphere capable of supporting Terran life; humans cannot, however, subsist on Rehmal food due to differences in protein structure.

"Rehma has one massive super-continent—"

"Oscar, interrupt." The machine would reel off ever finer detail until it ran out of databank entries. That could take days. "Oscar, query: Does Rehma have associations with the Far Being Retzglaran; answer it now." Because if his dream of the previous night were more than just a dream, then—

"Yes." It paused briefly, presumably while its program determined which sentences from the reference banks it should include. "The Far Being Retzglaran is the traditional deity of the planet. Legend has it—"

"Oscar, interrupt." Better and better. He could query Oscar in greater detail later on, but for now he would just close his eyes, concentrate, visualize, feel, know, and—

PING

The orange walls beamed down at him, while the grey carpet yielded to his feet. The notocactus in the hologram had opened two new flowers in the last day.

This time he stopped at the receptionist's desk, and asked the simulacrum if Walking Mule was free.

"One moment, Mr.— Feighan."

It vanished, then reappeared. "Go right ahead, Mr. Feighan."

"Thanks." The door opened before he reached it, and closed without his laying a finger on the knob. "New software, hey, Walking Mule?" He tugged off his boots before he left the patch of clear carpet by the doorway.

"New software?" The director frowned at Feighan. "No, I—you mean the self-opening door?"

"Yeah, it's never done that before."

"You never checked with the receptionist before."

"Oh." Chastened but not subdued, he moved into the middle of the room. "In that case, your old software has a bug in it. Your receptionist fades out of view when it checks if you're available."

"Damn." Walking Mule slapped the top of his table in annoyance. "Does it disappear completely, or just go dim for a second?"

"You lose it completely."

The director shook his head. "That gizmo's been nothing but trouble since I took over here. Had the techs up half a dozen times in the last month alone."

Standing on a fat red cushion, Feighan shifted his weight from one foot to the other. It was like having his feet massaged. "Why don't you get a human?"

"A human? Say, boy, you been out in the sun too long? You got any idea what a living, breathing receptionist costs?"

"Haven't the foggiest. Your predecessor had one, though."

"And my predecessor damned near bankrupted the NAC."

"There is that. Anyway. Sorry to bother you, but the reason I dropped in was because you asked me to keep you informed of my movements."

"You going somewhere?"

"On my own time, yes." At the older man's nod, he continued. "This weekend, Gina, Sam and I are going to visit Rehma."

Walking Mule brightened. "You're kidding!"

"No, why?"

He held up a sheet of paper. "The Hub just requested our assistance. Some sort of sickness is going around on Rehma and a bunch of the local Flingers have come down with it. They say outbound traffic's backing up something fierce. The Rehma consortia are looking to hire other Flingers on a temporary, fill-in basis. They are offering one helluva premium."

It seemed entirely too coincidental to Feighan that he should dream of Rehma just when that planet needed his Talent. "I said 'weekend,' Walking Mule. As in, 'on my days off'?"

"I heard you just fine, McGill—but how'd you like to spend a couple weeks there, starting Saturday?"

He knew at once that he wanted to—but his eagerness troubled him. He would be leaving just when Maccari would most need a friend. Would she understand? Or would she think he was rejecting her because of the cancer? The possibility that he might be doing exactly that, all the while hiding his true feelings even from himself, set off a pang of guilt. He had to admit that cancer scared him. "Well—"

Walking Mule fixed a shrewd gaze on him. "Gina, right?"

"What, do you know everything?"

"Not quite, but I'm workin' on it." He folded his hands on his tabletop. "Look, this here surgery's pretty much routine, McGill. Like having a tooth pulled, only quicker and safer. She'll be just fine—and besides, you can always Fling back to look in on her."

"Yeah, but—"

"McGill, they got close to a thousand tourists stranded on Rehma already, and the number's going up by the hour. They need help in a real bad way. As a favor?"

He could not refuse. His conscience still niggled at him, but Walking Mule was right. The Rehmal Minders could keep tabs on her, and Feighan could visit at will. "All right. Anything I should know before I leave?"

"Nothing your computer can't dig up for you." He rattled the sheet of paper. "I'll get you a copy of this; it's got the terms of your employment there, and the name of your local contact. I'll also scrounge around for a couple addresses and phone numbers of Terran residents on Rehma who might have some leads for you—which you will follow only on your own time, right?"

"Scout's honor, Walking Mule."

"You were never a Boy Scout."

"Are you saying I don't have as much honor as a Boy Scout?"

The Director made a face. "Okay. You better— oh, one other thing."

"What's that?"

"The Rehmal are a proud people—"

"Walking Mule, I'm not planning to take a book of bird jokes!" It offended him that the Director could think him so insensitive.

Walking Mule shook his head impatiently. "That's not what I meant. See, this situation sort of worries me. Something's going around Rehma that's incapacitated a whole lot of Flingers, and we're pretty damn tough. Hell, the FNC immunizes its people against more things than're listed in most medical dictionaries."

That had not occurred to Feighan. "Do you think they have something new there? Some kind of mutated virus?"

"Could be. If it is, they could be in real trouble. See, some cultures just don't like to admit that they've lost control, and they hold off calling for help till it's too late."

"You're making me nervous, Walking Mule. Is that what's going on?"

The Director shrugged. "Truth to tell, McGill, I don't know. But you'll be there on the scene. If you think they need help, and pride or whatever's keeping them from hollering for it, then get in touch with Thurndriddle, at the Hub. You remember ol' Thurny, don't you?"

"The Ylsslypn guest lecturer at the Academy? Sure, I do. I had to keep it wet that time its automatic mister broke down." Ylsslypni absorbed atmospheric oxygen through their skin, but the pores closed up if they dried out—or if they were totally submerged. Feighan had stood in a shower stall with the wrinkled grey alien for the better part of the night, adjusting the spray at its command. "But why get in touch with it?"

"Thurny's latest title is Senior Flinger for Emergency Assistance. It's in charge of dispatching all disaster relief teams. If things get out of hand on Rehma, talk to Thurny." He glanced at his watch. "And get to work, now."

"Right. And, Walking Mule, thanks, huh?"

He winked at Feighan. "My pleasure, McGill."

At lunch time he hurried home. Maccari had not yet called. "Oscar, order: Two ham sandwiches, on rye, swiss cheese, lettuce, brown mustard, mayo; do it now."

"Coming right up, Mr. Feighan. Something to drink?"

"Ah . . . milk."

"Very good, sir. Breakfast nook or dining room?"

"Breakfast nook."

"Yes, sir. In ninety-two seconds."

"Good. Also, Oscar, query: More information about Rehma; answer it now."

With the information it had gathered earlier still in its cache memory, the computer did not need to access a data-bank before replying. "The planet possesses one massive super-continent and hundreds of rocky island chains. Ninety-five percent of the one billion–plus population live on the mainland. Given the choice, the average Rehmal would rather eat grain than fish."

Feighan wandered into the kitchen, washed his hands at the sink and dried them on a towel that the apartment computer thoughtfully extruded from a slot above the faucets.

Meanwhile Oscar continued. "Culturally, the Rehmal share a common language spiced by scores of local accents almost distinct enough to be called dialects. The language has not diverged further because wings offer the natives a degree of mobility unknown to land-bound life."

"That makes sense," said Feighan, mostly to himself.

"Lunch is served, Mr. Feighan."

A panel in the wall hissed up to reveal a plate of sandwiches. Feighan took it, waited for the panel to close, and for it to reopen again with his glass of milk. He carried his lunch to the table and sat down.

"Will you require silverware, Mr. Feighan?"

"Only a napkin, Oscar."

"There is a fresh supply on the table, Mr. Feighan."

"So there is." He tugged one from the dispenser, unfolded it, and spread it over his lap. As he bit into a sandwich, Oscar proceeded with the briefing.

"The primary political unit on Rehma is the flock, which can number from a hundred to ten thousand individuals. A flock is ruled by a tripartite coalition of wise elders, strong youths, and educated intelligentsia. Though these individuals make all laws governing the flock, they possess only two means by which to punish lawbreakers: demanding community service of those who wish to remain members of the flock, and ostracism. Imprisonment, corporal or financial punishment, and execution are unknown on Rehma. The central government, meanwhile, is extremely weak. It is empowered only to handle planetary matters and settle inter-flock disputes. It is specifically forbidden to intervene in intra-flock matters."

"Now, that I've got to see to believe." He took another bite, and mumbled, "Good sandwiches, Oscar."

"Hundreds of religions, including dozens imported by Terran missionaries, co-exist in relative peace. The traditional deity of Rehma is the Far Being Retzglaran, about whom thousands of legends abound. Most natives believe that their planet is one of the Far Being's favorite places in the universe, and even if they no longer believe in Its divinity, they do believe in Its existence and Its near-omnipotence.

"The Rehmal celebrate the arrival of spring with a holiday most aptly translated as 'Festival.' Legend has it that the Far Being Retzglaran returns to Rehma during Festival, and those who fly a stretch of The River in Its company lead charmed lives thereafter."

"Oscar, interrupt." Feighan swallowed his mouthful and took a sip of milk. "Oscar, query: more detail about Festival; answer it now."

"The Rehmal year, though carefully calibrated in terms of days, is divided into ten seasons of unequal length and variable starting dates: Thaw, when the polar ice cap starts to melt and The River begins to rise in the 1200-kilometer-long gorges between The Cliffs; Flood, when The River overflows its banks and spreads across the fertile lowlands; Ebb, when The River begins to return to its banks; Sow, when the ground is finally dry enough that planted seeds will not rot—"

"Oscar, interrupt." He set down his sandwich and sighed. The damn computer could never distinguish between enough detail and too much. "Season names will suffice, Oscar; no definitions are required."

"Yes, Mr. Feighan. The remaining seasons include Grow, Fruit, Cool, Harvest, Chill, and, of course, Freeze."

"Thank you, Oscar."

"You're welcome, Mr. Feighan. Shall I continue?"

"Yes. Tell me more about Festival."

"In late Freeze, carefully selected observers fly to the south end of The Cliffs, where The River begins at the edge of the icecap. In Freeze this part of The River is dry; their duty is to watch for the first trickle of water from melting ice and then spread the word."

Feighan imagined what the observers must have to go through—the long flight south, with muscles straining against high winds and bitter cold; the lonely encampment at the feet of the glaciers; the hazardous patrol of The River's frost-rimed bed—and then, marveling at the vividness of those images, he wondered where they had arisen. The previous night's dream seemed even more like a message than before.

Oscar was still reading out the databank entries. "When the world learns that Thaw has begun, it celebrates. Everyone lays down its tools, and flies south to witness the miracle of the New Year. Even the youngest nestlings—those born during the previous Fruit, the season when all Rehmal are born—join the great flocks and arrow south. This year a billion Rehmal will converge in the air above the icecap, wheel about to fly north above the riverbed, light briefly and ceremonially somewhere on The Cliffs, and then return home."

"Oscar, interrupt." Feighan patted his lips with the napkin and pushed his empty plate away. "Oscar, query: What are the most common theories regarding Festival; answer it now."

"The River is the source of life on Rehma's super-continent, and Festival has become an integral, though un-intended, part of the planet's life cycle. Every year the River floods the vast, flat lowlands where the Rehmal raise their grain; it percolates through the soil to replenish the water table and spreads its silt across the surface. It is—"

Like the Nile, Feighan thought.

"—the flood which makes the lowlands so fertile. The Rehmal returning home from Festival fly in sun-blocking flocks above The River, shrunken by Freeze to a fiftieth its normal volume, for over 1200 kilometers. Their droppings fall into the trickle and along the exposed banks. As the spring runoff mounts into a torrent, it sweeps up the drop-pings, dissolves them into its waters, and then, in Flood, washes them across millions of square kilometers of grain fields."

He could see the rest for himself: Without Festival, the fields would yield less and less each year as Rehmal agri-culture exhausted the soil's nutrition. Without Festival (or massive petrochemical fertilizer industries), Rehmal agri-culture could never feed one billion beings. Without Fes-tival, an entire civilization would die.

But why did the Far Being Retzglaran *need* him?

Oscar interrupted his reverie. "Mr. Feighan, it is nearly two o'clock, and you promised Sam that you would pick him up."

"Thank you, Oscar." He set his plate and empty glass in the sink, where Oscar's attachments could reach and clean them, then—

PING

—stood near the front steps of All Saints School. Stepping out of the pedestrian flow, he leaned back against a sun-drenched wall. His stomach rumbled, complaining that he had not provided it with the usual handful of chocolate chip cookies. Embarrassed, he glanced around to see if anyone had overheard. No one seemed to be paying attention. He patted his belly gently, whispering, "Shut up, you had enough and you know it."

From the open building doors came the clamor of a school bell. A moment later, a stream of small children spilled down the steps. Clean-scrubbed and noisy, they all looked alike. Even the kids seemed indistinguishable from the general tumult of youth and energy and high, raised voices.

Except, of course, for Sam, who bobbed along in the middle of the crowd like a raft on a babbling brook. He caught sight of his guardian and lifted his tail in greeting.

Feighan stayed put, and waited for Sam to detach himself from the current and make his way to shore. "How ya doing there, kiddo?"

"Pretty good, McGill. We did fingerpainting today!" He held up his hands and spread wide the six fingers on each. A rainbow of pigments outlined the delicate scales of his skin. "Mr. Szcechlowski wouldn't let me use the paint remover 'cause he doesn't know if it's safe for Rhanghans or not, and figured he better not take any chances without talking to you."

Feighan consulted his watch. He had almost three hours till he had to report back to work—more than enough time to confer with one of Sam's teachers. "Is he still here?"

"No, he went home, but he said he'd call you this afternoon."

"Okay. Are you ready?"

"Any time you are, McGill."

Feighan looked up. At the top of the steps stood Sister Mary Margaret. He snapped his fingers. "Just remembered something, Sam. I have to talk to your principal."

Sam rolled his eyes. "I'll wait here, okay?"

"Chicken."

"Uh-huh."

Feighan approached the nun alone. "Afternoon, Sister. Do you have a minute?"

"Of course, Mr. Feighan. What can I do for you?"

"I just pulled TDY to Rehma, and—" At her blank expression he caught himself. "Sorry, Sister. The jargon gets to be a bad habit. I've just been temporarily assigned to the planet Rehma, I'm not sure for how long but probably not for more than a few weeks, and I wanted to find out what Sam should be studying so that he keeps up with his school work."

She raised one eyebrow. "Are you planning to take him with you?"

"Well, sure," he said, puzzled.

"I do not approve, Mr. Feighan. Sam has just started his course of studies here. Even a week-long absence will have a detrimental effect on the child's education."

"You don't think it's beneficial to expose him to another culture?"

"Of course that's beneficial, Mr. Feighan. The question, though, is whether the benefits will outweigh the costs—and frankly, I do not feel that they will."

He took a deep breath. Even chatting about the weather with a nun made him feel at a disadvantage. To have to argue with one—on the very steps of her school, no less—practically incapacitated him. "The problem, Sister, is that I can't leave Sam alone here in New York City while I'm way out there somewhere." He waved at the sky. "And it's only kindergarten, after all."

She tilted her head to one side. "Where is Rehma, exactly, Mr. Feighan?"

"Uh—" He spread his hands. "Sister, I'm a Flinger, not an astronomer. I know how to *get* to Rehma, but I couldn't for the life of me tell you where it's located."

"I see."

"Look. We leave Saturday morning. Can I get his assignments for the next couple of weeks tomorrow afternoon? I'll make sure he does his homework—I'll tutor him myself every day so he keeps up—and when we get back he'll fit right in."

"As the child's guardian, you have the final say, of course." She sniffed lightly, emphasizing her continuing disapproval. "If you insist on taking him, I'll make certain that his teachers provide you with his assignments. Two o'clock tomorrow?"

"I would appreciate it, Sister."

"Very well, Mr. Feighan." She turned and went back inside.

He descended the steps soberly enough to please any watching nun. "C'mon, Sam, let's get our butts outta here quick!"

The blue-white ball of Earth spun through the blackness overhead, and only the immaterial existence of the force-field dome bent its beams. Feighan liked the effect. It was good to see the planet as a whole just before leaving it.

He reached across the table and squeezed Maccari's hand. "I know you didn't want to talk about it in front of Sam, but we're alone now, and I'm worried sick. What did the doctors say?"

"The good news—" Maccari sipped from her wineglass. "—is that the twenty-year-survival rate for this kind of tumor—"

"Oh, Gina." So it was cancer, after all. He winced. "I'm so sorry—"

"McGill, McGill, don't be so upset. It's a very small tumor, and a very common one, and as I was saying, the twenty-year-survival rate is over ninety percent."

"But it's still cancer, Gina, and cancer—"

"It's part of life. We have to accept it as such. The oncologist was telling me that three out of every four human beings come down with cancer sooner or later."

"That's the bad news, huh?"

She looked into her glass. "No. The bad news is that I go into the hospital tomorrow night for Saturday surgery."

"So how long are you going to be in for?"

"Three days, that's all." Setting down her glass, she stroked the back of his hand with her fingernails. "The surgery itself takes less than an hour, but the blood-flushing and the immunotherapy take a day each. So I'll be out of the hospital Monday afternoon, but I'm afraid I'll have to miss the trip to Rehma."

"No, hey—" He interlaced his fingers with hers. "We'll postpone it. We'll wait till you're out—"

"You have to get there Saturday morning. You start work Sunday."

"I do?"

"Don't you read your mail?"

He forced a smile. "I don't need to. I have friends who read it for me."

"Cute, Feighan."

"Gina." He turned her hand over and traced the lines of her palm. He did not know what to say. He wanted to go, badly, but at the same time, and to the same extent, he wanted to stay till she had recovered. He felt like the rope in a tug-of-war game. "Gina, I—"

She giggled.

"What?"

"That image. You, a rope!"

He winced. "It came through?"

"Loud and clear." She leaned forward, bringing her face close to his. Her voice softened. "Don't *worry* so much. They need you out there. And even though I need you, too, the doctors and nurses and Walking Mule and everybody else will take good care of me till you get back. Go. You're not deserting me in my hour of need. I don't think that way, so don't you dare."

He kissed her. "Thanks."

"You're welcome." She kissed him back.

A simulacrum shimmered into being beside their table. Muted blues and greens rippled over the featureless oval of its face. Its machine-generated voice said, "Would you care to order now?"

At Maccari's nod, Feighan said, "Yes."

"You're packing a whole lot of books, McGill."

"And they're all yours, too, kid."

"Why'd you have to go and get my homework? I'm not going to be home."

Feighan suppressed a smile. "But you will be doing your schoolwork."

"Aw, McGill, do I have to?"

"Do *you* want to explain why you didn't to Sister Mary Margaret?"

The young Rhanghan paused a moment. He shivered; the knife-blade fins on his backbone trembled. "If I need more crayons, can we come back and get them?"

"If it'll keep Sister Mary Margaret happy, kid, you bet."

Maccari spoke from her chair in the corner. "And what are you taking to study, McGill?"

"Very funny."

"I wasn't trying to be," she said without sincerity. "How *will* you spend your free time?"

"Frankly, I don't expect to have very much. I mean, I'll be Flinging at least eight hours a day, and maybe more, depending on how badly backlogged Rehma is; I'll be tutoring Sam; and—" He had still not told her about the dream.

"You didn't need to," she said.

"I thought you weren't going to do that anymore."

"McGill, I promised I wouldn't read your mind—I *didn't* promise that I wouldn't listen to what your mind is shouting."

Sam said, "How come I never hear any of that? The only time I hear his mind is when he's gonna wallop me."

Feighan looked from one to the other. "I'm beginning not to believe this entire conversation."

"Our Talents are different, Sam," said Maccari. "I'm sensitive to thoughts; you're sensitive both to moods and to danger. I mean, you'd never step in a bear trap, right?"

He gave her an exasperated look. "You know I'd never do that!"

"Because you hear it, because you know it's there. But me, I wouldn't hear it. If I didn't see it, I'd step in it. You can sense moods, but you can't read minds unless they're broadcasting some kind of danger. I can't sense danger unless some mind is broadcasting it."

"And McGill can't do either, can he?"

"Nope." She shook her head solemnly. "He can't read minds like I can—"

"And he can't hear danger like I can—"

"Which makes me wonder how he survived to such a ripe old age without either of us on the scene, hey, Sam?"

"Yeah. Poor McGill. It must be like being crippled, huh, Gina?"

"It must be indeed, Sam."

For a moment the two grinned at each other, suppressing giggles.

Feighan cleared his throat.

Sam said, "Gina, I'm reading his mind."

"Isn't that funny? I just sensed danger."

Saturday morning, early, the sun laying horizontal bars of light down the streets of New York. Feighan yawned, hefted his suitcase, and blinked at his ward. "You ready?"

Sam had one eyelid open, and that just barely. "It's awful early, McGill."

"On Rehma it's almost noon."

Sam's other eye opened. "Lunchtime?"

"Uh-huh."

"Okay. I'm ready."

Taking Sam's hand into his, Feighan closed his eyes. He thought, visualized, concentrated, knew—

PING

They materialized in a huge openwork wicker cage. Through the holes in the floor they could see leaves, branches—and the ground a hundred meters below. A chill spring wind whistled through the walls. Sam clung to his guardian's hand. "I don't think I want lunch after all, McGill."

"It's okay, kid, this is just your standard issue Rehmal Flop Booth."

"I thought they were all white and tiled and—" The cage swayed in the wind; his tail wound around Feighan's leg and squeezed. "—and safe!"

"This is perfectly safe, Sam." He pointed to a haze that shimmered just beneath the woven floor. "See? A force field. Now come on, let go of my leg, we've got to clear out before somebody else Flops down."

They made their way through the archway, into a windowless wicker tunnel that spiraled around and down half a dozen times or more before they finally reached the ground. At the bottom they got in line behind a pair of marsupial Rii—edsch who did not speak English.

The line moved slowly toward the counter. An electronic signboard hung above the counter; across it flashed the words "Customs & Immigration" in script after alien script.

"I'm hungry, McGill."

"So what else is new, huh, kid?"

An hour passed, and thirty minutes more. Feighan's patience was wearing thin. At last they reached the head of the line and discovered the cause for the delay: Only four Customs Officers were on duty.

One of the birdlike beings beckoned them to its station, and pushed their luggage through the scanner. Predominantly blue and green, it had flamingo legs, great muscular wings folded carefully around a pear-shaped body, and a curving neck half a meter long. Its head came barely to

Feighan's shoulder. Apparently it was molting: As it reached to open Feighan's suitcase, a handful of turquoise feathers slipped off its chest and floated to the floor. Its thinning plumage gave it a faintly raffish, disreputable air.

He hated watching bureaucrats paw through his socks, and it irked him all the more that this one insisted on a manual search even though the scanner had found nothing. "Is today a holiday?"

With a cough, it straightened, and turned to him. Its beak opened, but it did not answer. Instead, it wheezed horribly, flapped its wings twice, reached for its throat, and keeled over.

▪ Chapter IV ▪

Saturday, 26 September 2105

For three months, now, Nathaniel Davis had controlled, though not possessed, more power and wealth than the average member planet of the Network. Not surprising, for Gryll had appointed him Chief Executive of the anti-culture—the criminal underworld—on ten entire planets.

Of course, if he failed to show a magnificent return on investment, the average beggar in the Inta Leina marketplace would wield more power and wealth than Nathaniel Davis. And have a much greater life expectancy . . .

But he would not dwell on that. Operation PlayGround would work. He himself would win for The Organization that which his predecessor had died attempting to seize. And anyone clever enough to pull off PlayGround would surely rise to rule an empire larger than any Terra had ever seen.

As he did before every meal, he asked the computer for the present whereabouts of his old enemy McGill Feighan. It flashed: REHMA.

Raising his eyebrows, he pushed the plate aside. Feighan had left his home turf? Davis chuckled. It was time to settle some scores.

▪ Chapter V ▪

**Saturday, 26 September 2105
—Monday, 28 September 2105**

"McGill, I'm starving!"

Feighan bent over to look Sam in the eye. "I don't understand you, kid—a Customs Inspector practically dies right in front of you and you still have an appetite?"

"I always have an appetite!" He put a dry, scaled hand on Feighan's shoulder. "I feel bad about the guy who got sick, but the paramedics came, right? He'll be okay, won't he?"

"I hope so."

"So how come I can't be hungry?"

The Flinger laughed and sat back up. "All right, all right—you can be hungry. What you can't do is eat. They told us to wait here till the Director could see us."

"Well, they coulda given us some furniture!"

Shifting uncomfortably, McGill Feighan sighed his agreement. A suitcase did not serve well as a chair, even for him, and he, at least, had approximately the anatomy for it. Poor Sam could either stand, or lie on the wickerwork floor. And given the white stains that splotched almost every strand of wicker, he could hardly blame Sam for staying on all fours. Once they got to whatever quarters had been assigned them, Feighan would have to make sure his ward scrubbed his feet.

Clearly, the Rehma Consortium's decorator had not expected wingless aliens to cool their heels in that airplane hangar of a reception room. Scores of perches adorned the walls, in sizes suitable for the largest known intelligent avians as well as for the smallest, but even if he could climb to one that would hold his weight, he would have to cover its white-crusted surface before he would dare sit. And as he had brought neither newspapers nor sheets of heavy-duty plastic, it would be pointless to clamber up those fifteen-meter walls.

"Even a stool would be better than nothing, McGill!"

"I suspect the hard part would be keeping it clean."

Sam looked around. "Yeah. This is pretty disgusting, isn't it?"

"To Terrans, yeah."

"I'm not a Terran, I'm a Rhanghan-American."

He tickled the side of Sam's belly. "I'm not talking whether you have scales or skin; I'm talking cultural background here—and your background, kid, much as you hate to admit it, is pure New York."

Wings fluttered at the far end of the reception room. An emerald green Rehmal half Feighan's size and built mostly of bony legs alit in front of them. It wore nothing but its feathers, and a pouch that hung from a string belt. Feighan stood. "Hello."

The alien's aquamarine crest stood at attention as it focused on them bright black eyes smaller than marbles. Half bowing, it snapped its long beak shut, bent forward, and ran the edge of that beak along each of Feighan's cheeks. It then repeated the gesture with Sam.

"McGill—"

"That's how the Rehmal shake hands, Sam."

"You could have warned me."

"I didn't know I needed to."

The Rehmal, having waited till they finished speaking,

opened its beak again. Music spilled out.

"I'm sorry, " said Feighan. "I do not understand the language of Rehma."

"It's pretty, isn't it, McGill?"

"Hush." He kept his gaze on the Rehmal.

Its head bobbed. Its wings spread just a little. Scratching at the wicker floor, it seemed to concentrate—

O*click*flyer of *click*world, welcome, welcome, six billion times welcome! Long have you flown; tired must you be; deep must you ache to preen. Can with snarled feathers you bear in patience some little while longer? Our Lead would with you speak.

As the voice welled up inside his head, he thought, *The staff telepath.*

It nodded. *Just so.*

Aloud he said, "The Director would like us to wait a little longer?"

On her branch, just so.

Tired of waiting, and hungry to boot, now that Sam had reminded him of how long it had been since their last meal, he nonetheless restrained his temper. Shrugging, not caring if the Minder thought him a bit rude, he sat back down. "All right, we'll wait."

"McGill, why are you talking to yourself?"

"Shh." He pointed to the Rehma. "It's a Minder. It doesn't speak English, so it's 'pathing me direct."

The Rehmal ducked its head beneath its right wing. *O*click*flyer of *click*world, our minds on different courses soar, and through the dark of first strangeness have passed without touching beaks.*

He shook his head. "I'm really sorry, but I don't know what you're talking about."

Just so! It danced backward, away from them, then paused and extended its wing. *If you will deign to wing my Lead?*

"Not here, huh?" He stood up again, and grabbed his suitcases.

"Is he taking us somewhere there's chairs, McGill?"

"God only knows, Sam."

Still facing them, it backed away with a slow, regal step, pausing every now and then to hop, bow, and flourish its wings.

"I wonder," said Feighan, "if this is their version of the red carpet treatment."

Just so! And after the words came an image of a short, fat cartoon character with a sparkly gold crown and ermine robes and a dainty, brass-buckled shoe poised on the edge of a scarlet runner. *Just so!*

"In that case, thank you."

It led them, step by prancing step, out of the reception room and onto a sun-dappled balcony. A cool breeze brushed Feighan's hair and rustled the leaves above their heads. Birdsong filled the air.

Sam stopped, rested his snout on the balcony railing, and gawked out at the trees and the towers of Stonehills City. "Wow!"

"Nice view, huh?" The city sprawled across two hundred square kilometers of the rugged granite hills that gave it its name. Six- and eight-lane roads ran along the ridges and leapt the valleys on graceful stone bridges. As far as the eye could see, buildings rose sixty and seventy stories high, each wrapped in perhaps a hundred acres of manicured parkland, each roofed with a heliport and bank upon bank of glittery solar panels. Overhead, helijets lifted and stooped like falcons. "You like it?"

"Yeah . . . but how come they have all those skyscrapers? I thought Rehmal lived in trees."

"They do." He pointed down to the wickerwork shelters scattered through the boughs of a fifty-meter-tall tree across the way. "See? Those are Rehmal houses."

"Uh-huh." It was Sam's turn to point. "But what are all the New York kind of buildings for?"

"Tourists, mostly, and all companies that depend on them. Remember, Stonehills City is the major tourist center on the planet. Plus there are diplomats, traders, manufacturers, uh . . . ?" He spread his hands. "They've got everything here. Except farming." He peered over the edge. "See how barren and rocky the soil below is? Back at the Academy they taught us, if I remember correctly, that this used to be pretty much a desert. They put the Rehma Consortium Headquarters here because they knew they couldn't use the land for food."

Just so! The Minder stretched its wings to the sun. *Just so!*

Sam looked puzzled. "Why not? The trees sure grew."

"Only because they transplanted each one here individually, and hand-watered it for years until its roots reached deep enough to find the underground streams."

"You mean they *wing*-watered them, don't you, McGill?"

"Nope." He shook his head in mock dismay. "And here I thought you were an observant little kid. For shame." He turned to the telepath. "If you would be so kind—?"

The Rehmal spread its wings. From the joint closest to the shoulder on each wing sprouted a thin hand with three delicate fingers and a thumb.

Sam rocked back on his haunches and lashed his tail in astonishment. "How come I didn't see them before?"

"Got me, kiddo. But—"

O *click*flyer of *click*world, the day turns on toward night.

He nodded. "I'm sorry," he said. "Let's go, then."

The Minder gestured for them to step onto a rope-and-plank suspension bridge that dipped over to a gaping hollow in the trunk of the next tree. The underlying force field, though transparent, distorted the view between the boards. Feighan stepped onto it; Sam's tail slapped down and he dropped his bags. "No way, McGill!"

The Flinger froze. "Do you smell a trap?"

Sam hissed.

"What is it, Sam?" Moving carefully, he retreated to the balcony.

"I'm not going out on that."

"Is something wrong with it? Is the force field defective?" Feighan had learned to trust his ward's instincts, and if Sam thought someone had tampered with the bridge or its mechanisms—

"It's too high!"

Feighan looked down. A hundred meters below, huge gnarled roots muscled their way into the boulder-strewn hillside. Small furry animals with giant ears scratched at the soil. "Sam, it's like the thirtieth floor, huh? Our penthouse is a lot higher up than that."

"The penthouse doesn't wobble in the wind!"

"It's just swaying a little. I'll go across first; then you'll see it's safe."

"I want to go home, McGill."

"Hey." He squatted to put his face on a level with the child's. "We can't, Sam. I have a job to do here. It's only for a couple of weeks, but in the meantime, you can't let a little thing like a bridge scare you."

"I can't do it, McGill."

"Okay. No sweat." He closed his eyes, visualized the far end of the bridge, concentrated, felt, knew—

PING

—and they stood on the other side, looking back at the reception room's balcony. "Is that better?"

Sam shuddered. "Yes."

The Minder squawked loudly. Flapping its wings, it rose into the air.

"Over here!" called Feighan.

It banked, and spotted them. *O *click*flyer of *click* world, for one long moment did this balding fish-eater think it had offended you to the point of *click*flying home to *click*world.*

"I'm sorry." He bowed as it landed by their side. "Sam was a little, um, perturbed by the bridge, so I Flung us across."

Just so! Its wings opened and made forward-sweeping gestures. *Within our Lead doth perch, and would with you your gift discuss.*

"My gift?"

From the shadows within came a lilt and a trill. Sam darted inside, leaving his suitcases in the entranceway. "McGill! Chairs! And a couch!"

The Minder stepped to one side and gestured for Feighan to go first. He bowed, said, "Thank you," and went in.

Sunlight spilled through openings in the wood and fell on Sam, who had already sprawled out on a long sofa upholstered in soft beige leather.

On a perch facing the doorway rested a large Rehmal with an orange crest and burnt umber tail. The whirling color bands of an energy tunic obscured the rest of its feathers, but they seemed to tend mainly to the yellow, with here and there a brilliant glowing scarlet. It dipped its head as Feighan came into the room, then glanced sharply at the Minder.

O *click*flyer of *click*world, our Lead greets you as the morning.

The orange-crested alien hopped off its perch, glided the short distance to Feighan, and laid Rehmal beak to Terran cheek as the Minder had moments earlier. Then it turned to Feighan's ward.

"Sam!"

The young Rhanghan scrambled to his feet and presented his snout. "Pleased ta meetcha," he mumbled, before crawling back onto the sofa.

Our Lead begs pardon for this fishreek poking into the nest of your mind, but the two-tongued singer lies ill abed and needs must I serve.

He blinked, nodded, and almost let it pass but thought he ought, perhaps, to double-check. Just to be certain he understood. Comprehension should never be taken for granted. "Excuse me, but are you saying you're filling in because the Director's translator is sick?"

Jut so!

"Ah. Well, an oral translator would have made things easier, but I think you'll do fine. Please tell the Director that I am pleased to meet him."

Her.

"Ah. I missed that."

Subtle indeed is the distinction, unlike *click*worlders who—

It flashed him an image of a Terran woman who surely brought her bras at a hammock store.

We people of the sky mark our sex in our feathers.

Feighan wanted to pursue the matter, but the Director's chirp cut the conversation short.

Our Lead begs leave to leave undanced the stately minuet of chat. Matters momentous ride her back like a coat of ice and force her down from custom's heights. With your good will, O *click*flyer of *click*world?

"Sure," he said, bemused.

The Minder spoke to the Director, whose translated reply came back at once: *As well you know, O *click*flyer of *click*world, a sickness stalks our world, a sickness so insidious that our own *click*flyers number one where once they numbered two.*

Startled, he said, "Half your Flingers are out sick?"

Just so! Hence our plea to the centermost city for *click*flyers willing to gift us with their Talent. We asked; you came; we cover crests in embarrassment and love and gratitude.

"You're welcome." He began to wonder about the time-and-a-half Walking Mule had promised him. If the Rehmal thought he was *donating* his time, the potential for misunderstanding—

Our answer gift to your gift, 'pathed the Minder. *The merest trifling token of our underlying appreciation. But.*

"Yes?"

Our Lead begs leave to beg a gift of different texture. The greatest doctor of the sky people scraggles feathers in his frantic search for the source of the stalking sickness. This noble inquisitor into minuteness, a proud-tailed flyer named—

It sang a sound.

"Th'hweet?" said Feighan dubiously.

Sam shot Feighan a scornful glance, and replicated the sound perfectly. "That's how you pronounce it, McGill."

"No, Sam, that's how *you* pronounce it. It's even how *they* pronounce it. It is not, unfortunately, how *I* pronounce it." He turned to the Minder. "Will it offend the doctor or the sky people if I call him Th'hweet?"

Ah no!

"Thank you."

The wondrous researcher of the smallest life seeks the assistance of a *click*flyer, that he might more rapidly from outbreak to outbreak travel. Our Lead begs leave to beg you gift us with such assistance.

"Well—" He frowned. "If I've got this right, Dr. Th'hweet wants a Flinger to help him get around the planet quickly."

Just so!

"I'll be more than happy to help, but there is a problem: I can't Fling to a place I've never been and never seen. Perhaps a na— one of your own people could be of greater assistance."

The Director gave a rude squawk.

Our Lead, alas, did such an observation make, and her heart still bleeds from the backstabbing of Th'hweet.

"What was the problem?"

As the teachings say, "'Tis a nut best left uncracked."

"Well, if Dr. Th'hweet won't take one of your people—"

The doctor most specifically a *click*worlder demanded.

"Okay." He held up his hands. "Look, I'm here to help. If your Director thinks I can help best by being Th'hweet's chauffeur, no problem, that's what I'll do."

We cover crests in gratitude. And they did.

Unfortunately, what they could not do was track down

Dr. Th'hweet, who was apparently spending the day in the field. Through the Minder the Director explained that she had to get back to work. With a good-bye chirp, and a wave of a wingtip, she Flung all three of them to the high-ceilinged lobby of the Stonehills Plaza, a tourist hotel reputed to be the best in the city.

O *click*flyer of *click*world, here will be your over-night nest, be that agreeable to you.

Sam's magenta tongue was already tasting the air, scented with tantalizing aromas from the open-air restaurant beyond the reception desk. Feighan looked around the lobby. A well-groomed Rii—edsch sat in one of the overstuffed armchairs reading a newspaper. An Edbargian, a long-necked, twelve-legged being with a tortoise-like shell a meter in diameter, made its slow way toward the high-speed elevators. "This will be fine."

The Minder led them to the desk. *Here sing a good many workers with two tongues; should aught you want, just ask.* It leaned across the counter and let out an imperious melody.

A clerk hurried over, spreading its wings a hair between steps to cover ground a bit faster. *"Hai! Chotto matte kudasai."* It bowed and brought out a stack of registration cards.

Feighan and Sam looked at each other and sighed. Then Feighan said, "Uh . . . do you speak English?"

The native's beak clacked. *"Eng-aw? Sumimasen, Eng-aw dekinai. Chotto matte kudasai."* It turned away, presumably in search of someone who could speak English.

"How come you never learned Japanese, McGill?"

"Cause all the Japanese speak English, Sam."

"Then how come the Japanese still speak Japanese?"

"I think they're waiting for us to catch up."

"I ought to learn Rhanghan."

"You probably ought to. We'll go visit your mother sometime and see what she thinks."

"Okay." A moment later, he said, "I'm hungry, McGill."

"Soon, Sam. Real soon, now."

"If we were in New York I could snack on a roach or something, but I haven't seen any here."

"Well, if you do, don't scarf 'em up, huh? Rehmal proteins and Rhanghan proteins don't mix."

"What's that mean?"

"Means we can't eat the food here, kid."

"We gotta go hungry the whole time we're here?"

"No." He scratched Sam's skullbone just the way the child liked it. "It means that we eat stuff imported from home. Like we did on Actu."

"How come I don't have to do that back in New York?"

"Same reason I didn't have to when I was on Throngorn."

"That doesn't tell me the reason, McGill."

"I don't know what the reason is." He shrugged. "Terra and Throngorn have similar proteins, so we can eat each other's food, but *why* the proteins are similar is out of my league, kiddo."

A plump clerk with a great deal of scarlet in its feathers landed in front of them. It dismissed the Minder with a wave of its wing. "Right, then." It looked Feighan up and down carefully. "That'll be a double?"

"Yes, but with twin beds, please."

"Well, I didn't bleeding think you were queer for scales and tails, guv."

Feighan's jaw dropped.

The Minder ducked its head beneath its wing.

Sam said, "McGill, what did he mean by 'queer for scales and tails'?"

"He meant, ah—" For the life of him, he could not think of a tasteful explanation.

The clerk bent over so its beak came within centimeters of Sam's snout. "I meant I see one bloody pouf after another come prancing through here 'and in 'and wiv such as they wasn't meant to be 'olding 'ands wiv, eh? And I can see at a glance, it being as plain as the nose on 'is face, that the guv'nor 'ere ain't no bloody pouf."

"And what's a pouf?"

"A pouf, me fine—"

Feighan cleared his throat. "I think Sam's a little too young for that."

The clerk swiveled its head in his direction. "You're 'aving me on."

"He's just a kid, okay?"

"Cor!" It opened and shut its beak several times without a sound. "'E's got more to grow?"

"Much."

"Then I don't think I'll be visiting 'is world any time soon now, eh guv'nor? 'Oo's 'is teacher while you're 'ere?"

"Ah . . ." Feighan scratched his head. "He doesn't have one."

The clerk clacked its beak twice and stared hard at the Flinger. Then it let its breath out with a hiss. "Gawd, you Terrans are strange." It produced registration cards, showed Feighan where to sign, and summoned a bellboy for their bags. In a confidential tone, it told Feighan, "'E don't speak the Queen's bloody English, 'e don't, nor 'is own 'arf as well as 'e ought, poor fish, but 'e's as 'onest as the night is long—"

"Day," said Feighan.

"Eh?"

"That's 'as honest as the *day* is long.'"

"Bloody idioms!" It made a harsh, cawing sound that Feighan decided, after a few moments, had to be laughter. "Just the other day somebody was asking for something I couldn't quite remember, and I said, ''Arf a mo', it'll come to me, I've got it on the knack of me head.' And didn't that proper confuse 'em." It laughed again. "That's wot happens when you learn your bleeding English from old telly shows."

"Telly?" said Feighan blankly.

"The 'olovision's ancestor. Only it's two-dimensional, 'ey?"

"Uh-huh . . . you were saying about the bellboy?"

"Oh yes, oh yes, 'e's as 'onest as the day is long—" It gave a small snort of triumph. "—so if you'd like to go straight outside to the terrace restaurant, which I see your young friend there is staring at with what you might call a certain intensity of expression, why, just give the bellboy 'arf a fancy, there's a love, and 'e'll take your bags on up for you, and bring the key back to the restaurant."

Feighan allowed as how that sounded good and parted with half a Flinger Network Credit. Then he caught himself, and turned back to the clerk. "Maybe you can help on something else. My girlfriend's going into surgery this afternoon, and I was wondering if this Minder could, um, sort of keep me posted on how she's doing? Her name's Gina Maccari, and she's the staff telepath for the North American Consortium."

"No trouble, guv'nor." It sang aloud for a minute or so.

The Minder sang back, then turned to Feighan, hopped, bowed, and spread its wings wide.

"That does mean 'yes,' doesn't it?"

"That it does, guv. 'E says 'e'll leave a message for you at this desk every morning and every evening, so's you can put your mind at ease before you start your day, and before you tuck in for the night."

"Thank you." Feighan bowed to the Minder. "You've been very, very helpful." The Minder hopped again, flourished its wings one more time, and flew out the door.

Feighan followed his ward to the restaurant on the patio. Sam did not wait to be seated; spotting an empty table in the shade at the far end, he scampered over and wriggled into a chair.

Feighan smiled at the obviously harried maître d', took the seat opposite Sam, and opened the menu laid across the ornate placemat. The courses looked familiar and uninspired. The prices made him groan.

"What's the matter, McGill?"

"They're paying me time-and-a-half to work here, but charging me triple to eat here ... I suspect we're not going to make much of a profit on this trip, Sam."

"Did we come here to make a profit?"

"Actually, no." A cylindrical robot waiter set a plate of French bread on the table. "Freeze, kid!"

Sam drew back his hand. "Why?"

"Table manners. Let the robot get out of the way, first."

The young Rhanghan mumbled something that might have been, "I would if it weren't so slow," but then again, might have been something entirely different.

Feighan decided to ignore the comment, whatever it was.

They ordered, were served just as Sam finished the last slice of bread, and, famished as they were—for the bread had whetted Sam's appetite, not dulled it—cleaned their plates within seven minutes. Leaning back, Feighan smiled satedly. Cocking his head slightly so the sun slipping between the branches hit his shoulder and not his eye, he pressed the waiter's call button and asked for a cup of coffee.

"Me, too!" said Sam.

About to argue the point, Feighan changed his mind. "Him, too."

"Good lunch, huh, McGill?"

He patted his stomach in answer.

"Are we going to have dessert?"

Feighan closed both eyes, opened one up halfway again, and studied the child. "You are kidding."

"No! They have strawberry shortcake with whipped cream. It was on the menu."

He permitted his right eyelid to drift shut. "Kiddo, I think you're about ready for the record books. You've been in kindergarten for all of three weeks, and already you can read 'strawberry shortcake with whipped cream.' Now that's what I call instant erudition."

"Are you making fun of me, McGill?"

"Me? Make fun of you?" He shifted his head so the sun could wash his face. A pleasant drowsiness crept over him. "Why, yes, Sam, I suppose I am."

"That's not nice, McGill."

"Nor is it nice to tell me you read something you couldn't possibly have read."

"But I know my alphabet! Wanna hear me? A-B-C-D-E-F-G—"

"I know—" Feighan yawned. "—you know your alphabet, Sam, and I'm very proud of you for knowing it, but simply knowing the alphabet doesn't mean you know—"

"S-T-R-A-W—"

He opened his eyes in surprise. "Go on."

"—B-A-R-R-Y—"

"E-R-R-Y."

Sam sighed. "B-*E*-R-R-Y. S-H-O-R-T-C-A-K-E. W-I-T-H. W-H-I-P-P-E-D. C-R-E-A-M." He sat back, tongue flickering in the air, and grinned. "What do you think, huh, McGill? Gonna take it back?"

He nodded. "I'm going to do more than take it back, Sam. I'm going to apologize. I'm sorry that I doubted you. You really do know how to spell 'Strawberry shortcake with whipped cream,' and that's pret-ty amazing, kiddo." He frowned. "Where'd you learn how to spell that?"

Suddenly Sam seemed uncomfortable. "That doesn't matter."

"Sure it does. Where'd you learn?"

"You'll just get mad."

"No I won't. Tell me."

He dropped his snout. "Off the box at home."

"What box?"

"The one that used to be in the freezer."

"Used to be?"

"You said you wouldn't get mad, McGill."

"You're right. I said I wouldn't get mad. I won't get mad. *Used* to be?"

"I got hungry ... and I had to learn how to spell it so I could replace it."

"Well, that was very thoughtful of—"

"May we join you?"

Feighan looked up into a bearded face with merry brown eyes. Next to the man stood a tall, extremely attractive woman in her late thirties. He got to his feet even as they motioned him to stay put. "We've finished eating, but if you'd care for a cup of coffee—"

"Or dessert, McGill!"

"—or dessert, please, have a seat. I'm McGill Feighan, and the one with the sweet tooth is my ward Sam."

"Ernest Williams." The stranger held out his hand. A centimeter or two shorter than Feighan, he had a bit of a paunch but a powerful grip. "And my wife, Celeste Quandala."

She wore a white dress and flat-heeled shoes. She used no makeup, but with her complexion she needed none. Her blue eyes gazed directly into his; she smiled. "Hello, Mr. Feighan." She had white, even teeth.

"Pleased to meet you." He truly enjoyed shaking her hand. "Are you tourists?"

"Missionaries," said Williams, holding a chair for his wife.

"Oh, Ernest." Quandala shook her head in apparent exasperation. "My husband is a missionary, Mr. Feighan—"

"Call me McGill."

"Thank you, I will. But I'm only a teacher."

"Only a teacher!" Williams rolled his eyes skyward. "Celeste, you're doing the Lord's work. Not in the way I do, yes, but you make it possible for me and the others to spread the Word of God. Don't say 'only a teacher,' don't ever say it."

"Ah—what do you teach, Ms. Quandala?"

"Please—Celeste. Or it's back to Mr. Feighan." Her smile by itself made Feighan believe in heaven. "I'm an instructor in conversational English at Rehma Rebirth College." She paused, as if waiting for him to recognize the name.

"I'm afraid I just got here, so I don't know the school. Rehma Rebirth College. Is that a translation of the native name?"

"No," said Williams, "it's from the original English. We witness, you see, for the Rebirth Church."

He spread his hands. "I feel sort of embarrassed, but the name doesn't ring a bell. Does the Rebirth Church have many, uh, adherents?"

"We call them 'communicants,' McGill," said Williams. "In America alone we have over fifty thousand communicants. Network-wide, a million, a million and a half, perhaps."

"So you're spread across the Network."

"Oh, absolutely." He leaned forward, thrusting his beard almost into Feighan's face. "We have the Truth, McGill. God's Truth for the community of souls. Our basic—"

"Ernest." Quandala patted her husband on the wrist. "McGill's just arrived here; he's surely tired after the trip, and the last thing he wants is to have to be polite to two strangers—even strangers bearing God's Truth for the community of souls."

Feighan made a small noise which he hoped would suggest that while he thoroughly enjoyed being polite to strangers, especially those of Quandala's quality, perhaps they could choose for their topic of conversation something other than "God's truth for the community of souls."

Williams nodded once. "Of course." With a fingertip he stroked the back of Quandala's hand. He smiled. "So what brings you and Sam to Rehma, McGill? Tourism?"

"No, I'm on temporary duty here, filling in for some of the local Flingers who came down with this bug that's been going around. I guess I start tomorrow, although it's a little confused, what with so many administrative types out sick."

"How long will you be here?" asked Quandala.

"That's sort of up in the air." He made a face. "Sorry, I didn't mean to pun."

Williams narrowed his eyes in puzzlement, gazed into the distance for a second, and then winced. "You're forgiven. *This* time."

"Thanks. Anyway, they told me back in New York it'd probably be two or three weeks." He held out his hand, palm down and fingers spread, and waggled it from side to side. "More or less."

"So you'll be here for Festival!" said Quandala.

"I will?" He found it hard not to stare at her. *Thank God she's married*, he thought. *Otherwise I could be thinking that what Gina doesn't know—*

"Oh, yes, definitely."

A red-headed Terran in greasy coveralls approached their table. A short, muscular man, he said, "'Scuse. Found the problem with your heli. Carburetor. Have it fixed in an hour."

Williams said, "You will bill it to the Mission?"

"Course." The mechanic nodded, turned about, and left.

"What a relief," said Quandala. "We can get back tonight. Anyway, McGill, as I was saying, today's—" She bent her head and pressed a button on the casing of her wristwatch. "Today's Saturday, September 26 back home. Isn't it?"

Feighan nodded.

"Here it's late Freeze; Thaw is *probably* going to start in two weeks, give or take a couple of days. And of course Festival starts the first day of Thaw. So figure it could start, um . . ." Tilting her face to the sun, she half-closed her eyes while she worked out the dates, in the process giving Feighan a good opportunity to study her marvelous profile. "As early as October 8, I think, and as late as the 12th or the 13th. You *will* be here then, won't you?" She seemed very anxious that his answer be "yes."

"As far as I know, yes."

"Oh, good." She actually clapped her hands and beamed. "We'll be taking the helijet for the trip; if you are around, please join us."

"Thank you," he said, "but I suspect I'll be working then."

Williams laughed out loud. "Nobody works during Festival. The whole planet shuts down."

"In that case, thank you, I'd like that." Quandala and

Williams seemed very knowledgeable about local customs, and that delighted Feighan. For him, the hardest part of interstellar travel was always finding someone who could explain what was going on, and why, in terms he could understand. "What about you, Sam, want to go see Festival from a helijet?"

The Rhanghan looked up from his dessert. He had whipped cream all over his snout—and a great big grin.

As soon as he got out of bed the next morning, Feighan phoned the desk for the latest message from the Rehmal Minder. The previous night the note had been brief: "Maccari fine; operation successful," and he was hoping for more detail. "Hello, this is McGill Feighan in room—"

"Of course, Mr. Feighan, of course. 'E just called wiv the progress report, so to speak. The lady's doing fine, resting comfortably. It's night over there now, innit?"

"Yes. Or very early in the morning, at any rate."

"Ah. Well, 'e said as soon as she wakes up they'll swap her old blood for new blood, and you are not to worry. 'E'll call again tonight."

"Thank you." His voice trembled with relief. "Thank you very much."

"Just doing my job as best I can, Mr. Feighan. Which is something as you might keep in mind when it comes time to check out."

He chuckled. "Right. 'Bye." To Sam, he said, "Gina's doing fine."

The Rhanghan looked up from his coloring book. "Good!"

Feighan made himself comfortable in the armchair, and poured himself a cup of room-service coffee. A minute later someone knocked on the door. Ensconced in soft cushions, cradling warm wakefulness, he did not want to move. "Can you get that, Sam?"

"Sure." He scampered across the room, his swishing tail carving an S-shaped wake in the pile of the carpet. He opened the door and said, "Good morning."

A high, thin voice said, *"You* are Mr. McGill Feighan?"

"No," he said scornfully, "I'm Sam."

"The clerk at the desk informed us that Mr. McGill Feighan was staying in this room."

"Yeah, he is. You wanna talk to him?"

"If we might."

"Okay." Without closing the door, Sam turned his head. "McGill! Two people here wanna talk to you."

Feighan sighed. Another fifteen minutes and the coffee would have driven the early morning fuzzies from his mind, but he was clearly not going to get those fifteen minutes. At least he had gotten the good word about Maccari. He put his cup on the table and stood up. God, he hated having to make intelligent conversation before coming fully awake. It was like trying to row without oars. "Invite them in, Sam."

"Okay." Sam turned back to the strangers in the hall. "Come on in."

Two Rehmal came through the door. The short blue one struggled with an oversized briefcase. The taller marched briskly across the room. Unlike every other Rehmal Feighan had encountered, it wore clothes. Sort of: A sleeveless white lab coat hung over its violet feathers.

Trying not to react to the sight, Feighan braced himself for a beakswipe across his cheeks.

Instead, the native reached for his hand. *"You're* Mr. McGill Feighan."

"Yes." He tried hard to keep the surprise—and the feeling of reprieve—off his face. "And you must be Dr. Th'hweet."

Th'hweet released Feighan's hand. "Precisely." Around his neck looped a loosely knotted tie of a crimson nearly the hue of his crest. "My unparalleled assistant—" He made a sound, sharp and rising, and repeated it twice more. "I suggest you pronounce it 'Sree?sree?sree?' We have a number of things to do today, and we should commence immediately."

"Ah . . ." He shrugged. "You're the boss."

Th'hweet bobbed his head in a way that was more than a nod and less than a bow. "Precisely." He reached into a pocket of the lab coat and drew forth a sheet of stiff paper. Striding to the table, he unfolded the paper and smoothed it out. "These are the settlements we will visit today, listed in the order in which we will visit them. Any questions?"

"Well . . . yes, frankly. How familiar are you with the way a Flinger works?"

Th'hweet fastened his unblinking gaze on Feighan. "You have the ability to transport up to 918 kilograms of mass from any spot in the known universe to any other spot in the known universe. You are able to do this as often as ninety-six times a day, nine days out of ten."

"A hundred and ten, actually," murmured Feighan. "There is, however, a limitation you didn't mention: I can only teleport to places I've visited."

"Or seen." Th'hweet made it a statement, not a question.

"Well, yes," said Feighan. "I can Fling to places I've only seen."

"Then the limitation is not a limitation." Turning his head slightly, he trilled four notes in Rehmal. Sree?sree?sree? laid the briefcase on the table and unlocked it. It opened into a flat-screen display with attached keyboard. "A direct link to our weather satellites, Mr. Feighan."

"Oh." He studied it with interest. "I didn't know Rehma had weather satellites."

"In fact you rather assumed we didn't, yes?" said Th'hweet sharply.

Caught off-guard, Feighan floundered. "Well, I, um . . . I hadn't really thought of it before, I mean—"

"I wish I understood why a race of mediocre technological sophistication instinctively believes other races to be even less sophisticated. Your own aphorism would have it that 'Experience is the best teacher.' One would think that having been discovered by the FNC, rather than discovering it, would have taught you not to underestimate aliens."

Feighan took a deep breath. *This would sure go a lot easier if I were awake* . . . "Are you always this grouchy, or only in the mornings?"

Th'hweet's beak opened wide, and shut slowly. After a moment he made the raspy cawing sound Feighan had decided was local laughter. "My apologies, Mr. Feighan. My personality is normally abrasive, a tendency accentuated by my recent lack of sleep. I shall try to control myself."

"No problem." He waved a hand dismissively. "If I don't get enough sleep, I'm not exactly Mr. Nice Guy myself."

"You can say that again," said Sam.

Feighan pointed a finger at him. "Enough out of you, kiddo."

"Yes, McGill."

He turned back to Th'hweet. "About the weather satellites."

"We have twelve. In addition to the normal observational gear, each is equipped with a reconnaissance camera directly controllable from this portable, battery-powered console. Given clear air, the reconnaissance cameras provide resolution fine enough to permit reading a newspaper from space."

"Now that is impressive." Feighan meant it.

"And I must confess that we did not build them, but rather bought them from a world of nation-states that suddenly found itself in need of massive amounts of capital for reconstruction."

Feighan blinked. "Did you buy them from the winners or the losers?"

"The appropriate term, I believe, is 'survivors.'"

"Uh-huh . . ." He stared at the console for a few seconds. "So what you're planning is, you'll type in the name of the place you want to visit, the satellite will flash back a close-up of the place, I focus on the picture, and then Fling us there, right?"

"Precisely."

He could do it. It would be hard to judge the differences in angular momentum accurately enough to guarantee that they did not sway when they materialized, but nobody would go skidding across the pavement. "All right," he said at last, "when do you want to start?"

"In a moment." Th'hweet went to the window and looked out. "An epidemic is loose on my homeworld, Mr. Feighan."

"So I understand."

Th'hweet looked back over the top of his right wing. "What you might not understand is that I am the only board-certified epidemiologist on the entire planet."

Feighan said, "I'm not quite sure what you're leading up to, Dr. Th'hweet."

"Our leaders are not particularly alarmed by the present state of affairs because we Rehmal are a hardy people, and because our leaders lack expertise in this area. I, on the other hand, have expertise."

"Yes?"

"I received my M.D. from Harvard Medical School, and performed post-doctoral research in epidemiology at Massachusetts General."

"That's impressive, but—"

"Mr. Feighan, I am terrified by the situation, and I have no one to turn to for assistance except the admirable Sree?sree?sree? I am confronted with an epidemic of unknown origins, with unknown degree of contagion, transmitted by an unknown vector. I must identify every aspect of this disease, and then must eradicate it."

"But isn't that what epidemiologists *do?*"

"Of course!" Th'hweet clacked his beak once. "But there is this which you must understand about my people: They have little, if any, concept of public health measures, and they cling to tradition like vines to a tree. My investigations are going to offend them—upset them—even outrage them—"

"Why?" he asked in honest bewilderment.

"Because to find the truth we shall have to violate some

rather strong taboos. And in all probability, the public health measures we are going to have to propose will fly in the face of ten thousand years of traditional teaching. Which leads directly to my next question: How long does it take you to recover from a Fling?"

"Anywhere from thirty seconds to five minutes, depending on how tired I am."

"Can you tell in advance how long it will take?"

"Not to the second."

"I see." Th'hweet bobbed his head up and down. "In that case, are you able to determine—without actually attempting to Fling—whether or not you are capable of Flinging?"

"Oh, sure. Except," he said thoughtfully, "toward the end of a very long day, I sometimes have trouble Flinging a max mass a long distance. Not that I can't do it, or that I screw up the momentum, just that it sometimes takes two tries."

"I see, I see. Very well. After we arrive in a village, please inform me the instant you feel confident that you can teleport us away. I shall avoid controversial subjects until you so notify me."

"Dr. Th'hweet—" Feighan cocked his head. "Am I correct in feeling that you just might say the sorts of things that would make it necessary for us to Fling out on a moment's notice—or less?"

"Precisely, Mr. Feighan." The Rehmal blinked his bright eyes slowly. "I confidently expect that at least a few of my people will try to kill us today."

Feighan sighed. "If nothing else, that should keep me awake . . ."

Feighan yawned as they arrived at their eighteenth stop of the day, a rocky, desolate island off the west coast of Rehma's super-continent. While Sam scrambled to the top of a sun-drenched boulder, and the haggard Th'hweet flew toward a group of reed-roofed nests, the Flinger turned to

Sree?sree?sree? "What did he call this place?"

Th'hweet's assistant tilted back his head and trilled nine bars of an intricate melody.

"Uh . . . yeah. I don't guess I need to know how to pronounce it, anyway . . . Where did you learn to speak English?"

"I work for American post-doc seven years ago." From the leather pouch at his waist, Sree?sree?sree? took first a small knife, and then a dark blue object that looked like a peach pit. "Now she is Ornitholoju— logical Consultant to Philadelphia Zoo. Nice lady. She find pen pals for my children."

"You're married?"

"Oh, many years now. Four broods, nine children. Maybe brood five come this Fruit, I think." Scratching at the rocky soil, he spread his wings and twitched them in a way that fluffed the feathers out. He settled down with a companionable chirp. "Take sun, Mr. Feighan." He began to carve a face into the big blue seed.

"It does feel good, doesn't it?" He sat on a basalt outcropping and yawned again. "Is Dr. Th'hweet married?"

Sree?sree?sree? cawed in delight. "Him? Who going nest with bad-mouthed genius like him?"

Feighan suppressed a smile. "Right . . . Tell me, what exactly is he doing today? We're not spending much time in any one place, but he doesn't seem to be stirring up any mobs, either."

"He draws a map of sickness, Mr. Feighan. Much of today he just wants to find how many folks sick here, how many folks sick there. He looks for a pattern, he says. And what he looks for, he finds. Is very, very good researcher."

Lab coat flapping in the breeze, Th'hweet swooped over the rise and landed before them. "Are you ready, Mr. Feighan?" He sounded testy.

Half-closing his eyes, he turned his attention inward. Yes, his Talent pulsed strong and bright, eager for exercise. "Any time you are, Doctor."

Sree?sree?sree? had already returned knife and sculpture to his pouch, and opened up the console. He waited attentively for Th'hweet's command.

The epidemiologist stood on one leg while he consulted his list. After a moment, he sang out a place name. Sree?sree? sree? tapped a string of keys, then spread his wing over the console to keep the sun off the screen. Feighan squatted down and peered at the overhead view of a snowbound forest. "Where's the village?"

Sree?sree?sree? pointed to bulges on tree branches that, on closer inspection, proved to be nests. "All through area."

Feighan shook his head. "The branches and twigs and all are obscuring my view. Can you find me a clearing or something?"

Sree?sree?sree? toyed with the controls; the camera panned to the northeast slowly until an opening in the forest canopy appeared. "Is two klicks from village."

"It's fine by me. Dr. Th'hweet?"

"If you can't do better, Mr. Feighan, I'll have to live with it, won't I?"

He did not comment. "Hey, Sam!"

"Already?"

"Yeah, come on." Pebbles clinked as the young Rhanghan slid down from his perch. Feighan thought, visualized, concentrated, felt, knew—

PING

"Here we are." The late winter wind bore a hint of thawing rot.

"McGill, it's cold!"

"Sorry, kid. We won't be here long."

Th'hweet let out a high-pitched cackle that drew a responding screech from the treetops surrounding the clearing. A moment later four villagers glided down from nests thirty meters up. Feighan stepped back out of the way; Sam moved with him. Sree?sree?sree? twisted his neck around and began to scratch the middle of his back with his beak.

Th'hweet greeted each of the strangers, starting with the

largest and ending with the smallest. He opened his mouth to speak.

A corpse hit the ground twenty meters away.

The four villagers covered their crests with their wings for a moment, then broke into a conflicting gabble of song.

Feighan bent his head to Sree?sree?sree?'s and whispered, "What's going on?"

Sree?sree?sree? unwound his astonishingly limber neck. "They say sorry for bad omen. Many folks here sick."

Th'hweet flared his wings and cried out.

With a soft noise of distress, Sree?sree?sree? sidled closer to Feighan. "Doctor losing temper. Says sickness folks own fault. Says folks here very stupid."

The villagers flared their own wings; the largest, with emerald head feathers and orange body plumage, sang a quick, sharp response.

"They tell doctor to close beak." He paused while Th'hweet replied. "Now doctor says even nestlings know not to foul own nest. He says sickness comes from droppings, flock must learn to do right."

All four locals cawed hugely, in unison.

Bouncing on his talons, Th'hweet screeched at his audience.

"Now doctor says same thing. Big orange one says she is Greenlife Teacher to flock, and knows Nest Forest needs um, um, food, you know? Droppings make nest trees tall and branches thick. Doctor says droppings make nestlings thick and folks sick. Teacher says folks who hide feathers in groundstumper clothes are thick ones. She says many years of history prove her right."

Th'hweet ignored them. Stretching his wings, he lifted off. The villagers followed. The five disappeared into the leafless forest.

"What's up?" said Feighan.

Sree?sree?sree?, listening, seemed to tense. "You ready to Fling?"

"Yes, but where?"

"Hotel, I think. Sam, you stay close with us, okay?" He touched the pouch at his waist absently, as if to make sure he still had it.

"I'm too cold to go anywhere."

A moment later the teacher's high, skittering screech whipped across the clearing. A moment later a hundred voices joined it, like hounds baying as they find the scent. Sree?sree?sree? said, "Ho boy. Greenlife Teacher told 'em get doctor. Get ready, Mr. Feighan."

Th'hweet appeared in the distance, zig-zagging through the thicket of immense tree trunks like a slalom racer. Twenty or thirty members of the flock followed in hot pursuit.

"They're gaining on him!" said Sam.

"Is coat," said Sree?sree?sree? "Extra weight; slows him down."

"Why does he wear it?"

"Says he needs pockets."

Feighan squinted into the murk. None of the pursuers seemed to brandish a weapon of any sort. They would have to catch Th'hweet physically, then—and if they came too close, perhaps a small Fling could save the doctor.

Sree?sree?sree? checked the console latches, fidgeted, and let loose a low impatient whistle. "Th'hweet is old, but healthy. I think should win."

"He better," said Feighan. "Say 'Go!' the second he touches down." Closing his eyes, he concentrated on visualizing their hotel room. He grabbed Sam's hand.

Wings beat at the air; feathers slapped his face.

"Go!"

PING

With a snort of disgust, Sam pulled loose from Feighan's grip and bounded onto his bed. Sree?sree?sree? said something to Th'hweet that the doctor answered with a beaksnap and a toss of the head.

"What was all that about?" demanded Feighan.

Spreading twigs and feathers on the table, the exhausted

Th'hweet began to poke them into plastic bags that Sree? sree?sree? held open. His hands trembled; his voice rasped harshly. "If it's any of your business, Mr. Feighan, I was gathering samples."

"With the whole-hearted cooperation of the local flock, huh?"

"Did you fail to understand me when I said we would be violating some taboos?"

Feighan sat in the armchair. "Doctor, I'm not too familiar with your local customs, but I have discovered that no matter where you go in the Network, diplomacy helps."

Th'hweet whirled around to glare at the Flinger. "And just what the devil is that supposed to mean, you young pup?"

He laced his fingers behind his neck. "Look, Sree?sree? sree? translated what you were saying, and frankly, when you insulted the teacher—"

"Fools deserve to be insulted!"

"Maybe so, but they'll be more helpful if you flatter them."

"Feighan, you know nothing of the culture or the discipline, so mind your own business!"

Tired and exasperated, he tried he keep his voice calm. "Now, listen, Doctor—"

"I do not listen to idiots!" Th'hweet flared his wings. "One more word and I'll drive my beak through your heart!"

Feighan leveled a finger at the epidemiologist.

He tweaked his Talent.

Th'hweet vanished.

· Chapter VI ·

Nathaniel Davis could hardly believe he had once valued his cleverness and his organizational skills at the pittance of a salary that the North American Consortium of the Flinger Network paid its Director. And the aggravations he had borne in the New York office staggered the imagination!

Whereas now, if he wished a problem eliminated, he had only to pick up the scramblerphone carved of polished wood. He did just that. "The Terran Flinger McGill Feighan is on Rehma. Have him killed."

The always-polite voice at the other end said, "Yes, sir."

Davis hung up, smiling. He had designed the procedures himself. His Executive Assistant would speak to the Executive Vice-President, Contracts, who would send a specialist to Rehma or, if one were already on-site, would use that one. Sometime later a memo would rise up the chain of command, and Davis would learn how and when the deed had been done.

How nice to have in-house aggravation relievers.

How brilliant to avail himself of them.

· Chapter VII ·

**Monday, 28 September 2105
—Wednesday, 30 September 2105**

The phone rang. Feighan turned to his dead father and said, "It's for you," but Patrick Sean Feighan said, "Sure and who would be after calling me, now? It's someone wanting to talk to the Greystein lad, so be a good boy and call him down." Feighan went to the foot of the staircase and shouted, "Greystein, telephone!" until the dead Flinger, dark hole in his chest, swooped down the stairs on the back of a great golden bird, but since he could not move his arms, or even his mouth, for that matter, he could only look helplessly at Feighan, who grumbled, "God, I have to do *everything* around here," and woke up.

The phone bleated again. An intensely irritating sound, that. And who the hell could it be? The wake-up call was not due for another two hours. Unless—

A chill ran through him. Could something awful have happened to Gina? According to the previous night's report, she was resting comfortably after a successful session of immunotherapy, but Feighan knew damn well that the process had shown serious, delayed side effects on a few people. Could she— *Oh, God, no, please!*

Adrenaline surged in his veins. He rolled out of bed,

stubbed his toe on a chair, hopped, cursed, grabbed the receiver. Sound only—who needed to *see* the bearer of bad news? Beyond the drawn shades the world lay dark and slumbrous.

"Mr. Feighan?" said a high, taut voice.

Pulse racing, he said, "Yes."

"Dr. Th'hweet here, Mr. Feighan."

Though fright had shocked him to the edge of wakefulness, it had pushed him equally close to panic. At the word "Doctor" he thought, *My God, something* did *go wrong!* The name "Th'hweet" took longer to percolate through an anxiety fuzzed with the last wisps of sleep. When it did, he flushed with anger. He lowered the handset to its cradle, and returned to bed. The pillow had barely cooled; the resilient force-field mattress hugged him to its bosom.

The phone rang again.

He decided it could ring itself hoarse.

On the seventh ring Sam awoke. "Hey, McGill!"

"Go back to sleep, Sam."

"Phone's ringing!"

"I know, go back to sleep."

"I can't, it's too noisy."

"So don't go back to sleep, just lie there and be quiet."

"Aren't you gonna answer it?"

"Uh-uh."

"Why?"

"Because it's that idiot Th'hweet, and I don't want to talk to him."

"He didn't mean it, McGill. I know he didn't."

"I don't like to be threatened."

"Well, if you're not gonna answer it, I will."

"Be my guest." He rolled onto his stomach and buried his face in the pillow.

•Briefly there whispered a susurrus of scales on sheets. Four feet hit the floor with a thump. A tail slapped on the carpet. The phone cut off in mid-ring as Sam said, "Hello?"

Far, far in the distance a tiny voice squeaked.

"He doesn't wanna talk to you."

Feighan tugged the sheets up over his head.

"'Cause you threatened him. He doesn't like that."

The air under the sheets got stuffy quickly, so he poked his nose back into the open.

"All right, I'll tell him. 'Bye." Sam hung up the phone, yawned loudly, and plodded over to the side of Feighan's bed. "Hey, McGill."

"Go away, I'm asleep."

"No, you're not."

"Am too."

"Dr. Th'hweet's on his way over."

So much for sleep. He turned over and sat up. "Thanks a lot, pal."

"McGill!" Injured innocence wailed in Sam's tone. "Don't blame me."

"Why not? You're the one who answered the phone."

"That's not fair." He beat the rug with his tail for emphasis.

"It's not, huh?"

"No!" The young Rhanghan grabbed Feighan's sheets and pulled them down. "Get up."

"My, aren't we bossy this morning?"

Sam clacked his teeth in annoyance.

"You're picking up bad habits from the natives, kid." Wearily, he swung his legs over the edge of the bed and sat motionless for a moment. "You're going to break a tooth that way."

"I'm gonna call room service."

"Order me a large pot of coffee and some toast, okay? Oh, and call the desk, find out how Gina's doing."

"Say please."

"*Sam*—" He took a deep breath. "Sorry. I shouldn't take things out on you. Please order me the coffee and toast. Please call the front desk. Okay?"

"Okay." But he sniffed to show that his feelings were still hurt.

• • •

Th'hweet and Sree?sree?sree? arrived half an hour later. The epidemiologist's out-puffed violet feathers and stiff movements suggested that he simmered with complaints about having to fly over. Apparently not daring to voice them, he confined himself to a terse, "I regret taking so long."

Feighan's mood, which had been buoyed by a favorable progress report on Maccari, sank again. He answered the Rehmal with a wordless glare.

Th'hweet's crimson crest bristled. "Mr. Feighan, I— dammit, man, but you're difficult to talk to!"

The Flinger raised his eyebrows. "Oh?"

"Surely you didn't take me seriously yesterday?"

"I didn't Fling you to the lobby because I thought you were kidding."

Short Sree?sree?sree? sang a few bars in Rehmal; Th'hweet appeared to listen closely. Then the doctor's shoulders slumped and he turned back to Feighan. "My assistant informs me that my behavior has been even more, er, irascible than normal."

The blue one cawed happily. "I tell him he been twice the fisheater he usually is." He opened his pouch to get his knife and his carving; sharp pointed ears set off the face, now, which also wore a rough-scraped smile.

Th'hweet's head twitched; Feighan got the impression the doctor was struggling not to snap at his chuckling assistant. "Mr. Feighan, I am a proud man, and even in the best of times I find it difficult to take the feelings of others sufficiently into account. These are not the best of times; indeed, they may well be the worst of times. Clearly I have offended you, and I regret it immensely."

Sree?sree?sree? paused in mid-whittle to twitter at his boss again.

"Oh, very well." Th'hweet smoothed the front of his white lab coat. "I apologize. I am sorry, Mr. Feighan."

Actually, he had little choice. He had accepted the posting

to Rehma, and the Director of the Rehma Consortium had assigned him to Th'hweet's staff. He had to work for Th'hweet whether he still wanted to or not. But did he have to let Th'hweet know that? *No...*

"All right, Dr. Th'hweet, I'll accept your apology. This time. But I warn you: I don't take death threats lightly. The next time you threaten me you're likely to wind up in the heart of Rehma's sun."

"Mr. Feighan, you must understand my position." The tips of his wings fluttered slightly as he moved across the room. He stood on one leg, and with his beak picked moodily at the talons of his free foot. "I have not yet announced this, because of the panic it would surely engender, but my race trembles on the brink of extinction."

Feighan's jaw dropped. "What?"

Th'hweet nodded sadly. "I have yet to isolate either the infectious agent or its vector, but I have developed some statistics which I believe to be valid." He spread the claws of his right foot, examined them, and set the foot back down.

"And?"

"The disease seems to be contagious only during a six-day incubation stage, before the symptoms manifest themselves. During that period, my demographic studies seem to show, the average infected individual encounters sixty-one other Rehmal—seven of whom will display symptoms of their own six days after the encounter. That's an infection rate of 10.8 percent; of those, nearly 30 percent will die from the disease."

Feighan performed a few rapid mental calculations. "But that's only a little over three percent of the population—granted, thirty million is a huge number, but it's not extinction."

"Unfortunately, Mr. Feighan, that is not how it works." He told his assistant something in Rehmal. Sree?sree?sree? immediately opened the console and plugged it into the

telephone jack. A few minutes on the keyboard filled the
screen with numbers. "Let me show you, Mr. Feighan."

Cycles	Carriers	Encounters	Infectees	Deaths	Eventual Surviving Recoveries	Population
1	1	61	7			1000000000
2	7	402	43	2	5	999999998
3	43	2648	286	13	31	999999985
4	286	17447	1884	86	201	999999899
5	1884	114947	12414	565	1319	999999334
6	12414	757309	81789	3724	8690	999995610
7	81789	4988971	538772	24537	57252	999971073
8	538772	32846558	3545851	161632	377141	999809441
9	3545851	215407717	23195860	1063755	2482096	998745686
10	23195860	1376307551	145769090	6958758	16237103	991786928
11	145769090	7352833090	692585206	43730727	102038364	948056201
12	692585206	5672946979	111124845	207775562	484809645	740280639
13	111124845	156894965	554735	33337454	77787392	706943186
14	554735	764447	2639	166421	388315	706776765
15	2639	3636	13	792	1848	706775973
TOTALS	977413423		977413434	293224027	684189402	706775979

The Flinger went over to the screen.

"We start with one infected individual." Th'hweet tapped
the first number in the second column. "He will meet sixty-
one people—" He pointed to the top of the third column.
"—of whom six-point-five-eight-eight, rounded to seven,
will contract the disease." His finger touched the fourth
column, then dropped down a line and moved to the right.
"Symptoms will appear the following week. Two of the
infectees will die; five will survive."

"I'm following you so far," said Feighan.

"Very good. However, before the disease manifests itself,
these seven people will spread it." He indicated the second
number in the "Carriers" column. "They will encounter four

hundred two other individuals." His finger moved to column three, tapped the number there, then moved to the "Infectees" column. "Forty-three of them will become infected. Thirteen of them will, eventually, die, but first the forty-three will infect two hundred eighty-six, who will infect eighteen hundred who will in turn—don't you see, man? Every week, nearly seven times as many people carry the disease as did the week before."

Feighan looked closely at column four, counting off the cycles between the top and the bottom. "Is this saying that after eleven weeks—"

"A bit less than ten of your weeks, actually. These are six-day cycles." His crest drooped. "But what does it matter? By the end of the eleventh cycle, eighty-six percent of my species will have come down with the disease. After fifteen cycles, nearly ninety-eight percent will have caught it."

"And thirty percent of them will die?"

"At an absolute minimum. On this round of the disease alone."

The implications of the phrase "this round" sank in slowly. Feighan's cheeks went cold. "Oh. My. God."

"Precisely." Th'hweet seemed very, very tired. "Although this chart is based on the reasonable supposition that surviving the disease confers a certain amount of immunity, I have found no proof of this. It is conceivable that a dose of the disease does *not* immunize one against further contagion. And if this be true, then the disease will pulse through Rehmal civilization again and again, striking down thirty percent of all who contract it, until such time as no one is left alive to infect or to be infected."

Feighan envisioned a world-sized scythe sweeping through an ever-diminishing field, felling a third of the remaining grainstalks at each pass, while the field shrank and the stubble browned in the sun. "This is—" He had no words for his horror.

"It is even worse, Mr. Feighan."

"How could it possibly be worse?"

"Are you familiar with Festival?"

"Sort of." He spread his hands. "I've heard of it, I know a little about it, but—"

Th'hweet touched a wingtip to the screen. "The ugly details are right here, Mr. Feighan. By the first day of Festival, one and a quarter million Rehmal will already have died."

Feighan grimaced.

Th'hweet went on relentlessly. "Twenty-three million will be contagious as they begin to fly south. They will infect nearly one hundred fifty million more within six days—and *those* beings will infect an additional seven hundred million. Which is to say that unless something is done quickly, virtually the entire population will have fallen ill before the end of Festival. Over two hundred million of them will die of the disease itself—but with eight hundred fifty million Rehmal sick and far from home, the final toll will be immense. Mr. Feighan, I sincerely believe that sixty percent of my planet's population will die within the next twenty-eight days."

Feighan wanted to vomit. Six hundred million people—yes, people; though they had feathers and wings, they also had humor, and thus had to have souls—six hundred million people, dead within a month. The number was just too large. "But what can we do?" He did not mind that his voice trembled as he asked the question.

"You said 'we,' Mr. Feighan." Th'hweet regarded him impassively for a moment.

"Well, ah . . . I'm on your team, I guess, but—"

"We can go to the Glade in the Forest of the Tallest Trees, Mr. Feighan." His long beak swung as he sang a few bars to Sree?sree?sree?.

The assistant pouched his knife and his carving, and bent over the console. In an instant the numbers dissolved into memory. The image of a clearing ringed with trees that would dwarf redwoods took their place. Sree?sree?sree? looked up. "This is Glade."

"Why are we going there, Doctor?" asked Feighan.

Th'hweet blinked, ducked his head beneath his wing for

a moment, then whispered, "We must ensure that Festival is canceled this year."

Feighan inhaled sharply. "That's sort of a tall order, isn't it?"

"There is none taller, Mr. Feighan." Somberly, he scratched the carpet with his right talon. "We must go now."

"Okay. Ready, Sam?"

"Just a second." Balancing himself on his tail, the young Rhanghan lifted up on his hind legs and inspected the room service tray. "I thought so." Triumphantly he scooped up the last two muffins. He held one in his left hand, said, "All set!" and popped the other in his mouth.

The Flinger shook his head. "You're getting crumbs all over the floor. No, don't lick them up, we've got to go. C'mon!" He held out his hand and waited for Sam to take it. Once Th'hweet and Sree?sree?sree? had stepped up to him, he closed his eyes, concentrated, visualized, felt, knew—

PING

Sunlight dazzled their eyes; the wind slapped their ankles with the young grasses of spring. An antlered animal not much larger than Sam lifted its head in surprise and sprang away. Three graceful bounds carried it into the shadows of the surrounding forest.

"What was that?" said Feighan.

Sree?sree?sree?'s kelly green crest feathers perked up. "Is *ch'ruch'row.*"

Th'hweet said, "Our equivalent of the antelope."

"*Ch'ruch'row* eats much grain; we chase away but always come back. Greatest sport is catch and ride. As teachings say, 'Make them work for what they steal.'"

He cocked his head. "How do you ride one of them?"

Sree?sree?sree? spread his wings and mimicked swooping in for a landing. "Must come in silent from upwind side, calls for great skill. If *ch'ruch'row* hears, *ch'ruch'row* runs. But if you get claws in shoulder fur and hands on horns, *ch'ruch'row* can't shake off, and you get good long ride till *ch'ruch'row* fall down tired."

"Is it dangerous?"

Th'hweet said, "Should it lift its head just a fraction of a second before you catch hold of its antlers, it is likely to impale you. Since it will then run for cover, the hapless sportsman has almost no chance whatsoever. It is said to be a remarkably unpleasant way to die."

"I can believe it." Feighan looked around. "Where are we?"

"As I said before, we are in the Glade in the Forest of the Tallest Trees, Mr. Feighan. This is where the Flock of True Lore nests."

"The Flock of True Lore?"

Th'hweet gave an annoyed-sounding trill. "My apologies for translating so literally. You would call it a . . . a Council of Elders? It is our central governing body, but even that is misleading, since our central government has no powers comparable to yours."

A shadow swept across them and all four looked up. Overhead, a large grey Rehmal banked in a wide circle and glided over to the opposite side of the clearing.

Sree?sree?sree? threw back his head to let loose a long, haunting cry.

Feighan eyed Th'hweet, who bent slightly in his direction and whispered, "Sree?sree?sree? is requesting the pleasure of an audience with anyone who will speak for the Flock of True Lore."

The circling grey Rehmal replied with a minor-key plaint that dopplered down as it headed for the trees.

"Now what?" asked Feighan.

"A representative of the Flock of True Lore will join us shortly." His gaze jerked away from Feighan's face and fastened on something in the grass behind the Flinger.

Sam hissed.

Startled, Feighan froze. He was not alarmed: If danger lurked at his back, Sam would tell him. Rather, curiosity gripped him. Surely, whatever provoked both Sam and

Th'hweet into staring so fixedly, so intently, had to be fascinating indeed. But he was hesitant to turn: Even a small motion could frighten off a shy wild creature.

Out of the corner of his eye he caught a glimpse of Sree?sree?sree?. The assistant focused on the same spot, and slowly let his beak fall open.

What are they all gaping at? Feighan turned his head— gently, so as not to scare whatever it was away—and then swallowed hard.

Four meters away, swaying upright like a cobra, a giant green snake dappled with brown regarded Th'hweet through cold, unblinking eyes. From a mouth larger than Feighan's curved long yellow fangs; a clear orange liquid dripped off their points. He quelled a shudder. The grasses hid most of its length, but he guessed that if it struck, it could reach him without half extending itself.

The question was, did it want to reach him?

He tried to calm himself with a very deep breath. If the snake meant to strike him, Sam would surely have sensed its intentions and warned him. Since Sam had made no sound beyond that first hiss, then . . .

He wondered if he dared ask Th'hweet or Sree?sree?sree?. Experimentally, eyes still focused on the huge, arrowshaped head, he cleared his throat softly.

It did not so much as glance in his direction.

In a whisper, he said, "Dr. Th'hweet?"

The epidemiologist took an unsteady step forward, almost as if he were stopping himself from falling on his face. He ignored Feighan completely.

Still motionless, Feighan said, "Sree?sree?sree??"

The assistant did not answer, either.

Panic began to rise in Feighan. His Talent trembled with the desire to Fling away. His muscles ached with a desperate need to bolt, to run for the shelter of the looming trees. He squelched his instincts hard. "S-sam?"

The Rhanghan stood like a statue. "Yeah, McGill?"

Thank God one of them can talk. "Are we in trouble here?"

"You're not."

"You are?" he said incredulously.

"It's pretty stupid, McGill. It's not sure what I'm doing here. It wants Dr. Th'hweet—"

At the mention of his name, Th'hweet tottered a pace closer to the snake.

"Sam, why is he walking toward it?"

"Don't ask *me*, McGill. Sree?sree?sree? isn't moving, though."

The breeze fell away. The sun blazed so strongly that the temperature seemed to shoot up by ten degrees in as many seconds. Now into Feighan's nostrils came the scent of the snake: It stank of dried blood and rotting meat. "Sam, do you figure there's any chance anybody would be offended if I, uh, made that thing disappear?"

Sam rolled his eyes and twitched his head. "McGill, do you really think I—"

Like an arrow from a bow, the snake launched itself at Sam. Blurring, stretching, it—

PING

Sam looked at Feighan. "That took you long enough."

Giddy with snapped tension, he shrugged. "I didn't know what was going on. For that matter, I still don't."

"What'd you do with it, the sun again?"

"Uh-uh." He pointed high into the sky, at a barely visible black dot. "I just put it about fifty thousand meters up."

Sam squinted in the direction Feighan was pointing. "It's falling, but not wiggling."

"The air pressure's pretty low up there. It might have exploded."

"Good!" A savage smile flitted across Sam's face. "I didn't like it much."

"Yeah, I noticed, kiddo. You looked just about ready to go for it."

"I coulda taken it, McGill."

"I believe you." He scratched Sam's skullplate. "But I'm glad you didn't have to prove it."

"Me, too."

Feighan turned to their companions. "Hey, Dr. Th'hweet."

The epidemiologist stared at him blankly for a moment, then twitched, fluffed his feathers, and clacked his beak. "My goodness," he said slowly, "that was a near thing. Was it you who removed the *k'see:k'see?*"

"The snake?"

Th'hweet bobbed his head. "I had never encountered one in the wilds before." His usual brisk turn of speech had softened into thoughtfulness. "Or a hungry one, either. We are, of course, taught of its hypnotic powers, but I had always discounted the teachings as mere legends..." He shivered. The tips of his violet wings thrashed in the grass. "Well done, Mr. Feighan."

"Believe me, it was my pleasure." He glanced over to Sree?sree?sree?, who seemed to be coming out of his trance, too. "Doctor, uh, not to be indelicate or anything, but, ah ... that was not the smallest snake in the world, and it seems to me that the guy Sree?sree?sree? spoke to earlier—the grey one, that was circling overhead?—should have seen it, and told you about it. Unless getting past the snake was some sort of ritual test?"

Th'hweet blinked. He swiveled his head to study Sree?sree?sree?, then swiveled it back to Feighan. "That had not occurred to me, Mr. Feighan. Indeed, the Watcher for the Glade should have espied the *k'see:k'see* and alerted us to the danger. I cannot think of a reason why it did not."

"Could it have been a set-up?" said Feighan.

"Do you mean a trap?"

"Yes."

Th'hweet lifted his wings. "But who could know in advance of our arrival? And beyond that is the more elemental problem of positioning the *k'see:k'see.* I assure you, Mr. Feighan, for those who lack your Talent, transporting a monster of that size is no easy task."

"Coincidence, then, I guess," said Feighan, though he was unhappy with that analysis. "Or—"

A wild soaring wail cut him off. All four of them glanced up.

Three magnificently feathered Rehmal fanned their wings and came to a stop just in front of them. The middle avian, feathered in flame-red and crested with ebony, took a pigeon step forward. Taller than its colleagues, it had a vulturish cast to its face. It bowed, cocked its head to one side while its bright eyes drank them in, and cooed a tune so obviously of greeting that Feighan needed no translation.

Sree?sree?sree? stepped forward to reply. With small movements of his wings, Th'hweet urged Feighan and Sam to fall back a meter. The Flinger looked sharply at him.

The epidemiologist sidled closer. In a very low voice he said, "That my assistant must sing for me is a source of particular embarrassment, Mr. Feighan."

"Why don't you sing for yourself, then?"

"The modality of the songs appropriate for addressing the Flock of True Lore can be learned only during a certain stage in the maturation process, Mr. Feighan. No, more than 'learned'—obtained, let us say, for the modality depends on an unnatural ductility of the vocal cords, and that ductility can only be achieved by appropriately stretching the vocal cords when they are most plastic, that is, during the fourteenth to eighteenth years of one's life. Unfortunately, I was pursuing my undergraduate studies at Princeton when that particular stage came—and went."

Feighan raised an eyebrow. "Are you serious?"

"Mr. Feighan, were I to open my beak right now, I could attempt to reproduce the proper sounds—on an intellectual level, I know them well, after all—but my voice would crack; I would sing off-key. The Watchers of the Glade would promptly tear me wing from wing for the insult to the Flock of True Lore. Therefore the noble Sree?sree?sree? speaks for all of us."

"So what's he saying?"

Th'hweet bent an ear to the proceedings for a moment. "He is just now concluding the preliminary formalities of courtesy." He paused. The red one said something. "She invites us to be seated."

At Feighan's nod, Sam lowered himself to his belly. The Flinger sat cross-legged in the grass, while Th'hweet made himself comfortable between the two off-worlders. He continued to translate. "Sree?sree?sree? is now beginning to explain our findings, their import, and our recommendations."

The assistant sang on uninterrupted for some fifteen minutes. Meanwhile Th'hweet explained that the three were members of the Flock of True Lore, and authorized to speak for it at this hearing. "The fat indigo male on the left," he said quietly, "is named Huu'leie. He convinced the Flock of True Lore to pay for my education on Earth many years ago. I am optimistic that he will give us a fair reception. I do not know the imposing female in the center, nor the yellow-crested blue male on the right. Their features express neither hostility nor warmth, but they are listening closely."

When Sree?sree?sree? finished, no one spoke for a minute or so. Feighan inhaled the fragrances of spring while the sun soaked into his bones. A gentle breeze brushed by like a lover leaving.

Huu'leie offered the first reply, and Th'hweet again translated: "You sing a dark tune, and it troubles us greatly, but we can do nothing."

Yellow-crest said, "It troubles you, perhaps, my legalistic friend, but for those with faith the honorable Sree?sree?sree?'s story offers naught but joy and hope."

The tall female said, "Death offers joy, K'rala?"

"Always! In the words of our teachings, if I may quote the relevant passage: 'In death we become one with the universe.' In this case especially, we must see death as the illusion it is."

"Six hundred million victims rings to me most coarsely

of reality, K'rala," said Huu'leie. "How does it suggest illusion?"

Blue-tailed K'rala made a rude noise. "The great piles of bodies belong not to the future, my dry-witted friend, but to one possible future. Can you honestly believe that Our Shield and Our Solace would permit us to suffer that future?"

"Considering what the Great-Winged Retzglaran has permitted us to suffer in the past, yes, I find it possible to accept Its willingness to test us once again."

"Nonsense! Oh, the sickness now passing through our flocks has taken its toll, and will claim more, but it is merely a call to the lax of spirit reminding them of their duties to their God."

Huu'leie said, "Between us lies a nut worth cracking, K'rala, and I predict a good many nights will pass before we have reached the meat, but for the here and the now we can ignore it. The honorable Sree?sree?sree? has asked us to fly to the stars, and we clearly cannot. The Flock of True Lore has neither the right nor the power to prohibit Festival."

"Of course it lacks the right, Huu'leie! Did the Flock of True Lore claim either the right or the power it would be living blasphemy, a stain upon the soul of our race."

The red female spoke directly to Sree?sree?sree?. "As you can see, my colleagues will vote to deny your request, each for his own reasons."

Sree?sree?sree?'s talons dug into the soil. "Will you sing to them for us, Elder Eewhie?"

She shook her head slowly. "Each of us is steeped in a different lore, honorable Sree?sree?sree?. K'rala is our Master of Theology; Huu'leie, our Teacher of the Law. I am our Songstress of Times Past, and from my own learning springs my own denial of your plea."

Undaunted, Th'hweet's assistant said, "It would honor us to hear the causes of such denial, Elder Eewhie."

"Sicknesses have ebbed and flowed through all our recorded history, honorable Sree?sree?sree?. Now another sickness flows. Eventually it will ebb. Such is life. So are we taught."

Sree?sree?sree? leaned forward eagerly, but before he could say anything, Eewhie raised a fiery wingtip. "I realize that the renowned Th'hweet and your alien companions may consider my reasoning to be the product of an uneducated mind—and, who knows? perhaps it is—but the logic seems sufficiently sophisticated to me. Listen, then: Plagues have fallen on us before, with great suffering and loss of life, but always have they ended long before a tenth the people have died. The diseases spring from the small life within us, from the small life which is part of us, and they must be seen as part of an evolutionary process. Those of us who develop a resistance will survive; those of us who do not, will die. It is the way of life that the strong and the adaptable survive, honorable Sree?sree?sree?. It is not for the Flock of True Lore to interfere with the growth of the people of the sky."

Th'hweet tensed, and moved as if to rise to his feet. Feighan seized his left ankle as discreetly as he could. Pitching his voice low, he said, "Didn't you say if you tried to talk to them they'd have you killed?"

"Yes, but—"

"Sit down and be quiet. And please keep translating."

Th'hweet settled back but did not relax. "Sree?sree?sree? is floundering. He does not know what to say. Ah, now he asks if they realize what will happen if they have made the wrong decision."

Huu'leie said, "Right or wrong, we cannot nest beneath the waves. The Flock of True Lore has not the power to prohibit Festival."

"And a good thing, too!" said K'rala, with a riffle of his chest. "Only by honoring Our Shield and Our Source can we do that which is right, so we must uphold Festival."

Sree?sree?sree eyed Eewhie but said nothing.

The tall female said, "If I am wrong in my estimation, honorable Sree?sree?sree?, our race will die, and I with it, and I will pass tormented by the knowledge that because of me, there will be none to curse me for all time." Spreading her wings, she bowed. "Should the renowned Th'hweet encounter new facts concerning the sickness, facts that disprove any of the assumptions we the ears of the Flock of True Lore have made, he should return to the Glade in the Forest of the Tallest Trees immediately, and make known the new facts in his possession." That said, she took wing, and headed for the trees.

K'rala and Huu'leie waited long enough for her to open a fifty-meter lead, leaped into the air, and followed after her. One blue feather fluttered in their wake, then drifted lazily to ground.

With an apologetic gesture, Sree?sree?sree? turned to his employer and whistled in Rehmal.

Th'hweet waved a wing at him. "It is at times like these, Mr. Feighan, that I wish I had a Terran's anatomy."

Puzzled, the Flinger said, "Why?"

"I wish to shake a fist at those pompous fools," said the doctor, "but my hand is so small that any fist I make is ludicrous. Ah, you Terrans with your thick bones and huge knuckles. You have come so far with so little that I feel for my people nothing but shame, that they who have so much more have fallen so short of your accomplishments."

Feighan and Sam looked at each other for a moment. "Doctor," said the Flinger, "I think you just insulted the human race, but I'm not sure, so I'll let it pass."

"You see?" said Th'hweet. "Come. If the Flock of True Lore chooses to cower beneath their wings, we must act on our own. Sree?sree?sree?!"

Patting his pouch, the assistant opened the console.

Th'hweet announced their destination, Sree?sree?sree? brought it up on screen, and Feighan made ready to teleport them.

After thirty-six hours of nearly constant Flinging, Feighan could barely focus his eyes on the screen—but once he had, he recognized the clumped shapes in the bushes. Corpses. Three of them. No, four, five—

"God! Why don't they take 'em away?" Physically close to his limit, he suspected he had already exceeded the amount of emotional stress he could absorb. Thank God the latest word on Maccari was good. It was the only thing keeping him sane.

Th'hweet said merely, "Are you ready?"

"Not just yet."

"We must identify the infectious agent!" Mounting desperation shrilled the epidemiologist's voice. "I still have no idea whether it is a virus, a bacterium, a spore..." He whirled to Sree?sree?sree? and snapped out four quick bars.

The blue-feathered assistant looked up from the wicker lab bench with its force-field surface. He replied wearily, in English, "No. You take samples from hundred flocks and more. How you expect me to culture all of them so quick? Hard enough to keep them straight."

Th'hweet tapped his beak against the glass door of the three-meter-tall incubator cabinet. "I risked my life obtaining those!"

"At least sixty times," said Feighan, who in each of those instances had had to Fling them back to the lab a heartbeat ahead of pursuers. His shoulder still ached from a stone an angry villager had dropped. He closed his eyes. The researchers' bickering had lost its tone of good-natured joshing, and the atmosphere in the lab had turned poisonous. "Don't you think you're pushing all of us just a little too hard?"

Th'hweet flared his wings. "No!" He drew a great, shuddering breath. Slowly he lowered his wings, brushing Sree?sree?sree?'s shoulder gently. More quietly, he said, "Our people are dying, Mr. Feighan."

"Okay." He sighed, stretched, and stood up. "Let's go."

This trip reprised the patterns of the last hundred some: first the Fling, then on arrival the studied head-turnings to ignore the bodies in the undergrowth. What Feighan could not ignore was the smell of death that permeated the clearing. And the rustling of small scavengers as they burrowed between lifeless feathers to claw at the meat beneath.

Th'hweet took to the air; Feighan and Sam sat down to go over a page or two in Sam's lesson book; Sree?sree?sree? carved the big blue seed and listened and told Feighan when it was time to teleport back before dropped stones crushed their heads. In the lab he ignored the scientists' temper tantrums while he recuperated. And then it was time to Fling to the next village . . .

The travels did help Feighan develop a mental picture of Rehma—or at least of its super-continent, where ninety-nine percent of the Rehmal lived. One huge mountain chain ran the length of the eastern shore, from North Pole to South and back up again through The Cliffs. Bleak, forbidding, and in certain areas nearly two thousand kilometers wide, the mountain ranges stood wreathed in cloud and whipped by treacherous winds that few Rehmal cared to ride. According to Th'hweet, not more than six thousand people lived there—the majority of them exiles and outlaws.

Most of the rest of the continent was given over to plains that truly deserved to be called "Great." Roughly rectangular, their very shallow bowl covered 240,000,000 square kilometers, extending from the northern ice cap to the southern jumble of rock out of which spewed The River. From the western foothills of the mountain chain they fell in a smooth slow descent to the choppy waters of the western ocean, 20,000 kilometers away. Here and there blossomed round lakes larger than Ohio, which Sree?sree?sree? said were craters left from giant meteorite strikes. More than anything else, the plains fed the planet.

They were ready for another Fling. Th'hweet was muttering under his breath again. Feighan opened his eyes, let out his breath in a whoosh of exasperation, and said, "Look, Dr. Th'hweet, if you're talking to me, I'd appreciate your speaking loudly enough for me to hear you. If you're not, would you please keep quiet while I'm Flinging? You don't really want to wind up half a meter underground, do you?"

Th'hweet stood on one leg, and sketched ducking his head under his wing. "My apologies, Mr. Feighan. The conundrum I face has me talking to myself. How is the disease spread? We have cultured dozens of fecal samples, yet nothing out of the ordinary has appeared. We have examined feathers, and nests, and talon scrapings—all to no avail. Clearly the disease is contagious, but until we can determine the agent we can manufacture neither vaccine to guard against it nor serum to cure it."

Feighan said, "I understand all that, but . . . look, I know next to nothing about epidemiology, but when I was a kid I read about the Black Death, and it just seemed to me like people were incredibly stupid back then. They didn't need drugs—I mean, they did, once they caught the plague, but all the healthy people had to do was kill the rats, and that would have solved the problem."

"Yes, but that is based on hindsight, Mr. Feighan. We know, now, that fleas carried the disease, and that rats carried the fleas, but the Europeans of the time did not know this. We are in a similar position: we do not know the vector of transmission, and until we do, we cannot stop the spread of the disease." He scratched the lab's tile floor absently with his lifted foot. "Sree?sree?sree? will accompany us on this trip. Are you ready?"

"I suppose." After one last glance at the screen, he closed his eyes, concentrated, visualized, felt, knew—

PING

They stood at the edge of a stubbled field that reached from the eastern horizon all the way to the setting sun. A kilometer to the north rose a forested ridge, a mirror image of the one behind them. The two wooded hills ran parallel for as far as the eye could see, perpetually overlooking the endless valley. The flock they had come to visit worked out among the browned, leafless stalks, moving in an apparently aimless fashion from one band of trees to the other. Here and there the sun glinted off the metal shell of a robot.

"What are they doing?" asked Feighan.

Sree?sree?sree? said, "They eat—"

"Hush!" said Th'hweet.

"They eat hush?" said Sam, turning from one Rehmal to the other. "What's that? Is it like mush?"

Sree?sree?sree? pointed his closed beak at Th'hweet and jerked his head, as if to say, "Ask him." He took out his knife and his sculpture.

The epidemiologist spread his violet wings. "If you'll excuse me—"

"Hold on," said Feighan tiredly. "What's going on here? Doc—"

But Th'hweet had already left the ground and was flying away.

Feighan turned to the assistant. "Would you care to explain what that was all about?"

Sree?sree?sree? paused in mid-whittle. "If you don't tell, okay."

"Promise."

"When Th'hweet go to Terra, to school, many schoolmates laugh at him because of what we eat, so now he not like Terran to know. He still thinks you laugh at him." Sree?sree?sree? looked anxiously at Feighan. "If you make fun of Th'hweet for our food, he know I tell you, and I will be in big trouble, okay?"

"I understand," said Feighan. He touched the Rehmal on the shoulder gently. "I promise I won't tell Th'hweet you told me, and I promise I won't make fun of him—but I'm dying of curiosity. What are those folks out there eating?"

"Bugs." Sree?sree?sree? winged-ducked briefly, then pulled his head back into the air and cocked it. "No reaction?"

The Flinger shrugged. "What's the big deal? Sam eats bugs all the time."

"Live bugs?"

Sam said, "When I catch 'em they're alive. Then—"

Feighan held up a hand. "I really don't care what anybody

else eats, but frankly, guys, I'd rather you kept the graphic details to yourselves. Okay?"

"Uh-huh," said Sam, switching his attention immediately to Sree?sree?sree?. "Can you tell me—"

From the field came a shriek pitched like a buzzsaw.

"Better get ready." Sree?sree?sree? began bundling up his equipment. "That Soul Life Teacher plenty angry."

Feighan said, "Right. Sam, come—"

"McGill! Watch—"

Bony feet slammed into his shoulder blades, driving him forward as huge wings flailed the air. He stumbled through three quick steps, almost but not quite losing his balance. Squawks and screeches rose from a hundred throats at once.

Jesus, he thought, *we've been ambushed!*

"McGill! Help!"

"Sam!" Feathers filled his mouth. He bit down hard; a nearby voice squealed in pain. Claws tangled in his hair. He groped for its ankle. A beak snapped shut on his wrist. The pain brought hot, angry tears to his eyes—and new strength to his body. He forced his way through the mob, kicking and biting and breaking every scrawny bone his fingers could grasp. Five meters he advanced, and ten, but the sheer weight of the ambushers bore him remorselessly to the ground.

He could Fling away, surely, but it was the end of the day. He had precious few Flings left in him, and those would have to be spaced at the longest intervals possible.

A mottled green tail slapped his knees. "Sam!"

"McGill!"

Feighan dove forward, into the squalling cloud of Rehmal attacking his ward. His hand touched rough scales. He held on for dear life, knowing that he had no time to do this right, he could only—

PING

They hit the carpet with a bounce, and slid a few centimeters across the hotel room. Sam groaned. Feighan spat out a mouthful of feathers. "You okay?"

"Yeah. I think so, at least."

He rolled onto his back. "You didn't warn me."

"Did too."

"Sam. A warning's supposed to come *before* the attack."

"It *was* before."

"By about a second."

"That's still before."

"All right, all right." He sat up. "I have to go back."

"For Sree?sree?sree? and Dr. Th'hweet?"

"You got it, kiddo." Gingerly, he explored his face with his fingertips. It surprised him that the Rehmal had not gone for his eyes. Not that he minded their omission. "I am not looking forward to this."

"You're going alone, huh?"

He spread his hands. "I can't take you, Sam. It's too dangerous."

"I know." The young Rhanghan reached out to Feighan. "Come back, okay, McGill?"

"I'll do my best." He concentrated on materializing about five hundred meters from the site of the ambush. He closed his eyes, forced himself to visualize the spot—

PING

He stood near the base of a tree. Feathers littered the site of the battle, but the attacking flock had moved on. Someone—Sree?sree?sree??—lay beside the console. He looked around.

Overhead, at least a hundred Rehmal, silent, now, and grim, pursued Th'hweet down the field. The doctor zigged into the forest. The hunters followed without hesitation.

Feighan crossed his fingers and ran to Sree?sree?sree?.

Just as he got there, Th'hweet burst out of the woods and broke directly toward him. Feighan waved his arms, grabbed the console, and knelt by the assistant's side. Already he was forming and holding the image of the hotel room—

Th'hweet snapped his wings wide and touched down half a meter from Feighan.

PING

"You made it!" Sam ran to Feighan and hugged him.

"Yeah." He squeezed the kid hard. The young life in his arms seemed suddenly very precious. He looked over Sam's head to the epidemiologist. "Are you okay, Doctor?"

"I endure." Th'hweet rose from his assistant's side. His crest drooped; his tail sagged. Tears welled out of his dark eyes. "But the honorable Sree?sree?sree? does not. They have murdered him."

▪ Chapter VIII ▪

An oversized glass tank dominated the cabin of the space-liner. Inside flowed garish blue and gold gases that did not mix: Gryll, Davis' superior, who controlled all Organization operations on a hundred worlds.

It unnerved Davis to be summoned before the alien. He patted his forehead dry with a handkerchief. PlayGround had not proved out yet, so Gryll did not intend to congratulate him. Had something gone wrong? "Sir?"

The speaker on the tank's side crackled. "Order to execute McGill Feighan violates truce between Feighan and Organization."

He went cold. He had forgotten about the truce. Or suppressed the memory, not that it made a difference. "I'll cancel it at once, sir."

"Too late. First try failed. Also killed Feighan's native friend."

Oh, Christ. How had Gryll learned that before he had? "Yes, sir."

"Serious error. Have aroused attention and possibly anger of Far Being Retzglaran. Beware It—Gryll as well—if Retzglaran learns of PlayGround."

At times, Davis truly regretted his own cleverness . . .

· Chapter IX ·

The corpse lay behind the filing cabinets, beneath a sheet of black plastic.

Rehmal tradition called for Sree?sree?sree? to be taken home in a funeral flight led by eight dignified bearers. Highly trained, and even more highly paid, they were meant to play a solemn role in the ritual. With slow, steady beats of their wings, wheeling and banking in perfect formation, they would carry the leaf-covered deceased in a sling of vines to his resting place.

Tradition had to give way to necessity. An exhaustive and increasingly exasperating series of phone calls revealed that every team of bearers in Stonehills City was booked for the next week.

"A week? How can they expect me to wait that long?" Th'hweet stroked his lab coat, adjusting his mask of scientific detachment. "That would mean rearranging my entire schedule."

Feighan glared at the epidemiologist. "Your right-hand man is murdered by a mob and you're griping because it interferes with your work?"

"Mr. Feighan. I take for granted the undesirability of

104

dishonoring his family by not returning his remains promptly. I assume you share my distaste for the stink of a rotting corpse—we do not embalm, you know. But the crux of the matter is that as his employer, I must soar vigil over his body until I relinquish it to the care of his family. And I cannot do that and save my people from the plague at the same time." He fluffed his feathers irritatedly, then smoothed them out again. "And the headaches involved in hiring another technician..."

The Flinger's eyes itched from fatigue. Sitting on the edge of the lab bench, he studied Th'hweet with growing disbelief. Here the old bird's closest friend had just died, and all he could think about was getting the project back on schedule. Feighan wanted tears, rage, even hysteria— not bureaucratic nattering. "You really care more about finding some microscopic bug than you do about your friend, don't you?"

"Are you saying I should care less about six hundred million strangers than about one friend, Mr. Feighan?" The doctor spoke in clipped, dry tones.

"Jesus, no!" Angry, now, he hopped off the bench and stood up straight. "But you know what I think? I think finding the bug is more important to you than saving lives."

Th'hweet's crest flared high. "Can I honor my friend more than by finishing the task for which he gave his life?"

"No...I suppose not." Still the Flinger remained morally certain that it was the challenge that drove Th'hweet, not the stakes. He sighed. "Can you bring up Sree?sree? sree?'s home grove on the console?"

"Of course."

"Are there any, um, taboos against it?"

"Perhaps, but when helijets were introduced, the Teachers ruled that they could replace funeral flights under circumstances similar to this. We could request a ruling, of course, but that, too, would take more time than I can spare."

"All right. Sam, come here." When the screen image

had clarified, Feighan concentrated, visualized—

PING

Shivers of fear ran up and down his spine. He looked around, at first with alarm, then with confusion. What could possibly have frightened him? The clearing was empty. Clouds hung low and heavy. Spring rain fell on bright green grass. Nothing moved but Sam, who would sense any danger, and he merely took a deliberate three paces away from the corpse so he could turn his back on it. And then Feighan remembered. The last body he had Flung had belonged to Marion Jefferson Greystein, his roommate and his best friend. Closing his eyes, he said a quick prayer.

The rain blew harder, colder, across the meadow, as if determined to cleanse the air of the stench of unburied bodies. It did not. It could not. Feighan's stomach churned. He hated that smell.

Th'hweet tucked the bottom of the sheet under his late assistant's tail feathers. "Please wait here while I find someone of the honorable Sree?sree?sree?'s family."

Feighan turned up the collar of his jacket and pulled his head in like a turtle. "Sure—but hurry, please."

"As quickly as possible, Mr. Feighan."

"Thanks." He caught a faceful of spray as Th'hweet flapped mightily and launched himself into the air. "Damn. Do you have a towel, Sam?"

The Rhanghan looked back over his shoulder. "You want to dry off so you can get wet again?"

"I just wanted to wipe my face."

"Sorry." He rolled over and over in the wet young grass. "Besides, it feels good, McGill!"

"Only to Rhanghan scales, kiddo."

"I believe I can help you, McGill." Behind him, heavy footsteps squished in the mud. He spun around to stare in astonishment at a broad-shouldered, bearded Terran hunched beneath an open umbrella. "Reverend Williams!"

"Please, McGill, I thought we'd dispensed with the titles." He handed over a second, furled umbrella. "It won't dry your face, but it should keep it from getting any wetter."

"Well, thank you." He could not bring himself to call the missionary by his first name. It seemed . . . disrespectful, somehow, to treat a man of the cloth with such familiarity. Even the fringe nature of Williams' "Rebirth Church" could not lessen Feighan's instinctive deference to the clergy. He popped open the umbrella and raised it over his head. "Much better. Thank you."

"You're welcome indeed, McGill." He looked down at the corpse in the grass and made a sound of sorrow. "Alas, poor Sree?sree?sree?."

"You knew him?" Feighan instantly wished he had phrased it any way but that.

"Oh, I knew him, McGill. He—" Williams stopped, shook himself as one does when emerging from a daydream, and smiled apologetically. "He accepted rebirth at my hands a year ago, and has— had been a pillar of the church ever since. I'll miss him greatly."

"I think we all will," said Feighan in a soft voice.

"Do you know what happened to him?"

The Flinger nodded. When Williams raised his eyebrows in inquiry, he told him about the ambush. "I just wish I could have spotted him in the confusion, but it was a blizzard of feathers. The only reason I got Sam out alive was because I practically tripped over him."

Williams put his free hand on Feighan's shoulder and squeezed sympathetically. "I know you did the best you could, McGill, and that's all anyone could ever ask for. Sree?sree?sree? knew that working for Th'hweet would endanger him."

"Oh?"

"Word spreads quickly in an avian society, McGill." Tilting back his umbrella, he made a broad, sweeping gesture to the cloudy skies. Rain beaded in the curls of his beard. "Most of the flocks know that Th'hweet has asked for an end to Festival—"

"That's not true. He only wants to cancel it this year,

because of the epidemic."

"Ah, but he's earned a reputation as a fanatic modernizer, and no one believes him when he says it's only this year he's concerned about." From the woods came a keening, a high wild dirge for the dead. Williams folded first his umbrella, then his hands. "It appears that they're ready to begin the funeral. If you and Sam would stand over there—" He pointed to a spot ten meters away.

"Oh, sure." Feighan started to move, but when Williams did not accompany him he said, "Aren't you coming?"

"Oh, no." Williams flashed a smile that faded almost simultaneously. "I am, after all, the minister."

Eight Rehmal came over the treetops, circled the clearing, and glided into gentle landings beside Sree?sree?sree?'s body.

Th'hweet, at Feighan's side, provided a running commentary on the ceremonies. "The flock is surely mortified to be burying a member so inadequately."

The Flinger made a small noise of puzzlement.

"You surprise me, Mr. Feighan. Did you not notice the raggedness of the bearers' flight, and the splashes they raised on landing?"

"Frankly, no."

"And note the design of the funeral sling: unequal diamonds, and frayed at the edges." Th'hweet snorted softly. "The noble Sree?sree?sree? deserved better than this."

The bearers laid the open sling on the grass and hoisted the corpse onto it. Listless blue feathers broke off to whirl away on the wind.

Th'hweet groaned. "His poor widow."

"What?" said Feighan.

"The clumsiness! The funerary rites are a dance of great intricacy, but these rude fellows have yet to find the rhythm. They should move as one hexadecipedal creature—when one leg lifts, all should lift; when one hand closes, all should close. But watch. They stumble around independently, out of step and out of time."

"I thought funeral teams were supposed to be highly trained," said Feighan.

"Yes, but this is . . . a pick-up squad, in your idiom. The flock's regular team returned this morning from a three-day flight to the Great Swamps, and declared itself incapable of performing for at least two days."

"Can they do that?"

"Really, Mr. Feighan. Since they have, they obviously could. Your real question is *should* they have done it, and the answer is, of course, no." Th'hweet swung his beak from side to side. The bearers hurled themselves into the air, dragging their burden behind them. "They are, however, the flock's only flight team, so— gaakk! I can watch no longer." Crimson crest drooping, he bent his great head in sorrow.

"Now what's wrong?"

"Look for yourself, man!"

Feighan looked up. The bearers had abandoned all pretense of precision. They flew at different heights, and flapped at different times. The braided vine ropes now tautened, and now hung slack. Sixteen wings rippled awkwardly across the sky, their tips sometimes striking each other. Leaves blew off the sling and spiraled down to the ground. And from the underside of the sling, through one of the gaping holes left by the uneven diamond pattern of the weave, stuck Sree?sree?sree?'s clenched right talon.

Feighan winced. This struck even him, an alien, as less than professional. And undignified, too, for that matter. Poor, noble Sree?sree?sree? . . .

"My people!" Williams thrust an arm into the rain and held it high above his head, one finger extended. "Sree?sree?sree? leaves us in flesh but not in spirit, for while he was among us he achieved rebirth. Yes, truly he did. As he cracked the speckled egg of life when he was but a chick, so did he crack the dark egg of sin when he was a man. Yes! He broke out of that dark egg into the community of souls—to which he still belongs! Yes!"

Overhead, the bearers banked into a wide, rough circle with Williams at its center. Watching, Feighan thought of a carousel—up and down and around, up and down and around—but no carousel could move so unevenly without spilling its riders—

Someone's wing snagged a vine. The sling lurched. Sree?sree?sree?'s head lolled to the side and hung over the edge.

Th'hweet shuddered audibly.

Twenty meters away, a slender Rehmal flanked by a handful of children gave a short, sharp cry and keeled over.

Williams continued to evangelize.

The flight crew broke out of its circular path and headed west.

"Where are they going?" asked Feighan.

"To a large tree in a distant forest, Mr. Feighan. Not a particular tree, mind you, merely a large one. An old one, with leaf mold mounded high around its knobby, rooty knees. A far-reaching one, whose branches so shade its trunk that no light ever breaks through to shine on beetle-picked bones. They will sweep the leaves aside with their tails, lay the noble Sree?sree?sree? wings-down on the damp ground, and cover him with a blanket of humus. Then they will return, and we will all know, no matter what that blithering idiot of a foreigner spouts, that we have lost a friend for now, and for all time." A tight, harsh sound escaped him, and he looked away.

By the time the funeral crowd had dispersed, Feighan had come to a decision. He waited till Th'hweet flew off in the direction of Sree?sree?sree?'s family's home, then turned to Sam. "We're pulling out, kiddo."

"Back to the lab?"

"Back to New York. I'll drop Th'hweet off wherever he wants, then we'll get our stuff from the hotel and go home."

"Why?"

He looked blankly at his ward. "You aren't serious, are you?"

"Sure I am. Why do you want to go home?"

"Sam, we agreed to help save Rehmal lives, not risk our own. We just buried Sree?sree?sree?, remember? If I'd been a couple minutes slower, we'd be burying you, too."

The Rhanghan shrugged. "I was doing okay."

"Aw, come on, we were ambushed. And outnumbered a hundred to one. It's crazy to have to put up with that. When we signed on, hostile natives were not part of the picture."

"You should be used to that, McGill." Sam swished his tail from side to side, flattening the short wet grass. "The Organization's been after you for a long time, now. And you haven't tried to quit life, have you?"

"Why don't you argue like a three-year-old?"

"Because I'm a Rhanghan, McGill, and we get smart quicker than Terrans do. You know that."

"Yeah, but—" Picking up the thread of his argument again, he groped for the right words. "I mean, the Rehmal don't want us here! They don't even want Th'hweet to be trying to help them." He knew he was giving in to bitterness, but he no longer cared. If the Rehmal wanted to die of the epidemic, that would be fine with him.

Sam flickered his magenta tongue in Feighan's face. "Th'hweet needs us bad, McGill, and you know it."

"He can get one of the local Flingers."

"Hah! Just before— just before it happened, Sree?sree?sree? told me most of the Rehmal Flingers are sick, and probably going to die."

"Is that my fault, or what?"

"Don't be stupid, McGill. Th'hweet needs us because he hasn't got anybody else."

"Th'hweet doesn't need us. What he needs is a top-flight emergency assistance team."

"You're right." His tail whomped the soggy soil in assent. "So as soon as the team gets here we can leave."

"Oh, Jesus." He scowled at his ward, but he had to consent. "All right, I'll talk to Th'hweet."

Th'hweet joined them, then, and Feighan Flung them to the lab. Sam scampered to the refrigerator for something to eat. Feighan dropped into a chair. "Dr. Th'hweet, we can't go on like this. It's one thing for you and me to risk our lives, but Sam is a child. We have no right to endanger him."

"I agree whole-heartedly, Mr. Feighan. We shall leave him behind on our next excursion. I have in any event engaged a tutor for him. She should be here shortly."

"You what?"

"Your ward is an intelligent, articulate youngster, Mr. Feighan, and to neglect his education during these formative years—"

"He's in kindergarten back home."

Th'hweet lifted his wingtips and bobbed his beak. "Drudru will instruct him in silence, patience, and self-control, Mr. Feighan—topics clearly not covered in kindergarten."

"Now, wait a minute."

"Oh, come. Must you be as childish as Sam? He can no longer accompany us on our voyages, it would be foolish to leave him alone and unsupervised in a laboratory so full of attractions for young eyes and hands, and Drudru is already on the payroll of the Rehma Consortium. Given that we shall be relying on your services for some time to come, this is the only sensible solution."

"I won't argue the point any more. You're right, he could use some tutoring, and God knows I haven't got time to do a good job. But what you said about relying on my services for some time to come—" Feighan rolled his eyes toward the ceiling. "Look, doctor, you don't need me. You need competent emergency assistance, and you can get it from the Hub. Why don't you request a team—"

"I have. Half a dozen times. Unfortunately, Flinger Network Control maintains that it hasn't the appropriate resources available right now. According to the official replies to my requests, widespread medical emergencies on other Network worlds have tied up every one of the FNC's floating medical teams."

"Oh, God." Slouched in the chair, he lowered his face to his hands. Th'hweet *did* need him. And Rehma needed Th'hweet: For all his brusque, authoritarian style, he was, as he had said, the only board-certified epidemiologist on Rehma—and very nearly the planet's only hope.

"Mr. Feighan?" Th'hweet tapped him on the shoulder.

"Yeah, I'm okay." So they would have to stay. Sam's uncanny ability to sense danger before it happened should probably protect them. Probably. When he was with them, and not in the lab with his tutor. Feighan would just have to resign himself—and survive until the end of Festival, by which time the matter should have been resolved one way or the other . . . and by which time also, it occurred to him, he just might have met the Far Being Retzglaran. Which was a much brighter thought than any other that had crossed his mind lately. "I guess we'll just have to do the best we can."

"That is all we can do, Mr. Feighan."

He snapped his fingers. "Give me a minute, okay? I just had an idea."

Th'hweet opened his beak—

PING

Feighan stood in the clearing near Sree?sree?sree?'s home grove. After one quick look around to orient himself, he headed into the woods.

A few minutes later he came across a smaller glade. In its midst squatted a bright orange tent; before the tent smoldered a cookfire engaged in warming a coffee pot. He cupped his hands around his mouth and called, "Ernest! Ernest Williams! Are you here?"

From the forest came "Hal-loo!"

"I'm at your tent!"

"Coming!"

Celeste Quandala emerged from the trees almost immediately, and behind her came Williams. "McGill! How nice to see you." She hurried over and took his hand. "What brings you back?"

"This epidemic." He was not sure, but he thought Williams' eyes had chilled; he extracted his hand from Quandala's grasp. *No sense getting the husband upset.* "It just struck me that your mission might be able to provide some medical assistance."

Williams stepped forward. "Actually, McGill, we are. We've brought four doctors here in the last two weeks. They're working eighteen-hour shifts up in the mission hospital, trying to save the sick."

"Could any of them work with Th'hweet?"

Quandala shook her head dolefully. "They're practitioners, McGill, not researchers. We have calls out to all our member churches Network-wide, asking for lab technicians or clinical researchers, but so far, we haven't attracted any volunteers. We think we'll be getting some nurses next week, but—" She spread her hands apart helplessly. "But no experts."

He sighed. "Oh, well. I should have known that you'd be doing everything you could, but . . . Thank you. I'd better be going."

Williams said, "Will you be back this way?"

"Only if Th'hweet thinks there's a need."

"Well, if you are, stop in for a cup of coffee and some human conversation. We're almost always within earshot of the tent."

"Thanks, I will." He nodded, smiled at them, and stepped away.

PING

Th'hweet cocked his head at Feighan's reappearance, but said nothing.

The Flinger stretched. It had already been a long day, and it was just beginning. "That didn't pan out, but something else might. I'll be back soon."

"But—"

PING

He materialized in a large reception room on the Hub. A holo of an Ylsslypn seashore filled the entire left wall: in it, surf crashed against the giant black rocks to which the natives clung; spray gusted into the air so realistically he could almost smell it. The holo provided most of the lighting in the room, with the rest coming from a Tiffany-style lamp on the sleek force desk before the door to Thurndriddle's office. Behind that desk sat a grizzled Timili Flinger, who lifted his giant ears at Feighan's appearance and said, "Yes?" The ritual scars of his clan showed livid and hairless on his furry chest.

Feighan knew the Timili people well—they shared the planet Throngorn II with Sam's race, the Rhanghan. He had traveled there just three years earlier; indeed, ritual scars adorned his own chest. He walked forward, feet sinking deep into the rich blue carpet that covered the metal plates of the floor. In the other's own language he said, "Good day to you, sir."

The Timili cocked his head in interest as he stood. With his seashell ears and huge round eyes, he looked like an elongated lemur. "Good day to you, sir. You speak our language well, for a Terran."

"Thank you. I am McGill Feighan, and I am here to speak with Senior Flinger Thurndriddle."

"Ah. I am Filoso, deputy to Thurndriddle. The Senior Flinger is on an inspection tour of our relief efforts on Feroeset at the moment, and is not expected back any time soon. May I be of assistance?"

"I have been assigned, temporarily, to the planet Rehma, where a fearsome plague rages out of control." Timili was such a *stuffy* language. Every time he spoke it he felt he should be wearing a morning coat and striped pants. "I have come to beseech medical assistance."

"Ah, you assist the good Doctor Th'hweet, do you not?"

"Yes." That surprised him. "How did you—"

"The doctor has requested emergency aid teams several

times. Unfortunately, we have none to spare at the moment."

"But the FNC has dozens of teams!"

Filoso nodded gravely. "Forty-six. And all labor in the starry field. Sixteen on Feroeset alone, where political dissidents have destroyed thirty-eight cities with thermonuclear devices in the last three weeks, and vow to continue their campaign of terror if the planetary government does not hunt down and execute all Talented Feroesetti, from the most powerful Flinger to the weakest Minder."

He sank into a chair. "God."

"This office estimates Feroeset actually requires thirty-four teams. But we do not have them to spare. Eleven teams, you see, attempt to mitigate the suffering of the famine-stricken Leioleio, whose planet is presently wrapped in a blanket of dust thrown up by a giant meteor strike. A hundred teams might suffice, but this office has not the resources. Four on Inta Leina, where a plague imported by a Rogue Terran Flinger continues to wreak havoc."

Feighan winced. Greystein had unintentionally triggered the Inta Leina epidemic by Flinging someone without authorization. Greystein had paid for his sin. The Inta Leinans were still paying.

"Need I continue, Mr. Feighan? Three planets consume thirty-one of our teams. The other fifteen are on fifteen different worlds, and each demands reinforcements daily." Abruptly the Timili slapped his desktop. "Billions of sentient beings are dying unnecessarily and we can do nothing to save them because we do not have the resources! I weep in my cave, Mr. Feighan. I rage against the limits imposed by reality. But I can do nothing. Our granaries are empty."

"I— I see." And he did. Nature loved disasters. Earthquakes and floods and giant meteor strikes . . . Why did they all have to happen at once? He reverted to English. "I guess, uh, I'd better be going, then."

Filoso switched languages, too. "I wish I could help, Mr. Feighan. I assure you, Rehma has first claim on the next available team. But I have not the faintest idea as to when that team shall become available."

"I understand." He pushed himself out of his chair. His last hope for outside help, squelched. "Thank you."

PING

Th'hweet said, "Well?"

"Well, doctor, it does look like it's completely up to us, so we'd better get going."

It was one in the morning. Or maybe two. The bedside clock was supposed to glow in the dark, but Feighan could swear it only glimmered, at best. He leaned closer, practically pressing his nose against the clear plastic over the clock face. Two a.m. it was.

He yawned. Let his eyes fall shut. Laid his cheek on the pillow's warm spot and wiggled until everything found precisely the right position. Ah, comfort. Time once more for the long easy downhill run into sleep...

The noise came again. A heavy, stifled shuffling, as of massed feet fidgeting outside the suite door. Probably a couple of chance-met tourists cuddling in the corridor while deciding whose room to use.

He envied them. Given the research team's hectic schedule, he had barely had time to think about Gina Maccari, but now, in the quiet early morning hours of an alien planet, he missed her badly.

She was doing well, said the twice-daily updates. She had left the hospital and returned to work. The doctors rated the procedures a complete success.

A smile touched his lips. He had reached that stage of sleep where dreams would come easily, yet move at his command. He visualized Gina: her silken brown hair, sparkling eyes, infectious grin. A little misty around the edges, perhaps, but tangible enough to hug and to kiss and to—

The door burst in with a thundering crash. Sam squealed. Feighan sat up, groggy and confused. "Hey, what the—"

The lights flashed on, blinding him, but he pushed himself to his feet. Blinking against the painful brilliance, he stepped toward the intruders. Four of them, maybe five. One human. The rest Rehmal. Holding— guns?

"McGill! Danger!"

He jerked his head toward the child's frightened cry. Metal glinted. Pain exploded in the rear of his skull, blossoming outward in a fiery ball that swallowed all of him. Claws and beaks tore at his arms, his legs, his face.

He fought to remain conscious, but folded up slowly nonetheless.

"Check for money belts," said a strangely familiar voice.

He lifted his face to the speaker. Surely he had seen the man before. Tears of pain distorted Feighan's vision, blurring the attacker's broad features, smearing his red hair into a carroty haze. Feighan squinted, but the image swam away.

And into view came the carpet, rising up at him faster and faster until his face smacked it hard. Sam screamed again. And all was silent.

Feighan woke up naked on the floor. Groaning, he stood, and looked down at the scratches on his arms and legs. *They must have clawed me pretty good getting my pajamas off.* He hurt all over.

All the clothes he had brought to Rehma lay at his feet, their every seam ripped open, even the heels wrenched off the shoes and the boots. The scrap leather heaped in a corner represented all that remained of his and Sam's luggage.

The rest of the room also looked like it had been run through a shredder. Their assailants had cracked open the videophone, the holovision, the small room computer, and scattered broken circuit boards all around. They had reduced the full-length mirror to a pile of gleaming shards, and the artwork on the wall to scraps of unwoven wicker. Feathers carpeted the floor in dozens of sizes and colors.

In a mumble, he said to himself, "What the hell were they looking for? Did they think we had a lot of money here, or what?"

Sam limped out of the bathroom. "I don't know, either,

McGill, but you should see what they did in there! They even took the toilet and sink apart."

"This is crazy. Doesn't make any sense at all." He looked at the wreckage of the telephone. "And we can't call Th'hweet and ask for help." He scratched his temple; his arm ached. He did not at all feel like flinging back to the penthouse for clothes, but he would have to. "Sam."

"Huh?"

He waved at the mess of plumage on the floor. "Did we put up that much of a fight?"

"I didn't. They hit me over the head and knocked me out right away."

"Me, too," said Feighan. He was thinking even more slowly than usual that morning, but he seemed to recall something about feather loss being a sign of sickness. At least one of their attackers, then, and more likely a couple of them, had the disease.

In sudden suspicion, he stared at his scratches. Several were red and swollen. "Stand still." He knelt at Sam's side and inspected the child closely. Uh-huh. A few of Sam's cuts were also inflamed.

Feighan had a horrible hunch that he and Sam just might be providing Th'hweet with a new set of samples.

▪ **Chapter X** ▪

Friday, 2 October 2105

Even though Agent Silver had had himself Flung to the ship, Nathaniel Davis used the carved wood scrambler-phone. No matter how good its numbers, Operation PlayGround did not feel right. Should it not work out, the fewer people who knew his jowly face, the better. And Silver was a born snitch.

"Schoolteacher here, Agent Silver. Make your report."

"Sir, I'd hate to be thought of as a finger-pointer—"

Davis rolled his eyes to the ceiling.

"—but you should know that your order canceling the contract on Feighan did not reach Rehma till an hour after an extraordinarily stupid late member of Sub-operation *Needle* decided a phony assault-robbery would let us infect Feighan without drawing suspicion, and also help *Haystack*."

Davis absorbed the news in dismay. Feighan knew too many doctors. And if he drew in the Far Being, Gryll would kill him. "You said 'late'?"

"Yes, sir. If only because he should have cut Feighan's throat."

"Very well. Dishonor the corpse before disposal." *As Gryll will mine.*

· Chapter XI ·

Th'hweet hummed a lively tune as he fluttered from the lab bench to the equipment cabinet. Sam, still half-asleep, lolled on the sofa. Feighan lay on an examination table built for a shorter being with wings, not shoulder blades, trying to remember where he had seen the man with red hair. Th'hweet's air of delight kept distracting him, though, and he was growing irritated. The dull ache pulsing through every part of his battered body did nothing to improve his mood. "What are you so damn cheery about?"

The epidemiologist gave him a puzzled stare. "But is it not obvious?"

"Not to me it isn't."

"Ah. Well, then." There came a knock at the door. "That must be the tutor. She promised to begin this morning." He chirped merrily, hopped across the room, and opened the door.

A short, slender Rehmal with pumpkin-orange body plumage and an ice-blue crest spread her wings and trilled a few bars.

Th'hweet stepped back. "Come in."

In she came, hesitating just inside the doorway to cock her head and study first Feighan, then Sam, through bright,

121

unblinking eyes. After a moment she said, "Hello. I am Drudru. I am tutor for young born beneath different skies."

Feighan swung off the table and moved close enough to be beaked. "How do you? I'm McGill Feighan. This is my ward Sam, your new pupil."

Sam scrambled down off the sofa and presented his snout. "Hi!"

With two head bobs and a beak clack, Drudru said, "We start now."

"You may use my office, if you wish. Sam will show you where it is."

"Thank you. Show Drudru the office, Sam."

"Sure! Come on!" Tail swishing from side to side, he led her past the long lab bench into the small room at the back. "See you later, McGill!"

Feighan threw him a two-finger salute. "Have fun."

The door closed.

Th'hweet said, "Ah. Peace and quiet descend at last."

Feighan shrugged. "Little kids are noisy." He sat on the table's edge and let his legs dangle freely.

"Not with Drudru." He lifted a small, perforated box to eye level, then clucked in regret and replaced it on the shelf. "The needle, I'm afraid."

The Flinger lifted his head in alarm. "What?"

"This blood sampling device is designed for Rehmal fingers, Mr. Feighan. Yours would never fit through the holes. Sam's might, although I shall have to check. In your case, however, I must definitely resort to cruder means—which, I hasten to assure you, entail nothing more than a small needle to puncture the skin, and a glass slide out upon which to squeeze a drop of blood. Your ancestors made do with them for more than a century; they shan't harm you in the least. Now, where did I put them?" He whistled a complex run of notes. A panel popped open; a cylindrical machine perhaps twenty centimeters in height rolled out on rubber treads.

He blinked, and pointed. "What's that?"

"A robot. Surely, Mr. Feighan, you've seen robots before."

"Oh." His cheeks grew warm with embarrassment. "I didn't know you had any."

Th'hweet's tone cooled noticeably. "You assumed we Rehmal were too primitive to avail ourselves of such sophisticated technology?"

"Ah, no, no, not at all." *Jeez, he's touchy about this.* "The Plaza must have a thousand of them, at least, and I've seen some out in the fields. I just didn't know *you* had any *here,* in the lab."

The robot wheeled to the right and trundled down the length of the bench, dodging instruments and appliances with deft precision. Th'hweet followed it. "This was manufactured off-world, but the software was written on *Rehma,* Mr. Feighan."

"Doctor," he said in exasperation, "I didn't suggest it wasn't!"

The robot stopped, and so did Th'hweet. As a miniature mechanical arm telescoped out to pull open a drawer, the epidemiologist sighed. "I apologize, Mr. Feighan. When in the company of Terrans, I all too often find myself unwarrantedly defensive."

"You can say that again." He grinned to show he meant no insult. "But if I'm not prying too much, what are you so defensive about?"

"Your standard Terran assumptions about us." He flared his wings a few centimeters, and stood on one leg. "You see the surface, but not the depth, and so you look down on us."

Indignation blazed up in Feighan. "I do not!"

"Perhaps not you." Bitterness throbbed in Th'hweet's voice. "But as you may recall, I studied in Boston. I know from personal experience that many of you call us savages because we follow our teachings."

"Doctor, you're losing me. What teachings?"

Now he spoke earnestly, persuasively. "Our teachings promulgate self-reliance within the framework of the flock, and we interpret 'self' to refer to the unencumbered individual. From childhood our teachers exhort us never to rely on artifacts or outsiders unless we absolutely must. For a civilization as advanced as ours, we are singularly unmechanized."

"Well, yes, but—"

"Your people tend to measure a culture's worth in terms of motors and micro-miniaturization, Mr. Feighan. They call us backward. And barbaric." He gave a derisive caw. "We breathe air more pure than anything your world has known for centuries. No Rehmal ever goes hungry—never. Our literacy rate approaches 99.9 percent. Our written records go back seven thousand eight hundred of your years— and prove that we last shed blood in battle two thousand one hundred years ago. Can your oh-so-highly-advanced world match *any* of our claims?"

"Ah . . ." Feighan shrugged.

"I thought not. But that, in a nutshell, is the cause of my defensiveness. I resent condescension from my inferiors. I apologize for suspecting it where it did not exist." Turning his back on Feighan and on the topic, he rummaged through the drawer the robot had opened. "Here we are."

The Flinger was only too glad to change the subject. "Here we are *what?* And you never did say why you were so happy."

Th'hweet held up two small envelopes. "Here are the needle and the slide. As the labels make plain, the manufacturer sterilized both before sealing them in this impermeable plastic. If you would be so kind as to extend the index finger of your—you are right-handed, yes?"

The Flinger nodded.

"Fine, your left one then, please." Approaching, he tore open the two packages and reached for Feighan's hand.

The Flinger yanked it away. "First tell me why you were so pleased with yourself."

"Really, Mr. Feighan, you're an intelligent man. You should be able to see it without having it pointed out to you."

He propped himself up on his elbow. "I may be intelligent, but I am not a research physician. Point it out to me. In words of three syllables or less. Then you can stick me with that needle."

"Oh, very well." He sighed for dramatic effect. "We have all come to the conclusion that in the process of robbing you and ransacking your room, your assailants somehow managed to infect you and possibly Sam with the virus or other agent responsible for the present epidemic, correct?"

"Uh-huh. And you're delighted. Why?"

"Good heavens, man! Think about it! I have been flying my feathers off trying to isolate the infectious agent, and those thieves have just made me a gift of it!"

"But you've taken blood samples from hundreds of sick Rehmal. That didn't help you a bit. Why will this work?"

"You're not thinking, Mr. Feighan." Th'hweet paused, cocked his head, and clacked his beak. "On reconsideration, I apologize. You're a Terran, and so you take scientific medicine for granted. You may not realize it, but very few of the Network worlds have made such a fetish of studying and treating disease."

Feighan frowned. "Come on, there are doctors everywhere."

"Correction. On nearly every planet there are individuals whose profession has been translated into your native English as 'doctor.' This is, in part, because your Terran xenologists hesitate to use the terms 'shaman' or 'witch doctor,' given their rather insulting connotations in your language."

"I'm not sure what you're saying."

"Mr. Feighan, most intelligent beings throughout the Network maintain sufficient mental control over their bodies that they do not need doctors as you know them. You Terrans, on the other hand, require a great deal of external intervention to stay healthy. Without your doctors, your vaccines, and your medicines, most of you would die before the age of thirty."

"But *you're* a doctor, and—"

"As I have said repeatedly, I am the only board-certified epidemiologist on this entire planet, Mr. Feighan. I am also one of perhaps four Rehmal formally trained in Terran-style medicine, assuming the others are still alive. What we translate into English as 'doctor' actually means 'Wellness Teacher'—that is, one who teaches the mind's keys to the body, the mental way to health."

"Okay, fine," he said in frustrated confusion. "But what does that have to do with anything at all?"

"Simply this: The Terran bloodstream is the most thoroughly documented physiological system known to the Network. So much has been discovered that even the best of your researchers can add very little to the vast body of knowledge already extant. For comparison purposes, I have discovered more about Rehmal biochemistry than all prior investigators put together. And I really know very little about it, Mr. Feighan. Which is to say—"

"I think I'm beginning to understand."

"Ah?"

"Sure." He focused on the acoustic tile ceiling while he worked it out. "You run a sample of my blood through your machine, the computer analyzes it, anything that shouldn't be there is going to stand out like a sore thumb. But the bug can hide in your blood, because you don't know what's supposed to be there!"

"Very good, Mr. Feighan."

"And that's why you're so pleased about this." He laid his palm over the scratch on his biceps. The swelling was hot, and as red as his assailant's hair. Where had Feighan seen him before? "It's a short cut."

"A bad pun, but an apt observation. And every day saved," said Th'hweet in a murmur, "means, ultimately, millions of lives saved. Now be cooperative, and hand me your hand."

Feighan held it out and looked away. Something sharp

pricked the tip of his index finger; Th'hweet squeezed the finger's fleshy pad for an instant, then—

"Excellent, excellent. You can open your eyes now, Mr. Feighan."

"They were open all along," he said with a growl.

"Of course." Th'hweet slipped the slide into the maw of the analyzer and pirouetted about. His crimson crest stood straight up. "Five minutes and we shall know!"

A chill raced through Feighan. He glanced toward the door to the back office. Still closed. He lowered his voice anyway. "Uh, doctor, something just ... just occurred to me." He had to swallow hard before he could continue. "What you were saying about scientific knowledge of alien physiologies?"

"Yes?"

"What about Rhanghans?" Sudden worry nearly overwhelmed him. "I mean, Sam's scratched up, too, and if nobody knows Rhanghan biochemistry—"

"Mr. Feighan, you don't expect to become *infected* by this?"

"Well, uh, I mean, it hurts, it's hot—"

"Oh, Mr. Feighan, you disappoint me. Given the quantity of feathers shed in your room, we must assume that the cause of this inflammation is the agent responsible for the epidemic sweeping the planet. We Rehmal are highly susceptible to it. But it would be the height of coincidence if you were similarly susceptible. Remember, our biochemistries are not even similar, except in the grossest aspects. Naturally, your body is reacting to a foreign substance, and generating antibodies, probably at random, but I fully expect—"

Ding

"Hah! The analysis is complete." Talons clicking on the tiles, Th'hweet practically danced over to the machine. And said, "Damn!"

"What's the matter?"

"Nothing."

"You expect me to buy that? You just cursed, something has—"

"I cursed because it found nothing."

Feighan squinted at the squat, LED-eyed device in confusion. "But didn't we just agree that it had to find something?"

"Yes! Unless," he said in a musing tone, "your body has already digested— no, no, there should be *some* remnants. But there are none. There is no trace of anything not native . . . hmm."

"What?"

"A thought." He waved a wingtip distractedly. "Not even that; a mere fragment of an embryonic idea."

"Tell me."

"Mr. Feighan," said Th'hweet with some testiness, "I shall share my thoughts with you when I feel confident that they are worth sharing."

"But—"

"No. I can find nothing unexpected in the blood sample. You have nothing to worry about."

Feighan, who had already considered, then rejected as unfounded, suspicions arising from the fact that he and Sam had been attacked while Th'hweet escaped unscathed, abruptly changed his mind. He sat up on the table. "You're right. Because we're leaving. I want Sam to get medical attention back home."

"Oh, come, Mr. Feighan. If either of you begins to display symptoms, you can Fling the both of you back to New York in fifteen seconds. You must stay."

He bristled. "We *must* stay?"

"I order you to stay."

His stomach knotted; the muscles at the back of his neck tensed into hot cables. Through nearly clenched teeth he said, "You don't have the authority."

Th'hweet grunted softly. "Mr. Feighan, we can proceed through formal channels if you insist. I can speak to the

Director of the Rehmal Consortium, who has the authority, and who will use it at my request. But are you truly going to waste that much of our precious time?"

Rebellion ignited in Feighan's heart. He opened his mouth to make angry reply, but shut it again almost at once. He lowered his head and stared at his knees for a minute.

Calm down, Feighan, he told himself, but he had trouble following his own good advice. His pulse raced; his hands gripped the hard metal edge of the table until his knuckles turned white. *Calm, easy.* Damn, but he hated being ordered around. It was not the orders themselves, it was the way in which they were delivered. Th'hweet insisted on treating him like a flunky, and that drove him nuts. But . . . he took a deep breath. "Doctor, we've been through this before, and I have a hunch we'll go a few more rounds before I'm gone, but let me remind you that I'm a fully competent adult human being. I demand that you show me the respect you claim you don't get."

"Then you will stay?"

"Let me put it this way. I will concede that since Sam and I can get good medical treatment almost instantaneously if we need it, there's no reason for us to leave now. Unless you provide it by failing to accord me the respect I am due. And your people are dying; you clearly need assistance." To himself he added, *And if this really is one of the Far Being's favorite worlds, I better help out all I can.* "What I'm saying is that I will stay a while longer, but you had better develop some manners in a hurry."

"I shall make the attempt, Mr. Feighan."

"Good. Hey! Wait!" He closed his eyes. The redhead— now he remembered how they had met. He snapped his fingers. "Got it!"

"What?"

"I told you about the human with red hair?"

"Yes. Repeatedly."

"Well, he's the mechanic who fixed Ernest Williams'

helijet. The Reverend Williams ought to know where this guy works. So I go there, and, um, persuade him to explain what the hell he was looking for."

Th'hweet made a sound deep in his throat.

Feighan looked up. "Something wrong, doctor?"

"I had planned to visit some outlying villages, but—" Long neck twisting, he eyed the blood analysis equipment. "But I also have a few things to do here. I believe I could spare you for an hour."

"Fine. I'll be back then."

PING

A cool breeze blew through the small glade, lifting ash from the extinguished cookfire, picking lost feathers off the ground, and bearing, as always, the stink of death and rot. Feighan breathed through his mouth. In his extensive travels on Rehma, he had found that each place had its own scenery, but they all had the same smell. "Hello!"

The clearing seemed deserted, but he had the eerie feeling that someone was watching him. He wished he could have brought Sam. The Rhanghan's ability to sense moods—and danger—offered a great deal of comfort in situations like that.

He walked over to the bright orange tent. It was zipped shut, and its flaps were tied.

He made a megaphone of his hands. "Ernest! Celeste! Hal-loo!"

He paused a moment, heard nothing, then walked around the encampment. Every meter or so he came across another feather, sometimes a clump of them. Quite a few sick Rehmal had visited Williams and Quandala.

Blueness flickered beneath a low branch at the edge of the clearing. He tensed, Talent ready to Fling him out at a hint of trouble, and moved to the spot on the balls of his feet. He lifted the branch.

A fluff-tailed furry creature the size of a cat backed slowly away from him, half a Rehmal's wing in its mouth.

It growled. Its upper lip lifted away from sharp pointed teeth. It growled again, whirled, and fled.

Feighan looked down, gasped, and bit back a moan. Half-dismembered, the corpse lay in a pile of its own blue feathers. Scavengers had ripped away the kelly-green crest and torn great hunks of flesh from its body. The gaping wounds exposed tendons, bone, and viscera. Beetles scuttled along the edge of its beak. And maggots writhed in its eyes. Feighan shuddered, stooped to retrieve the sculpted blue seed, then let the branch fall.

He walked on shaky legs to the center of the clearing. He tried to catch his breath but the stink clung to him. Trembling, he clenched his jaws against the impulse to vomit. Sree?sree?sree? deserved better. He should have killed the damn beast when he had the chance.

A voice called, "Hi!"

Slipping the carving into his pocket, he scanned the ring of vine-covered tree trunks for movement. "Where are you?"

"Up!"

I keep forgetting . . . He tilted back his head.

A large blue Rehmal with gold tints on crest and wings and tail circled above him. It waved once to Feighan's upturned face, then arrowed down to land two meters away. It chirped, hopped in place, and finally stepped forward to stroke his cheek with its beak.

"Hello," said Feighan.

"Hi!" It opened its wings, seemed to fluff them out, and pulled them in tight again. "Preacher go. Teacher go. Back six dawns."

Feighan did not want to wait a week to locate the redhead. "Uh . . . do you know where the preacher and the teacher went?"

With a high, happy trill it said, "Tusirox."

"Tusirox?" He had never heard the name.

The Rehmal clacked its beak. "No. Preacher and teacher go Tusirox."

"Yes, I heard you." Feighan spoke with slow, careful enunciation. "Is Tusirox a city?"

"No, no." It adopted the same deliberate precision of speech he had. "Prea-cher and tea-cher go to Si-rox."

"Oh. He went to Si-rox." Not for the first time, he wished he had had time for some language training before coming to Rehma. Or that Maccari had come along—she could understand anybody, anywhere. "You mean, 'to see rocks'?"

Its head bobbed up and down. "Yass!"

He was not sure why anybody would want to see rocks, unless they were jewels of some sort. A mine, maybe? Or a geological dig—if geologists had digs like archeologists. Or maybe Williams was a climber.

"Is he mountain climbing?"

The Rehmal shook its head from side to side. "No, no. Prea-cher and tea-cher go to Roxincy."

Feighan snapped his fingers. "Rocks in sea. Sea rocks. Islands!"

The Rehmal cawed triumphantly. "I-lans. Sea rocks. I-Lans."

"Do you know where these islands are?"

It pointed due west. "Two dawn strong. Three dawn weak."

The Flinger nodded encouragingly. "Two days travel for a strong flyer; three days travel for a weak one, yes?"

"Yes!"

Closing his eyes, he visualized the map of the planet. And groaned with discouragement. Four hundred kilometers to the west sprawled a vast bay which held in its arms over a thousand small, rocky islands. With a little luck, and some cooperation from the natives, he could probably find Williams in less than a day—but he had to be back at the lab in half an hour. "Dammit." But maybe Th'hweet could help, if he knew the territory. He would have to go ask him.

PING

Th'hweet balanced on one foot before a meter-wide,

millimeter-deep monitor, the tip of his beak touching the electron micrograph projected on its screen. Feighan had no idea what the squiggly shapes represented. Bacteria? Viruses? He reached into his pocket for the seed. "Doctor—"

"Shush!"

He recoiled. "Okay." Maybe he should have left the carving there.

A second later Th'hweet screeched. "I've got it!"

He probably had broken a taboo. Best keep quiet. "Huh? What?"

"The agent. I found it."

"In my blood? I thought—"

"No. Yes." The epidemiologist made a noise of disgust. "I pondered the problem after you left. Despite the swelling, there was nothing in your blood stream that did not belong there. Why, I wondered, why? Perhaps, I thought, perhaps there is something in the Rehmal blood stream which does not belong there. So I gave the machine two samples, one of yours, one of a local resident's, and I asked it to look for similarities. This—" With the tip of his wing he brushed the screen. "This is the one."

To Feighan, the thing on display looked pretty innocuous. Hard to believe that it was causing the most devastating plague in the planet's history. "So I have been infected."

"Yes, oh definitely, yes. Thousands of times."

That staggered him. "What?"

"Don't you recognize this?" He touched the monitor.

Feighan made a face. "Sure. It's an electro-luminescent screen with a whole bunch of funny pictures on it. Come on, doctor, you know how little I know about your field."

"Influenza."

The Flinger squinted at the shapes on screen. "Flu?"

"Essentially, yes." He touched a button on his keyboard. One of the images grew to fill the entire screen. "It's a very simple life form, you see, and it's capable of almost endless

mutation. What we have here is a variant of Istanbul A—
that was the one that caused so much snuffling and sneezing
on Terra about three years ago?"

"But how can a common Terran disease infect you people? I thought—"

"Influenza is one of the few diseases capable of infecting
both avian and mammalian life on your planet. Certain
especially virulent forms of avian influenza are capable of
decimating entire flocks of chickens or ducks—and I speak,
here, of healthy, hybrid, well-nourished animals cooped
under optimum conditions. This seems remarkably similar
to some of the worst varieties of avian influenza ever isolated."

"But that doesn't explain why the Rehmal are getting
sick. Our DNA is so completely different—"

"Because the flu virus has such unstable surface proteins
that they can adapt to almost any genetic environment. And
this is definitely a variant. See here—" He used a plastic
pointer the size and shape of a knitting needle. "This is the
hemagglutinin protein; the one that penetrates the wall of
the host cell. This is the neuraminidase protein, which lib-
erates the virus's offspring once replication is complete.
Both are structurally quite similar to the proteins that enable
interaction with Terran DNA, but show just enough alter-
ation to permit them to operate upon ours." He leaned back
against his lab bench and beamed at them.

"So now that you've isolated it, can you develop a vaccine against it?"

Th'hweet opened his wings slightly, and pulled them shut
again. "Perhaps. That is to say, certainly a vaccine can be
developed. I cannot. I lack the facilities and the necessary
technical support. As soon as I have double-checked my
experimental procedures, I shall request the Flock of True
Lore to ask for off-world assistance in developing and man-
ufacturing the vaccine. But in the meantime, I have also
discovered the vector of transmission!"

"Pardon?" said Feighan.

"I have found the means by which the influenza spreads—the way in which one person infects another."

"Congratulations," said Feighan. "It's been a productive day for you."

"And I owe it all to you two. If you had not been attacked—"

"Yes, speaking of which—"

"Oh, the means of transmission, of course."

"No, that's not quite—"

"Beaking."

Feighan shook his head in confusion. "Say what?"

"You are familiar with our custom of beaking, are you not?"

"The Rehmal equivalent of our handshake?"

"Precisely." Crimson feathers flapping, Th'hweet's head bobbed pontifically. "As it turns out, when a sick person rubs his beak on a well person's beak, the vibration dislodges a cloud of dried, dormant virii which the well person inhales. The result, some eleven percent of the time, is the infection of the formerly well person."

"In other words," said Feighan, "to leap ahead a little, you can stop the epidemic in its tracks—if you can just convince people not to beak."

"Surely there won't be any problem with that," said Th'hweet. "I mean to say, mine are not a stupid people, and once they realize that their health—not to mention their lives—depends upon their avoidance of what is, really, nothing more than a custom—"

"Tell you the truth, doctor, if I were you, I'd put my money on the vaccine."

At Th'hweet's direction, Feighan Flung them to a northern forest where the infection rate was running extraordinarily high. The epidemiologist felt it was the best place to start. "So many people there are sick that statistically speaking, everyone in the region will catch the disease within two weeks unless we stop it now."

"Makes perfect sense to me." Feighan started to glance around the small clearing, then stopped. Lifeless talons jutted out from beneath a flowering shrub. And twenty meters further into the woods, that mound of bedraggled feathers, surely . . . He went back to breathing through his mouth, and wondered where he could find a gas mask. "Could we be too late?"

"No." The Rehmal pointed to the sky. "Here they come now."

A coughing native swooped down from the treetops to land nearby. A dozen followed it, and a hundred followed them, and within minutes so many had arrived that they filled not only the small meadow, but also every branch on every tree that overlooked it. Feighan quit counting at two hundred twelve. "This is your biggest audience yet."

"And my sickest," said Th'hweet grimly. "Do you hear the wheezing and hacking of congested lungs? Can I but convince them, we will break the back of the epidemic right here and now."

"Go to it." He stepped back, and once more wished he could have brought Sam. The child could read crowd moods better than a politician, and this crowd made Feighan uneasy.

The epidemiologist flapped his wings for attention. Millions of feathers rustled as the crowd stifled coughs and settled in to listen. Thousands of feathers fell to ground in a downy rainbow mist.

Th'hweet sang greetings, bowing and dancing and sweeping a wing toward Feighan as he introduced him. Applause pattered down on them like polite rain.

Then the doctor sang a question to the flock, and paused.

From the top of the highest tree, a hoarse, deep bass rumbled back a reply.

Th'hweet opened his wings wide. His voice rose till leaves deep in the forest shivered. His song soared and circled and—

The deep bass cut in with a few brief bars.

Th'hweet rapped back with two quick notes.

The hairs on the nape of Feighan's neck prickled.

As if the deep bass had pulled a trigger, the listeners surged off their perches. Diving, they bellowed hatred. A thousand beaks gaped, two thousand talons reached to claw, to rend—

PING

The laboratory materialized around them. Feighan shuddered with relief.

Th'hweet stood motionless, wings still spread wide.

Feighan touched the other's shoulder gently. "Doctor?"

Th'hweet let out a long, slow hiss, like a tire losing air. His violet wings gradually drooped, but he did not fold them around himself. He did not blink, or take his gaze from the wall.

"Doctor Th'hweet, are you all right?"

"Their Teacher of Rites and Manners spoke against me." He seemed in shock. "She said I lied. She said I wished to foment hostilities between individuals and between the flocks as well."

"Why would she accuse you of lying?"

"Jealousy? Fear? I do not know, Mr. Feighan."

Remembering his conversation with Reverend Williams at Sree?sree?sree?'s funeral, Feighan said, "You know, I've heard that the flocks believe you want to abolish Festival forever. That teacher probably thought you were trying to do her out of a job."

"Perhaps," he said dully.

"But what did the *people* say?"

"They would not listen." The epidemiologist swung his face around toward Feighan's. "They refused to believe me. The sick ones deny they endanger the healthy; the healthy will not accept the threat their ailing loved ones pose." There was pain in his eyes, and sorrow sharp enough to draw blood. "We are doomed. My entire ignorant, hidebound race has chosen suicide."

· Chapter XII ·

Friday, 2 October 2105

For the peculiar requirements of Sub-operation *Feather-duster*, Nathaniel Davis had customized a standard computer program designed to assist managers in scheduling work-flow. He sat now at his desk, nibbling eclairs, changing significant parameters one by one, searching for the single mesh of personnel and equipment that would yield the quick-est, cheapest job.

The numbers looked good, very good. A warm thrill of satisfaction shot through him. God, it took a clever man to manage an operation like this!

The scramblerphone purred; still smiling, he picked it up. "Yes?"

"Agent Silver returning your call, sir."

"Ah. Put him through." He waited for the double-click. "Silver."

"And a good morning to you, sir. What can I do for you today?"

"The one random factor in PlayGround is Feighan. What is he up to?"

"Absolutely nothing, sir." Silver chuckled. "I think you

can safely consider him, umm, de-randomized. He won't get in our way."

"Thank you." Hanging up, Davis really wished he could believe it.

▪ **Chapter XIII** ▪

Friday, 2 October 2105
—Thursday, 8 October 2105

Feighan, Sam, and Drudru stared at the impassive door to Th'hweet's office. Dismayed and disheartened by his people's rejection of his message, the epidemiologist had ordered the tutor and her pupil out of the room twenty minutes earlier, and immediately locked himself inside. They had pounded on the sheet-metal panels and shouted till their throats hurt, but nothing had provoked a response from within.

Worry gnawed at the Flinger. "You hear anything, Sam?"

The young Rhanghan cocked his head and listened. His inner eyelids swept shut as he concentrated. "Yeah, I do."

Feighan waited for details, but eventually had to say, "Well?"

"Oh! That's right, you're deaf." His tongue lashed the air derisively.

Drudru clacked her beak twice. "Not polite, Sam."

"I'm just kidding!"

"Not time for joking. Apologize."

"Okay." The tip of his tail lifted up into a circle and nearly touched his skull. "I'm sorry, McGill. I didn't mean to insult you or anything."

Feighan raised his eyebrows, impressed with how much Drudru had already influenced the child. "I know you have trouble remembering it, but human ears just aren't as sharp as Rhanghan ears. So. What's he doing in there?"

Sam fidgeted. "I don't know if I should say."

He pointed a finger at his ward. "Out with it."

"Well, he's walking around—pacing. Can't you hear his toenails clicking on the tiles?"

"Talons, Sam. Or claws. But not toenails." Shutting his own eyes, now, he listened hard. Odd, when you came right down to it, how at any given moment the human ear caught dozens of noises that the brain ignored. He filtered out the steady thu*thud of his pulse, the aimless whispering of the wind in the trees outside, the distant chirping of the natives . . . "Nope. I can't hear a thing. What else am I missing?"

"Uh . . ." Sam's face scrunched up as he tried to describe what he heard so clearly. "He's doing something with his wings, I don't know what. The feathers are, are . . . I don't know what they're doing, they're going 'ff-hwop! ff-hwop!'"

Feighan's concern mounted. "He's not hurting himself, is he?"

"No, it's like he's—" He flapped his arms wildly. "Like he's just sort of opening and closing them real quick."

Drudru said, "To vent emotion. Not dangerous."

"Is he saying anything?"

"No, he— he . . ."

"He what?"

"I think he's crying, McGill. That's what it sounds like, at least."

"Oh, geez." He plopped onto the polished wooden bench. Other people's tears embarrassed him—not because he equated crying with a lack of dignity, but because he did not know how to respond to the sorrow that provoked them. *I mean, what do you say? "Gee, I'm sorry y'all are going to be extinct in a month or two, and please let me know if there's anything I can do"? God, I feel so helpless.* "Well, let's leave him alone for a while, he'll be okay."

"I don't think so, McGill."

"Why not?"

"Because he—" Sam touched his chest, then held his hands before him as though cradling something round and delicate. He turned the imaginary globe over and around and then split it open to peer inside. He shrugged, and slapped his tail on the floor. "I'm not sure, McGill, but I think what he's gonna do is, he's gonna curl up and die."

Drudru gasped.

The tension in Feighan's stomach knotted tighter. "Can he?"

"He thinks he can."

They both looked at Drudru. "Can he really?"

"Yes." She snapped her beak firmly shut.

The concept itself did not surprise Feighan: A lot of aliens could let go of life at will. Terrans never understood it, but then, according to Th'hweet himself, Terrans were so far out of touch with their bodies that it would take a miracle to make them understand it. "Oh, damn it!"

"Yeah," said Sam sadly.

Feighan's initial reaction was to abandon ship. *I mean, when the captain gives up hope, what's the point of the crew hanging around?* A quick stop at the hotel to pick up their luggage and to check out, and then **PING**, back in New York.

But then he would be quitting, too, out of disappointment over Th'hweet's quitting, and anyone who is willing to quit has no right to be disappointed in someone else's willingness to quit, and . . .

If he went home, no one would rouse Th'hweet, so one billion intelligent beings would die of a disease that Terran medicine, if applied, could probably prevent, or even cure. One billion Rehmal would die, and rot where they fell because none would survive to bury them. McGill Feighan did not want that stench haunting his nightmares for the rest of his life.

Besides, how could he ever face the Far Being Retzglaran

if he let that happen?

Not, in all probability, that he would ever face the Far Being.

Oh, sure, Rehmal legend claimed It came to Festival every year. But that proved nothing. Nearly every world in the Network told folk tales about how the local divinities dropped in unexpectedly, to intervene, to inspect, or sometimes just to have a good time.

Only rarely did you meet anybody who claimed to have chatted with the divinity—and when you did, the claimant usually displayed enough symptoms of lunacy to cast serious doubt on its claims.

Feighan was positive that the Far Being Retzglaran did exist, but whether It was really a God in this universe, in another reality altogether, or only in the minds of those who believed in It, he could not say.

But what if It *did* come to Festival? So it was a one-in-a-trillion shot. Could he risk missing his chance actually—finally!—to meet It?

Did he dare let It come only to find a billion dying worshipers?

He touched the carving in his pocket. No way.

"Sam, Drudru, we have to get Th'hweet out of there and back to work."

The child nodded morosely. "But how, McGill?"

"I was sort of hoping Drudru could tell us . . ."

In a whisper, she said, "Teachings say, when one want start last sleep, is wrong to wake."

He stared into her bright eyes. "Do you really believe that?"

"Is teaching. But—" She chirped, and turned her head.

Feighan would not let her get off so easily. "But what?"

"Other teachings say, 'Flock always laugh at keenest vision, until wind storm finally strikes.'"

"You think Th'hweet sees farther than most, don't you, Drudru?"

"Yes."

"So you'll help us?"

"Yes."

Sam slapped the tiles with his tail. "Let's go! How do we get inside?"

"Uh—" Feighan ran his fingers through the multi-hued bands of his energy tunic. "I don't know where the key is, but I don't think we'll have much of a problem."

"And then we just make him feel better, and everything's okay?"

"Something like that." There had to be a key around somewhere. If only he knew where to look. "But how exactly do you propose we make him feel better?"

Sam screwed up his face in earnest thought. "We could tickle him."

"Get serious, kiddo."

"No, really! Like you do to me, you know—" He stuck his finger in Feighan's ribs. "Coochy-coochy-coo! It always makes me feel good."

Smiling, he pushed the small hand away. "I have a feeling a more sophisticated approach is called for here. Um . . ."

"McGill?"

"Hmm?"

"Why don't we get inside, first, and then figure out how to cheer him up?"

He patted his ward on the head. "I *knew* there was a reason I let you hang around all the time."

"'Cause I'm a genius, right?"

"And modest, too. Let's go." He rose to his feet and walked across the laboratory. The metal door still resisted his experimental shove. He bent to study the lock.

Sam touched his shoulder. "I thought you were going to Fling us inside."

Feighan straightened. "I changed my mind. I'm not sure how his furniture is arranged, but I know it's so cluttered that I might have to dodge two or three times. That's sort of iffy. Once is no problem, but twice . . . I'd hate to materialize us halfway inside a file cabinet."

"Oh." He squinted at the lock, too. "So what are you going to do?"

"I don't know yet."

"Well, why don't you just put a whole lot of momentum into the lock and blow it away?"

"I would," he said distractedly, "if there were bad guys on the other side, but I'd rather not hit Dr. Th'hweet with a high-speed lock, you know?"

"Send it the other way, then, McGill." Clearly, it exasperated the child that Feighan kept overlooking the obvious.

"So it can ricochet around in here with us?" He gestured to the centrifuges, microscopes, and sensors that cluttered the laboratory. "Even if it missed us, that's expensive equipment, and I really don't want to have to pay for any of it."

"Oh, yeah, that wouldn't be too good, would it?" Tail swishing from side to side, he lay on his belly and peered underneath the door.

"You see anything?"

"Uh-unh." He giggled. "But the floor's cold."

Feighan snapped his fingers. "Wait a minute."

"What?"

He stroked the door's aloof metal. "I really should have thought of this sooner, but I'm slow today, you know?"

"What are you talking about, McGill?"

"Hinges." He felt incredibly stupid. A juvenile delinquent would have seen it in an instant, and it had taken him half an hour. "The hinges are on this side of the door."

"So?" Puzzled, he sat up and wrapped his tail around himself.

"So—" Feighan touched the lower hinge, concentrated on the way the pin fit, visualized the pin climbing slowly to the ceiling—

PING

Sam gasped. "It popped right out!"

He caught it as it fell. It had a solid, no-nonsense heft to it. "And now for the other—"

PING

The second hinge eluded his hand and clattered onto the tiles. Feighan coughed; Sam snickered; Drudru said, "Politeness, Sam. Self-control, too."

"Yes, ma'am."

"Okay, folks. Stand back, because—" Concentrating, he imagined the now-free edge of the door swinging a few centimeters forward to clear the frame, and then sliding out of the lock—

PING

Door hit floor with a hollow boom. Sam yelped. Drudru bounced into a backward glide.

"I told you to stand back." Feighan smiled, but inside he felt sheepish.

"'Stand back' is not the same as 'stand in the next room.' That almost got me, McGill!"

The Flinger's cheeks grew warm. "My sincerest apologies."

"Hah!"

"Sam!" said Drudru.

"Was I rude again?"

"Yes."

He hung his head. "I'm sorry, I didn't mean it. Honest."

Feighan scratched his ward's skullbone. "Come on, let's see why our, um, lock-picking efforts didn't attract Dr. Th'hweet's attention." He stepped into the small office. The bright fluorescents overhead hummed softly to themselves.

Th'hweet perched on a horizontal bar behind a large desk strewn with open books. Neck bent, head and beak tucked entirely under his left wing, he looked the picture of despair.

Feighan cleared his throat politely.

The epidemiologist did not move.

"I think he's asleep, McGill."

Drudru spoke in a tone so soft Feighan could barely hear her. "He started last sleep already."

Absurdly, the scene reminded Feighan of a time in his childhood when he had insisted, with increasing desperation, that his parakeet was "on'y as'eep, Mommy!" while she shook her head in sympathetic silence.

A grin slipped over his face as he thought of an almost foolproof way to pull Th'hweet back from his "last sleep." The epidemiologist might come out of it spitting mad—no, not might, definitely—but better outrage than despair. "I don't know, Sam. I don't think Rehmal can sleep in the light."

The Rhanghan made a rude noise. *"Everybody* can sleep in the light."

"Not true, kiddo, not true at all. A lot of species are, um, whatchacallit, photo-sensitive? Exposure to light produces hormones that keep them awake; as soon as it gets dark the hormone levels fall off and they just conk out. The Rehmal are like that, aren't they, Drudru?"

"Yes." She eyed him curiously.

Sam said, "So if he's not asleep—"

"He's got to be dead."

Sam gasped.

Feighan glanced at the epidemiologist to make sure he still hid his head, then held a finger to his lips and winked at Drudru and his ward. Time for the assault on Th'hweet's dignity. If this failed to resurrect his fighting spirit, nothing would ever do it. "The only way to tell for sure," he said loudly, "is to give him a good shove. If he spins on his perch like a propeller, he's a goner, no question." He laid his palm on the doctor's warm, downy chest.

"Barbarian!" Fingers thin as pipe cleaners seized Feighan's wrist; the Rehmal's head snaked out of concealment. "How dare you!"

"The same way you did." He twisted his arm out of Th'hweet's grasp. "Are you about finished sulking in your tent here?"

"It's my office, not my tent."

"A literary allusion," said Feighan. "To a piece of barbarian literature three thousand years old."

Th'hweet lifted one leg and balanced on the other. "Twenty-eight hundred, maximum." He bent his head and picked at his talons with his beak.

Taken aback, Feighan blinked. "The allusion's still valid."

"Hardly, since my Patroclus died before I took to my tent."

"I thought you studied *medicine* on Earth."

The epidemiologist stretched his wings, riffled their feathers like a pianist running fingers down a keyboard, and shifted his weight from right foot to left. "I had to do something in my spare time."

"Right." He wondered if Th'hweet intended to make him feel intellectually inferior, or did it purely by accident. "Then you know what I mean. Even if the allusion isn't a hundred percent accurate. You're the only one who can save your people, but you stay perched here while the enemy mows them down."

"Oh, come, Mr. Feighan—if I could save my race by hoisting a sword and wading into battle, I would. But the 'enemy' is a mutant virus, not a Trojan in a crested helm. So go away and leave me alone."

A weird idea struck Feighan. Whether right or wrong, possible or impossible, did not especially matter. What mattered was keeping the epidemiologist's fire alive. He tossed his head back and laughed with a confidence he did not feel. "Shows how much you know."

"And what does that insult mean?" said Th'hweet.

"The virus isn't the enemy, it's the enemy's sword." The words poured out with smooth assurance, eliciting an internal astonishment that almost choked him. "Look, if any other Terran virus had caused the plague, you would have been astonished—but since it was flu, and—what did you call it? Highly unstable?"

Th'hweet extended his neck till his beak nearly touched Feighan's nose. He squinted hard at the Flinger. "Yes, I believe I used those words, but—"

"Hear me out. Since it was flu, your attitude was, oh yes, this makes sense because the virus mutates so easily. But really, what are the odds of its accidentally mutating in such a way as to be first—" He ticked the points off on his fingers. "—ah, capable of infecting Rehmal, and second, as extremely contagious as it is, and third, as fatal as it is? What are the odds of a random mutation's doing all that?"

"Astronomical, of course, Mr. Feighan. But it clearly happened."

"No. It did not. What happened was, because this is the only thing that makes sense, is that someone—probably an off-worlder, but definitely someone with access to Terran genes and Terran gene-splicing technology—created that particular mutant flu bug and brought it to Rehma. And the only reason they would do that is to eradicate all of you."

"Do you often indulge in such paranoid fantasies?"

Suddenly Feighan realized why his story had to be accurate. "No. No, I almost never do, at least not on someone else's behalf, but see, when I was on Actu—earlier this year?—The Organization was trying to incite a civil war because the husks of dead Actuni contain, um—" He spread his hands helplessly. "I forget what it's called, but it's addictive to you people."

"'Needledust' is the local slang name." Th'hweet clacked his beak once. "To call it addictive is like saying a nuclear warhead makes a noise when it detonates. And you say The Organization was trying to amass a considerable amount of it?"

"They had a whole harvesting operation set up, and—"

"Can you document this assertion of yours, Mr. Feighan?"

"Well, I . . . about all I could do is Fling you to Actu. If we can find H'nik—"

"You know H'nik?" Th'hweet straightened his legs and leaned forward even farther, almost toppling off his perch in the process. With a flurry of wings he caught his balance. "You know it personally?"

"Oh, sure, H'nik was the monk who invited me to come."

"H'nik invited *you* to its planet?"

Offended by the epidemiologist's tone, Feighan drew himself up to his full height. "Is that so surprising?"

"Frankly, yes." He stared hard at Feighan, as if seeing him for the first time. "Although it does tend to clarify certain things that had puzzled me . . . So you feel that The Organization deliberately caused our epidemic in order to eliminate all of us?"

"I wouldn't bet the farm, but I might bet the house."

"Well." Spreading his wings, he hopped from his perch and glided toward the door. "That does put a different complexion on the matter, doesn't it?"

"If you say so, doctor."

"Oh, yes." He landed in the doorway, and lifted his left leg briefly. He tweaked it with his beak. "Oh, definitely. Thwarting nature is one thing. Resisting an invasion is something else again entirely." He led the way into the laboratory and headed for the longest bench. "Let us get to it, then."

"To what?" said Feighan blankly.

"Why, to our counterattack, Mr. Feighan. What else?"

Dusk had settled over Stonehills City before Th'hweet turned away from his computer console. Wearily, he preened his chest feathers with his right hand. "Clearly, Mr. Feighan, standard public health measures will fail."

"Why?"

"To put it most simply, even if I could win over the various teachers, my people would not give up their traditional greeting. A simple analogy, if you please: For centuries, Terran physicians have advised that shaking hands spreads disease. Yet you persist."

"This is different," said Feighan.

"Oh?"

"Sure! You have an epidemic, here." He struggled for the right words. "I mean, shaking hands with someone and then touching your nose or your mouth is a good way to catch a cold, and everybody knows it, but number one, the infection rate's an awful lot lower back home, and number two, even though the common cold might make people wish they were dead, it almost never kills them. If an epidemic hit Earth, I'll bet people would stop in a hurry."

"Let me ask you this: Have you ever shaken the hand of someone you knew had a bad case of flu?"

"Well, yeah, I have, but—"

"Why?"

"Politeness, um, friendship . . ."

"And you didn't stop to think that you might be infecting yourself."

Exasperated, Feighan said, "Well, I don't *kiss* 'em."

"And do you immediately afterward wash your hands clean?"

"Of course not!"

"Politeness and friendship again?"

He squirmed. "Yeah, I suppose."

"So why should it be different here?"

"Because this is a killer epidemic!" He slapped the bench-top hard. "Doctor, when something like this is loose, the rules change—don't they?"

"Another question, Mr. Feighan."

"What?"

"Was the handshake the traditional greeting of the Asian world as well as the Western world?"

"The Asian world?" Nonplussed, he scratched his head. Asia . . . what he knew about the traditional Orient he could write on the back of his wrist. But he closed his eyes and tried to remember some of the samurai holos he had seen. "Ah . . . no, no, ah, to the best of my recollection, the Chinese and Japanese used to bow to each other. Come to think of it, maybe the Arabs did, too."

"My point exactly."

"Huh?"

"The handshake originated in one particular culture, and spread throughout all Terran societies because the culture that introduced it also achieved military and economic dominance. On Rehma, however, beaking has always been a universal custom. Though I can not prove it, I suspect that one reason we maintain our tradition lies in our genes."

That triggered Feighan's skepticism. "You're saying it's instinctive behavior?"

"I am saying that I do not know for sure. I suspect, however, that there must be sociobiological reasons why all Rehmal beak the people they meet. This is another area where far too little research has been conducted." He sighed heavily. "Mr. Feighan, I simply do not know. All I can swear to is that even I, this planet's sole epidemiologist, the isolator of the virus now killing my race, find it almost impossible not to beak."

"Oh boy." Feighan nodded sadly. "We have a major problem here."

"Yes. Preventive measures simply will not suffice. We must develop a vaccine to protect the uninfected, and produce anti-viral medicines in quantity to save those who have come down with the disease."

"But I thought you said you couldn't do that."

"We have no choice, Mr. Feighan." Closing his eyes, he shook his head slowly. "And we have so little time..."

"So what do we do first?"

"You, Mr. Feighan, and you, too, Sam, go to your hotel and get a good night's sleep. I will wake you a few hours before sunrise."

Feighan cleared his throat. "Uh—"

"We are in the western part of the continent, Mr. Feighan, and I wish to reach the Glade in the Forest of the Tallest Trees shortly after dawn breaks there."

"You're going to talk to the Flock of True Lore again?"

A grim look in his eye, Th'hweet nodded.

"Do you think this time you'll be able to convince them to cancel Festival?"

"Unfortunately, no. But there is something I would like them to do—something they *must* do if our race is to survive." He lifted a wingtip. "Two hours before dawn, Mr. Feighan. Sleep well."

• • •

Th'hweet had called ahead, so Feighan had risen and dressed, if not awakened, by the time the doctor reached their hotel room. With him came a short, stocky Rehmal with indigo feathers and an ice-blue crest. He chirped good-naturedly at the Flinger and his ward, and then stepped forward to beak them.

"My nephew Lu'reeng, Mr. Feighan." Th'hweet's voice held a trace of defensiveness. "You might recall my, er, inability to sing in the mode demanded by the Flock of True Lore?"

"I was wondering how you were going to get around that." He stood still while the Rehmal's cool beak swept across his cheeks. "So your nephew's going to sing for you?"

"As the noble Sree?sree?sree? did," said Th'hweet with a nod. "But one hopes Lu'reeng will sing to better effect."

Feighan stretched, covered his mouth, and yawned behind his hand. "Let me finish my coffee, call the desk, and I'll be ready to go."

"Please be quick."

"At this time of the morning, it's enough of an effort just to be, never mind quick." He returned to the tray on the small table. Cup in hand, he picked up the phone.

Sam stayed with the visitors. "How old are you, Lu'reeng?"

Th'hweet said, "My nephew reads English fluently, Sam, but he does not speak it." He warbled a question; Lu'reeng replied with three sweet notes. "He says he is nineteen—almost exactly nineteen of your years, as well."

"You mean Terran years," said Sam. "*My* years are Rhanghan years, and they're about twice as long as Terran years."

Ear to the receiver, Feighan set down his empty cup. "Throngorn years, Sam, not Rhanghan years."

"Aren't you ready yet, McGill?"

"The kid hates to be corrected," he said to Th'hweet. "And no, I— yes, hello? This is McGill Feighan; I'm calling for—"

"Got it right to 'and, guv'nor. The message reads, and

I quote verbatim, 'Gina Maccari is in good health and better spirits, except that she misses you very much and 'opes you'll be 'ome soon.' Good enough, guv?"

Feighan smiled. "Yes, thank you." He sat down the phone. "Now I am ready, so—shall we go?"

Th'hweet said, "Please."

"Sam, is Drudru going to meet you here, or at the lab?"

"At the lab, I think, but can't I go with you? She won't be there for *hours.*"

"Good point." He looked at Th'hweet. "Doctor, do you have any objections?"

"None at all, Mr. Feighan, except to further delay."

He nodded. "Hang on, then."

PING

Dawn filtered through the leaves to the east and washed the Glade in the Forest of the Tallest Trees with a pale light that cast no shadows. Dew clung to the young grass, and soaked Feighan's pants legs when he walked to the boulder at the center of the glade. "There aren't any snakes around, are there?"

Sam sniffed the air with his tongue. "Not nearby, not lately."

"That's a relief." Still he prodded the dead leaves at the base of the mossy boulder before he sat down on it. "Now what?"

Th'hweet said, "Now you get off the Rock of the Aged, and choose another position, one that will not offend the Flock of True Lore."

"Sorry." Wearily, he pushed himself to his feet and went to stand beside Sam. "And now?"

"We wait until the Watcher for the Glade flies overhead, whereupon it asks us our business, and we state our desire to see the Flock of True Lore, and we wait again."

Feighan stared off to the east. "Are you sure anybody's up this early?"

"Of course—we take the old Terran adage to heart."

The Flinger eyed him suspiciously. "You can't possibly

mean what I think you mean."

"But I do," said Th'hweet with a certain smugness. "I most certainly do."

Birdsong fell on them in liquid query; Lu'reeng threw back his head and trilled a reply. The Rehmal overhead circled the glade once before returning to the east.

"Was that the Watcher?" asked Feighan.

Th'hweet nodded. "The Flock of True Lore will be here shortly. Please stand when they appear, and remain standing until they have invited us to be seated."

"As long as you translate for us again."

"Certainly, Mr. Feighan." He gave a mournful sigh. "There is, unfortunately, little enough else for me to do here..."

Within moments, the three elders who had heard Th'hweet's previous plea soared regally over the treetops and came to earth. Eewhie, the flame-red Songstress of Times Past who bore a strong resemblance to a vulture, tossed off a snippet of song that suggested civility but not welcome.

Th'hweet tensed as Lu'reeng stepped forward. To Feighan he whispered, "They have prejudged us."

"How do you know?"

"Their poses; their gestures."

While Lu'reeng launched into cautious melody, Feighan squinted at the three. He blinked, then elbowed Th'hweet. "The blue one with the yellow crest's shedding."

"Elder K'rala?" After one glance, Th'hweet hissed in surprise. "The Master of Theology has the plague!"

Even as Feighan watched, a fourth blue feather lost its hold on K'rala's right wing. "Do you think he knows yet?"

"The vomiting commences two days before the initial molt."

"I meant, do you think he knows he has the plague?"

"The symptoms are quite distinctive, Mr. Feighan... ah, nicely put, my fine-crested nephew."

"What did he say?"

"He smoothed their suspicions: 'Guided by the wisdom of your earlier decision, we looked deeper into the causes of the worldwide sickness, and have news worthy of your attention.' Lu'reeng is in his element, Mr. Feighan: his life's ambition is to become a diplomat."

Eewhie whistled; Th'hweet translated: "It was thoughtful of you to bring us the news, but unnecessary, as all news reaches us eventually."

Lu'reeng bowed. "As the teachings say, 'The best time to hear of outlaws is before they stoop from the clouds.'"

"And that is well recalled," said plump Huu'leie. "Have you come to tell us of outlaws?"

"We have come to tell you that the disease of which we spoke before springs not from life, but from the laboratory."

K'rala, coughing, opened his wings in abrupt consternation. A dozen sky-blue feathers slipped free and danced on the wind. "You glide dangerously close to heresy, young spokesman, beware your tail."

Lu'reeng hopped from one foot to the other. "Your pardon, Elder K'rala, but I do not apprehend the danger. I beg enlightenment."

"One. Life comes only from life. That which is not alive cannot become alive. Two. You have previously stated that this disease threatens the existence of the entire race. The puny creations of a laboratory cannot jeopardize the beloved of the Great Winged Retzglaran. Even to suggest that they can verges on blasphemy."

Obviously out of his depth, Lu'reeng twisted his head all the way around to glance at his uncle, who whispered a few quick phrases. Then he faced his inquisitors again. "Please forgive me for the words that hid my meaning in fog. We have found the agent of the disease, an extremely small and simple virus. The virus is not native to our planet—rather, it is native to Terra, and has been especially modified to infect us."

Huu'leie extended his neck to its full length. His beak gaped wide, then snapped shut. "Who be these outlaws?"

"We believe them to be members of The Organization—"

"Hau'yeach!" Racked by another violent cough, and then a third, K'rala snapped his wings together and rocketed toward the trees. The sound of his retching carried all the way to the center of the glade.

Uncertain, now, Lu'reeng looked from Huu'leie to Eewhie. "Shall I wait for the Elder K'rala, or shall I continue?"

"Please, go on," said the female. She cocked her head to one side. Her ebony crest lay flat against her skull. "You blame The Organization—have you proof?"

"No, elder, none whatsoever. We do, however, have the testimony of this Terran—" He waved a wingtip in Feighan's direction. "—who says that recently, on the planet Actu, The Organization was attempting to amass a stockpile of needledust sufficient to addict us all. Through the intercession of the Great Winged Retzglaran, The Organization was thwarted, but they are nothing if not persistent."

"Which brings us to the second of K'rala's objections." Huu'leie, Teacher of the Law, spoke with a pedantic air that transcended language barriers. "To wit, that life forms from a laboratory can hardly threaten a people so loved by One so powerful."

"Ah, but consider, elders, the possibility that The Organization is attacking us simply to bring our Benefactor to our aid— so that It may, in Its turn, be attacked."

"You suggest that we are being used as bait?" said Eewhie.

"Yes, elder. Our legends sing of the love our Benefactor holds for us, and we all know the animosity The Organization holds for our Benefactor. What could be more natural than that Its enemy uses Its loved ones to lure It out of the trees and into the open sky? Although It might know of this danger, It might not be able to save us without great risk to Itself."

"On behalf of our missing member," said Huu'leie, "I

feel obliged to point out that your tail feathers will soon begin to smoke from the flames of heresy."

"Theology is not my strongest suit." Lu'reeng swung his tail imperturbably. "I will instantly recant any heresy I may accidentally utter, but I would die of shame should the Great Winged Retzglaran suffer injury because we did not use the means at our command to protect ourselves, but instead relied on Its beneficent intervention to save us."

The two elders regarded each other in silence for a while before Eewhie said softly, "Have we the means of self-protection at our command?"

"We do," said Lu'reeng. At a sound from his uncle he added, "That is to say, we have the knowledge, but to protect ourselves we must apply that knowledge in concrete ways."

"I take it," she said dryly, "that you come to us for assistance in the application of that knowledge."

"Yes, Elder Eewhie, that is why we have come."

"Please explain."

He gestured to the southwest. "There are many pharmaceutical plants which could quickly be converted to production of a vaccine against the disease. The one in River Mouth City, which now produces an anti-fungal powder, seems the choicest opportunity. The workers are skilled and the management is highly trained."

"And you would have us—?"

"Authorize the temporary expropriation of the plant, the diversion of its resources to the production of the vaccine and certain anti-viral agents that might prove effective against the disease, and the distribution of the vaccine and the medicines to as many of our people as are willing to be treated. We also ask you to encourage the people to accept the drugs."

Lawyer that he was, Huu'leie found the loophole in the plan. "We have no power to do that."

"But you are the Flock of True Lore."

"So we are, but I say it again, we lack the power. In all our history there is no precedent for the taking of production facilities, temporarily or otherwise, by the Flock of True Lore."

Eewhie looked ready to object to his venture into her specialty, but tilted her head thoughtfully and then, after a moment, nodded. "My esteemed colleague is correct. There is no such precedent."

To himself Feighan muttered, "Then set one, dammit!"

Eewhie impaled him with a vulture's hooded gaze. "Did the foreigner address us?"

Lu'reeng looked at his uncle, who whispered briefly. Then the youth opened his wings to the elders and bowed. "The foreigner poured his thoughts on the air, not intending to disturb these proceedings. His comment urges the typically Terran course of action: Where no precedent exists, one must create one."

"Impetuous people, these Terrans," said Huu'leie, rubbing his belly.

"Yes, they are, rather, but the suggestion is worth considering nonetheless."

Again Eewhie and Huu'leie stared at each other for an uncomfortable length of time. Before either said anything, K'rala emerged from the forest. He flew unevenly, losing feathers with each stroke of his wings. When he landed it looked more like he had stumbled on the wind and fallen to the ground.

"I have overheard some of what you are suggesting." He regarded each in turn through watery, filmy eyes. "Tell me, can this anti-viral medicine of yours cure me?"

As Lu'reeng began to nod, his uncle whistled one sharp note. The youth leaned back to let Th'hweet mutter in his ear. Then he straightened. "I am sorry," he said softly. "The medicine could save you, had it been produced already, but by the time the first batch comes off the production line, it will be too late to help you."

K'rala clacked his beak. A stray feather worked loose from his neck and skittered down his torso to the ground. His yellow crest drooped and splayed in all directions. "I consent," he said to the Songstress.

Eewhie nodded, and touched K'rala's shoulder with the tip of her wing. "We grant your request. Go directly to River Mouth City and explain to the authorities at the plant the powers we have—temporarily—granted you. We will spread our singers across the length and breadth of the continent, that they might inform the people of the steps you are taking and the reasons behind them. When the vaccine and the anti-virals are ready, our singers will disseminate information on how to acquire them." She waved a wingtip dismissively. "Go now; we have much to do."

Lu'reeng bowed low, thanked them, and stepped back. Th'hweet nodded to Feighan, who—

PING

—Flung them back to the hotel suite.

"Give us a few minutes to get something to eat," he told the two Rehmal, "and then we'll go commandeer this pharmaceutical factory of yours."

The next three days blurred past in a flurry of Flings to forest points near and far. Feighan never quite caught his breath. Th'hweet wanted to map the distribution of the disease with greater accuracy than he had earlier so that the initial batches of vaccine and medicine could be sent to the most infected areas. To do that, he needed to know what percent of every flock had the plague.

Each day started well before dawn, with a knock on his hotel door and Th'hweet's impatient, "Hurry up, Mr. Feighan, there's work to be done!"

Hauling himself out of bed, he would mumble incoherent curses as he wondered where the epidemiologist found the energy to keep moving at such a pace. Even Sam, who only traveled with them before and after his sessions with Drudru, began to drag.

While Feighan dressed, drank his coffee, and checked with the desk on the latest word about Maccari, Th'hweet would pace. Lu'reeng, on the other hand, would perch on a chair arm, and plug a read-only memory chip into a bank-memory section of the console. Though he spoke no English at the outset, his pouch bulged with bookchips imprinted with the Regency Romances he devoured. He flicked one on every time his uncle flew into another flock center, and at times refused to display the next village until he had finished the paragraph he was reading.

So it was Fling, and sit on the equipment box for a few minutes till Th'hweet came winging back to them, and Fling again, yawning, stretching, looking around at the fallow fields and the budding trees, and Fling again and again and again, a hundred times a day, once even teleporting a hundred eighteen times in one sixteen-hour stretch.

They materialized in a forest meadow; the ground seemed to lurch beneath their feet.

As Lu'reeng switched on his novel, Th'hweet squinted into the forest. "Tectonic activity. Strange. I thought this area was stable."

"Tec-ten-ic?" asked Sam.

The epidemiologist looked down with a tired smile. "Tectonic, ah, 'referring to the forces or conditions within the earth that cause movements of the crust' . . . like an earthquake, Sam."

"Wouldn't it be a Rehmaquake?"

Th'hweet nodded but Feighan said, "It's neither. It's me."

Sam's eyes widened. "You did that?"

"You bet, kiddo. I'm in bad shape," he told the epidemiologist.

"You are doing very well, Mr. Feighan."

"Not when I can't keep momentum straight coming out of a Fling, I'm not. It's about the easiest thing in the world to do, but when fatigue sets in this badly I just lose the control." He covered his mouth with a hand, noting again that his fingernails needed clipping, remembering that the night before he had simply been too tired to do them. "It's starting to get dangerous here, doctor."

"Please endure. River Mouth Pharmaceuticals is in full

production, now; the first batch of vaccine is due off the line tomorrow morning. We *need* this information, Mr. Feighan, and you are the one person on the planet who can help me compile it."

He stared at the doctor through eyes that felt like sandpaper. "That's a little much, don't you think? I mean, there *are* native Flingers—"

"Not any more," said Th'hweet simply.

Feighan did a double-take. "You don't mean—"

"Sick or dead. Each and every one of them. Until we can hire some off-worlders to take their places, you are our only functioning teleport."

If he had felt exhausted before, now he felt crushed. The weight of an entire planet on his shoulders? They were broad, but not that broad, not that capable. Dazed, he shook his head. "When are the alien Flingers coming in?"

Th'hweet shrugged. "They tell me there's a problem with that. Flinger Network Control maintains that there is a Network-wide shortage of trained teleports. The Flock of True Lore is offering triple-pay premiums, and still cannot find anyone to come."

"Your entire interstellar trade has come to a halt?"

"We never had much trade: the market for our traditional wicker art is small, albeit wealthy. Tourists and visiting scholars, yes, many of them—we avian races are few and far between, and you ground— unflighted species find us fascinating. As news of the epidemic spread, the tourists stopped coming. As for other imports, they were confined mostly to information and to food supplies for the off-worlders on the planet."

Fear stirred in the Flinger; his mouth dried. "Has the food stopped coming in?"

"Oh, heavens, no. There is no problem with imports, Mr. Feighan—you should understand that. The Flingers on other worlds teleporting goods and beings to Rehma have not sickened, and have not stopped sending what we need." His crest feathers drooped momentarily. "Except, of course,

for more Flingers and a medical emergency team and—"
He straightened abruptly. "Enough complaints. We have a
chance, Mr. Feighan, if you can endure just a few days
longer."

"I don't know," said Feighan slowly. "I'll do my best, I
promise, but this isn't something I can control. It's physiological. When I'm too tired, I lose it, and that's all there
is to it." He touched the Rehma scientist on the shoulder.
"I'll do my best."

"That is all I can ask, Mr. Feighan." He leaped into the
air and went looking for the local flock's village.

Lu'reeng gave a friendly chirp. At Feighan's glance, the
would-be diplomat gestured to the screen and twiddled a
control. Feighan yawned, and trudged over to him. "What's
up?"

Lu'reeng tapped the screen.

"You want something pronounced, huh?" Feighan peered
at it. Halfway down a page of arch dialogue glowed the
highlighted word Lu'reeng wanted to hear pronounced prop-
erly. The Flinger was used to the ritual by now—for five
days it had been about the only communication they had
had. "Fiddlesticks."

"Pittles Dix?"

"Fiddlesticks. Fiddlesticks." He pinched the bridge of
his nose, not really believing what he was doing. "Try it
again. Fiddlesticks."

"Fittles Tix."

"Fiddlesticks."

Lu'reeng nodded his head confidently. "Okay, sirrah.
Fid-dle-sticks. Okay? Gad! Rotter of a word."

Sam tongue-lashed the air. "Fiddlesticks? What are you
teaching him, McGill?"

"Just how to pronounce what he's reading, Sam."

"Did you have to teach him 'Forsooth'? He says it all
the time, now."

Lu'reeng glanced up and opened his beak in a grin.
"Forsooth!"

Feighan sighed. "Was not my idea, kiddo. Don't worry, sooner or later he'll start making sense."

The Rhanghan merely snorted.

"Fiddlesticks," whispered Lu'reeng. "Fiddlesticks!"

Feighan survived that day, though his control continued to slip. More than once they skidded out of a Fling with velocities of at least a centimeter a second. He fell into bed that night grateful that the day had ended before he had harmed anyone.

In the morning, tired, groggy, and out of sorts, he Flung them to River Mouth Pharmaceuticals. As they materialized inside the manager's office, the executive broke into a song full of quick sharp runs. Feighan knew something was wrong at once: Lu'reeng, ignoring his pouch full of bookchips, joined in a three-way trill with Th'hweet and the manager. The Flinger let it go a good five minutes before he touched the epidemiologist's shoulder. "Excuse me, but what's the matter? Did the process go wrong, or what?"

Th'hweet turned an utterly defeated expression to him. "Far worse, Mr. Feighan—at this moment, thousands of demonstrators are camped outside demanding that the factory cease production of the vaccine. And even as we speak, thousands more are flying toward us."

"But why?"

"They claim that this factory is an affront to nature, the teachings, and the Great Winged Retzglaran. They—"

Sirens shrieked. The manager bolted out of the office and flew to the site of the disturbance.

Th'hweet said, "Can you Fling us to the roof?"

He searched his memory. Yes, he had been on the roof once. The image wavered in his mind. "Sure." Closing his eyes, he concentrated, visualized, felt, knew—

PING

War sprawled below them. The demonstrators, breaking away from their picket lines, had attacked the unguarded factory. Technicians and researchers armed with whatever lay nearest to hand tried to drive them off, but faced a hundred times their numbers.

"This is not good, Mr. Feighan."

"Today's an understatement day, huh?"

Th'hweet pulled a bullhorn from their equipment box and sang into it ferociously. The mob paused, looked up, and split like an amoeba, with the larger portion continuing to invade the plant, and the smaller soaring up to confront Th'hweet's party.

Lu'reeng said, "Fiddlesticks!"

Sam groaned.

Feighan squinted at one of the Rehmal out ahead of the rest. It looked familiar. He was sure he had seen it before. But where? He had visited three hundred flock centers in the last three days, maybe more, and to associate one briefly glimpsed face with a name, or a place, or even a date seemed nearly impossible.

Below, the mob screamed in triumph. It was an ugly sound, feral and deep-throated, and Feighan's blood ran cold. He felt sick.

Smoke wisped up through the roof.

Th'hweet said, "They seem to have fired the building. There is nothing we can do here any more. The hotel room, I think, Mr. Feighan, if you—" His voice broke; he sobbed.

Feighan said, "Sure." Taking Sam's hand, he beckoned Lu'reeng and Th'hweet closer and—

PING

The suite materialized around them. He snapped his fingers. "The funeral!" His stomach twinged abruptly.

"A vivid image, Mr. Feighan, but incorrect." Th'hweet shuddered, and with a massive effort of will went on. "The Organization will conduct our funeral—with bulldozed graves and millions of tons of quicklime. Unless they simply wait a few years for the scavengers to pick clean our bones."

"No, no," he said impatiently. For a moment his vision blurred, but he blinked hard and it cleared. "Sree?sree?sree?'s funeral. Some of the leaders of that mob were Sree?sree?sree?'s, uh, pallbearers."

"You jest."

"No, I—" He clutched his stomach. Nausea pulsed through him in a blinding, irresistible wave. "Oh geez." He turned.

"Mr. Feighan, what is it?"

"I—" No time for speech. None whatsoever. He bolted for the john. Fell to his knees before the porcelain bowl. And vomited for what seemed like hours.

He wondered if the plague would make his hair fall out.

▪ Chapter XIV ▪

Even standing before the giant tank in which restless gases stirred irritably, Nathaniel Davis found it hard to keep the pride from his voice. He continued his report. "In sum, then, *Draft* maintains a 99.9 percent personnel effectiveness rate; *Needle*'s successful implementation did trigger a self-sustaining spread that falls within two-tenths of one percent of our operating projections; *SNAFU* has, to date, prevented institutional response from either the FNC or any member planet; and *Haystack* seems so far to have diverted the attention of the one entity capable of thwarting our plans. *Featherduster* and *Mintmaker* are plotted and awaiting implementation. They will be launched once the necessary preconditions have been met."

Gryll's speaker crackled and spat. "Sound surprised, Davis. Why?"

He sighed. Would the alien understand the phrase *Because it seems too good to be true?* "I'm not sure, sir, but I suspect it's because I thought that damn Feighan would cause us much more trouble than he has."

"Interesting premonition," said Gryll gloomily. "Pray it be false."

· Chapter XV ·

Thursday, 8 October 2105

McGill Feighan grabbed the towel bar and half pushed, half pulled himself to his feet. His knees ached from twenty minutes on the cold tile floor. He trembled all over, and not just from the disease.

Between his bouts of vomiting, he had had plenty of time to think, and not much else to do but gasp for air.

He had decided exactly what he had to do next, and he did not like it one bit. He would much rather Fling to the hospital in New York for treatment—but that would doom an entire race. Shivering, he leaned on the sink.

A pale, frightened face stared out of the mirror at him. It measured him, estimated his odds of surviving the plague, and paled even more. But it lost none of its determination. Not with Sree?sree?sree?'s carving in his pocket. He owed his friend that much.

Bending slowly lest wild dizziness swoop back to churn his gut again, he rinsed the sourness from his mouth. He splashed water on his soiled cheeks and dried his hot skin with the plush hotel towel. Then he returned to the sitting room.

Three glances met his: two anxious, one empty. Th'hweet

had surrendered. The eyes he lifted looked on death.

Lu'reeng said, "Egad!"

"Are you okay, McGill?" Sam hurried over and touched Feighan's leg. "You sounded *awful* in there!"

"Ah—" He held out his hand and waggled it from side to side. "I've been better. Right now I have to talk to Dr. Th'hweet."

"Home to New York, Mr. Feighan?" Weariness and resignation robbed him of all animation. "They should be able to treat you within an hour, and restore you to health within a week."

Health. The word evoked the cool, antiseptic corridors of the hospital, the friendly competence of the staff physicians, and the relief that would well through his entire being once he placed himself in their hands. Yet he had to say, "No." His voice shook.

Th'hweet's crimson crest rose perhaps a centimeter; his beak clacked faintly. "What, then?"

He needed a chair, badly: His legs no longer had the strength to support him. Lowering himself into the nearest armchair, he felt old, discouraged, utterly inadequate to the task of convincing Th'hweet to meet the problem head-on, with all his former fanaticism. "Let me just check: Do you have any hope of getting another pharmaceutical factory here on Rehma to manufacture the vaccine?"

The crest flopped back down. "None whatsoever, Mr. Feighan. After the destruction of River Mouth Pharmaceuticals, what executive would risk his own plant to produce our material? No, no, the people of the sky will fly no more."

"So we get someone else make it for you. Like the FNC."

Th'hweet made a guttural noise deep in his throat. "You know how many times I've requested emergency assistance."

"Forsooth!" said Lu'reeng.

"But this is different!" Sine waves of nausea rippled through his innards. He clamped his jaws and sat motionless until they passed. A trickle of cold sweat ran down the side of his face. "It is!"

"The only difference is that the probability of our extinction is higher than before, Mr. Feighan." He lifted a leg and picked moodily at his talons. "Probability, hah! Certainty is the word. Why should Flinger Network Control come to our aid now, when it has refused so often?"

He chose his words with care. "Because now we're not asking for the medical teams they've sent elsewhere. We're just asking them to produce your medicine in their labs. God knows they have more labs at the Hub than anywhere else. I can take samples there, and bring the product back once it's ready—I mean, it's not *that* heavy, is it?"

"I estimate a one-milligram dose of the vaccine should afford adequate protection." He paused, obviously waiting for the Flinger to extrapolate meaningful figures for himself.

Feighan held his stomach. Queasiness forbade him to do multi-digit arithmetic in his head. "How many Flings will it take, then?"

"At 918 kilos per Fling? With a million lives riding on each kilogram, Mr. Feighan? Two Flings, perhaps."

"Two? I can do it even in this condition."

"By the time it's ready I doubt if you will need even one entire Fling. For the vaccine, that is. The medicine is a bit heavier, though not significantly." He seemed exasperated by Feighan's unwillingness to let him curl up and die. "But why do you feel the FNC will cooperate this time?"

"There's a Senior Flinger named Thurndriddle who has the authority to provide the help you need."

"Oh? Where is he from?"

"*It* is from Ylsslyp."

Sam broke in. "It?"

He looked down at his ward. "Thurndriddle's race has three sexes, and it's in the middle. Now, hush." He turned back to Th'hweet. "Not only is it Thurndriddle's job to allocate FNC assistance in times of emergencies, it owes me a favor. Well, if I'm ever going to collect on that, now's the time. So, uh—" He clutched his stomach again. "While I'm being sick, why don't you get the samples?"

His resolution battered and just barely alive, he knelt in misery before the porcelain bowl. Behind him, scales slithered across tiles. A cool hand touched the back of his neck.

"Go 'way." His throat hurt from retching; acids burned at it from top to bottom. "Lemme die in peace."

"Don't be silly. When do we leave?" He turned on the faucets.

"We?"

"Yeah, McGill, you an' me. Do we leave as soon as Th'hweet comes back with the samples or do you want to take a nap, first? Here." He pressed a damp washcloth to Feighan's forehead.

"Thanks." While he wiped his flushed face, he tried to think. Could he, feverish and exhausted, deal with the bureaucrats at the Hub and look after Sam as well? "You're going home, kiddo."

"Back to New York? You're crazy!"

"Sam, this whole thing is crazy. I want you somewhere out of harm's way—like with Gina Maccari." It seemed safe to straighten up. He patted his ward on the shoulder, then used him as a crutch. "I might as well do it now. You don't have anything to pack, do you? Oh, your books. Well, get them together—"

"If you do, I'll run away."

He rocked back on his heels. "What?"

"You heard me. I said I'll run away."

"I thought you liked Gina."

"I do. I like her a lot—almost as much as you do. But if you think you can just get rid of me, and make me miss out on all the fun—"

"Fun?" He fought for control of his digestive system, and succeeded—for the moment. "Trust me, kiddo, this is not fun. It's painful is what it is."

"I'm not talking about being sick, McGill, and you know

it." He waved a hand dismissively. "I'm talking about the excitement—fighting The Organization and saving the Rehmal and maybe meeting the Far Being Retzglaran—*that's* what I'm talking about."

"Yeah?"

"Yeah." He bobbed his head so vigorously that it nearly made Feighan sea-sick. "McGill, I know when there's going to be any danger, and if you take me—"

"I'm going to the Hub, Sam, the *Hub*. It's the safest place in the galaxy for me, yes?"

"Well, yes, but . . ."

Through his fever came an idea. "You know who might be in danger?"

He folded his arms and looked scornfully at his guardian. "Are you going to try to convince me Gina's in danger?"

"Uh-uh. Th'hweet."

Sam frowned. "Why Th'hweet?"

"Because if anybody can save this planet, it's him."

"I gotcha, McGill. The Organization might try to kill him so the plague doesn't get stopped!"

"Right again."

"As usual."

"You're pretty cocky for a little kid, you know?"

Sam shrugged modestly.

"Listen, kiddo, I won't send you back to New York after all—I'll leave you here with Lu'reeng and Th'hweet as their bodyguard—but you have to promise me three things."

Sam looked skeptical. "What?"

"First, that if you get even a little bit sick, you'll find a Minder and have him get in touch with me at the Hub, so I can come back and get you to a doctor."

"I don't think Rhanghans can catch the plague."

"That's what I thought about humans—but your biochemistry isn't all that different from mine, and if I've come down with it, you might be vulnerable too. Be a good kid and promise. Or else I'll Fling you back to Gina's and if you run away, you run away. Think you could survive in

New York on your own?"

Sam gave an involuntary shudder. "Okay, McGill, I promise."

"Second, you keep on studying with Drudru."

He smiled broadly. "Good! I like Drudru. She gives me stuff to eat when I do my patience lessons right."

So that explained Drudru's influence on the kid. Feighan made a mental note of it. "And third, you'll warn Th'hweet and Lu'reeng of any danger."

"I'll do a good job, McGill. Nothing'll happen to them."

"Good boy. Now—" His stomach coiled like a cobra preparing to strike. "—if you'll give me a couple minutes privacy, there are some things that have to be brought up before I can leave."

Th'hweet set the bag at his feet. "Use both hands, please."

Feighan hefted it. "It's not heavy."

He fluttered his violet wings for a second. "Neither are you strong. Please. The vials are unbreakable and tightly sealed, but if you should lose them—"

"Oh, all right." He hooked his other set of fingers around the plastic handle. "You sure you don't want to cuff it to my wrist?"

The epidemiologist looked thoughtful. "I have no manacles, but there is some wire—"

"Just joking, doctor, just joking." He looked around. "All right, I'm off. Sam, be good, don't hassle Drudru or the doctors, and watch out for all of them, okay?"

"Sure, McGill." He hugged his guardian quickly, then stepped away.

"Doctor, to go over it one more time: First I talk to Thurndriddle and convince it to get the process underway; then I Fling to New York to see a doctor; next, I go back to the Hub and wait for the first batch to roll off the lines. Unless, of course, they won't let me out of the Infirmary, in which case I'll try to get Walking Mule to bring the medicines back here."

Th'hweet flourished his wings. "Thank you, Mr. Feighan."

He hoisted the bag. "See? Two hands. 'Bye all. See you soon." He closed his eyes, visualized the blue-carpeted, holo-lit reception chamber to Thurndriddle's dank office, felt, knew—

PING

"Don't move!"

He opened his eyes. And looked up the tunnel of a rifle barrel.

"Jesus!" Eyes snapping shut, he tried to Fling away.

And materialized in exactly the same place.

McGill Feighan was trapped.

▪ Chapter XVI ▪

Thursday, 8 October 2105

Gryll said, "Make self comfortable. Force-chair controls located under panel in table top. Order drinks, foods, dancing girls. Must celebrate."

Nathaniel Davis suppressed a frown. Dinner sounded like an excellent idea, but he did not drink, and as for dancing girls, well . . . He cleared his throat. "To my way of thinking, sir, that might be a bit premature."

"Come to me, report wondrous delighting events, and spurn celebration? Why? Must understand shadow of doubt attitude casts on report, Davis."

He chose his words carefully, cleverly. "Sir, I reported the status of an extensive, on-going operation as accurately as possible. To the best of my knowledge, the situation as it now stands parallels almost exactly the situation that our projections forecast for this point in time. Operation PlayGround is, however, by no means complete, and will continue to require nearly flawless management if it is to result in success. May we defer the celebration until the opening of the first casino?"

"Anxiety's persistence excellent sign, Davis. Might keep you alive."

• Chapter XVII •

Thursday, 8 October 2105

Panic flashed through Feighan's mind, blinding him, nearly disabling him entirely. The only thought he could complete said *Run-hide-quick-now!* A futile thought, that. Already weakened by the plague, further crippled by numbing fear, he could not move a centimeter.

Shock-released adrenaline surged in his veins. Its fire burned off some of the haze; his brain slowly cleared. *Wake up! Quickly!* Death waited in the ammo clip of that rifle. *Come on!* He took a breath. *And hang on to the case!* Fighting down the panic, holding it at bay with all the will power he could muster, he closed his eyes. Distress signals wailed up from his stomach. He blocked them out, too, and concentrated on his Talent.

Ah, there, at the fringes! Spinning and flickering on the edge of perception, four hungry vortices drained off his power.

Now he understood what pinned him down. Four natural anti-teleports—"Anchors," in FNC jargon—had opened their Talent-sinks to him, canceling out his ability to Fling, and forcing him to materialize at a point equidistant from them.

Short of putting a bullet through his head, it was the only

way one could strip a Flinger of his power. But who had let them loose in the Hub, the very heart and soul of the Flinger Network? Had the world city been invaded? That might explain the gun, at least.

Speaking of which . . . he opened his eyes.

Again, the rifle claimed all his attention; he had to wrench his gaze from its gape-mouthed menace to its wielder.

Filoso.

The Timili made an imposing warrior. He stood two meters tall and his muscles bulged. Half obscured by the interlocked color bands of his energy tunic, his clan scars gleamed white on his furry chest.

Feighan relaxed and lowered his hands. Whatever had happened at the Hub, he and Filoso fought on the same side. "Good day to you, Filoso." He spoke in the other's language. "You startled me. I have come to see Senior Flinger Thurndriddle."

The Timili cocked his head. His big ears opened to their fullest. His finger did not budge from the trigger. "Good day to you, Mr. Feighan."

"Thank you." Feighan bowed slightly—and carefully. Guns made him nervous, even when held by a friend. "What's this all about?"

"Ah." He waggled the rifle a bit—but not enough to spoil his aim. "You mean this?"

"Yes, that. Would you mind pointing it somewhere else?"

He peered at Feighan closely, great eyes narrowed, irises slitted against illumination from the wall-holo that to the nocturnal Timili had to be blinding. After a moment's consideration, he took his finger off the trigger and lowered the butt of the rifle to the floor.

"Thank you."

"You are most welcome. I apologize for the unpleasantries, which were prepared for someone else entirely."

"What are you expecting, an assassination attempt?"

"In a sense. It seems that a Rii—edsch Flinger went berserk, and cast a tax auditor. She will not reveal the point of the cast—she laughs, and says he is truly among his own kind, now."

"Probably in a shark pool somewhere."

The Timili smiled. "Naturally, she was declared Rogue. When she heard, she threatened to kill my superior. Thurndriddle is, frankly, terrified. As his assistant, I have taken precautions. As I say, I do apologize." He seemed sincere. "Please, have a seat."

Feighan gestured to the staid reception room. "You baited a lure in the entry to a Senior Flinger's office? Did you not worry about ricochets and stray bullets?"

"Not quite. We have reinforced the walls, floors, and ceilings of this room—and my superior has, of course, changed offices. It works in an entirely different sector of the Hub now."

Feighan nodded in relief. Rehma needed Thurndriddle alive. "Good fortune for the Rogue hunt. And as for me, I must see Senior Flinger Thurndriddle as soon as possible."

"Oh? We still have no medical teams to send."

"I bring glad news." Feighan grinned. "The need for the teams has passed." He held up the case. "This contains samples of a vaccine and an anti-viral medicine; we formally request the FNCN to produce them in quantity most quickly."

"Ah." Filoso shuffled his prehensile feet in embarrassment. "I'm afraid I haven't the authority to make that sort of decision—"

Feighan rolled his eyes to the ceiling. *Bureaucrats!* "Who holds such authority, then?"

"Thurndriddle, of course."

Hoping to gain a tactical advantage in the intricate game of getting past the secretary, Feighan switched to English. "That's fine, let's go see it." *And quick,* he thought, as nausea rose in his throat.

"Unfortunately—again I must apologize—my superior has grown physically feeble with age, and is terrified of the possibility of infection. Before I can permit you to enter the Senior Flinger's presence, I must insist that you document your clearance through Customs and Immigration."

"Are you kidding? I'm a Flinger. I came right here."

"Of course." He paused, then jerked his head upward and looked into the distance. He cupped his right ear with a six-fingered hand and appeared to listen to it intently.

A micro-earphone, Feighan decided.

"Clearance can wait. The Rogue approaches. We must go."

"Getting out of the crossfire is fine by me."

He raised his right hand, fingers spread, and made a fist. "Follow my cast to safety."

*PI—

Before Feighan could react, Filoso's Talent awakened his own. His reflexes swept him away like the surf seizes a board. Energies shifted all around him, but with Filoso guiding him, he did not need to measure their quantities. He let instinct balance him as he rose the wave to shore. The sheer smoothness of it exhilarated him.

—NG*

"God, that was *great!*"

Filoso backed away. "Wait here!" He disappeared.

"But— damn." He spoke to an empty room. Tiles covered it in a blanket of white—floors, ceiling, and walls. The only contrast came from discreet black printing on each ceramic square, printing that varied from tile to tile so as to repeat the word in a thousand languages. He found the English translation in seconds. It read: "Quarantine."

When he tried to escape, Anchors held him fast.

"Dammit! Filoso, what's going on here?"

The bare room echoed back his roar, and wrapped him in imperturbable sterility.

"Hello?" He could not spot a door. Eyes on the ceiling, he started to cross the room. An invisible resilience barred his way. He touched it; it took color from his skin and instantly appeared as an octagon raised a meter off the floor. A force field. Propagated, probably, by machinery built into the floor. He assumed it to be a bed. Or a table. Or a chair.

Depending on what the occupant needed at the moment. He looked around more carefully. The room held nothing else but a metal-rimmed hole in the corner with a black tile just in front of it. It looked like a drain.

He stepped on the black tile. A chrome-colored force field spun up from the hole and opened into a bowl. Through a narrow pipe woven of convoluted energy streamed water that swirled down the inside of the bowl and disappeared back into the drain.

For a minute he watched in bemused admiration. Trust the FNC to buy the finest technology available, even if a standard hotel-issue toilet would have cost a fraction of the price. Although this probably stayed cleaner. The thought triggered a spasm of nausea, so he used the gadget.

It worked exactly as intended.

Finished, he paced the perimeter of the room, tracing the narrow walkway between the force-bed and the wall. His legs trembled, but he stooped to examine the tiles closely for switches to other devices—or better yet, locks to concealed doors. Three steps. Turn. Three more steps. Turn. Three more . . .

His stomach seethed with the flames of tension, the acids of illness. Bending over began to hurt. He sat on the edge of the force field. After a few deep, shuddery breaths, he lay back. The field adjusted to his mass, to the contours of his long body. It took on, too, the colors shooting through his energy tunic. It was like lying on a rainbow.

"Why doesn't somebody tell me what's going on?" he said loudly.

The silence that answered did not know.

An hour passed, and during that hour he tested the Anchors' hold twice. He could not break free: not by brute force, since they drank down every bit of power he could generate and clamored for more; nor by stealth, either, for his own Talent triggered theirs. He suspected, as he used the force drain for the fourth time, that if it came to a struggle, he would give up long before they did.

So he stopped trying. To conserve his strength, he told himself. And to figure out, if he could, what the hell Filoso thought he was doing.

He racked his brains in vain.

Another hour passed before a metal panel in the wall retracted to reveal the grill of a speaker. Through it poured the jabber of two beings; Feighan did not even recognize their language, much less understand it. No matter. If they spoke no English, they could surely find a translating gizmo around somewhere. This was, after all, the Hub.

He sat up. "Hey! Hey, you out there!"

The jabbering stopped. Paper rattled. The cool hiss of an alien voice said "This is Dr. F'taox, Mr. Svensson."

"My name is Feighan, doctor, McGill Feighan. What in hell is going on here?"

"We have analyzed the airflow in your chamber, and have determined that you have, unfortunately, fallen victim to an utterly unknown disease."

He touched the bag. "It's not unknown. Dr. Th'hweet on Rehma—

"Remote diagnostic examination has discovered the following symptoms: fever, nausea, and hallucination. Does your head ache, Mr. Svensson?"

"My name is—"

"Please, if you help us do our jobs, we will heal you more quickly. Does your head ache?"

"Look, this is crazy! My name is McGill Feighan."

"We have your file in front of us, Mr. Svensson. The delusion that your name is McGill Feighan is a symptom of your disease. Your real name is Carl Josef Svensson."

"It is not!"

The two voices conferred in their own language for a moment. "Would it make you feel better if we called you Mr. Feighan?"

"It's what I'm called, dammit!"

"Fine, Mr. Feighan. Does your head ache?"

"Oh, geez, yes, I have a headache, but why don't you

just let me go see Senior Flinger Thurndriddle?"

"Because we have determined that you are contagious. You must spend at least six months in Quarantine before we can release you. Do your muscles hurt?"

It took a while for the enormity of the statement to sink in. "Six months! Every person on Rehma will be dead in six weeks!"

The two outside chattered in their own language; eventually F'taox said, "The Rehma plague is the responsibility of an entirely different department, Mr. Svensson."

He reined in his anger. "I said my name is Feighan!"

"My apologies, Mr. Feighan. Do your muscles hurt?"

"Look, Dr. F'taox, I'll leave the Hub, just let me—"

"We regret that we could not permit such a contravention of the regulations, Mr. Feighan. Subsection 82, paragraph 46C, clearly states—"

"All right, all right! Let me have a phone, though, huh? I have to talk to the Senior Flinger right away."

"Oh, of course." Another panel in the wall retracted to reveal a standard-issue all-languages telephone. "Be our guest."

"Thank you." He meant it to sound sarcastic, but suspected F'taox would miss the nuance. He walked over and picked up the receiver. "What's Thurndriddle's extension?"

They gabbled with each other briefly. "Nine-five-five-nine-eight-two-six-ten thousand."

He tapped the number in and waited for the earpiece to crackle to life.

He heard nothing.

"Hey!"

"Yes, Mr. Sven— Feighan?"

"This doesn't work."

A chitter whispered through the speaker; from its faintness, he assumed the one further from the microphone had spoken. "Try jiggling the buttons."

He pushed the slick plastic tabs in and out to no avail. "Any other bright ideas?"

The two discussed that at great length. At last, F'taox said, "Our apologies, Mr. Feighan. A repair tech will come in a short while. In the meantime, is there anything else we can do? Something to eat, perhaps?"

His stomach lurched in alarm. "Ah, no, no, and I'd be grateful if you didn't mention it again."

"Of course, Mr. Feighan. It should only be a few minutes." The speaker clicked off.

More like forty minutes later, it clicked back on.

"Yo, hey, you in there!"

He sat up on the bed. "Yes?"

"I'm the technical specialist—repairman, to you. Futtocks says you got trouble with your phone."

"Yeah, I do."

"So what's the problem?"

"The line's dead." *And I don't know why Filoso mousetrapped me, and I can't get a hold of Thurndriddle, and a billion intelligent beings are going to die. But that's somebody else's department, right?*

Metal clattered. The tech hummed to himself. A moment later, he said, "Looks okay out here."

"But it doesn't work!"

"Well, ya gotta pick it up," he said with weary patience. "You wanna try that, see does it work if you pick it up?"

"All right, all right. Just— just give me a minute, okay?" Dizziness assailed him every time he moved his head; an undulating haze kept distorting his vision. To top it all off, his leg muscles quivered so badly he was afraid they would give way, and tumble him to the floor. But he reached the phone eventually, and pressed his sweat-drenched forehead to the cool wall tiles. He lifted the receiver to his ear. Silence still filled it. "Hello?"

"Works now, huh?" boomed the intercom.

"No," said Feighan, "it *doesn't* work." A sudden liquid rumbling in his gut doubled him over. The receiver clattered to the floor as he clutched his belly.

"Hey, whatcha trying t'do there, break it?"

A softer voice whispered in the background.

The tech spoke again in a subdued tone. "Hey, sorry, buddy, I din't know . . . Lemme see what I can do out here. Can ya put the receiver back in its cradle, though?"

"Yeah." Straightening against the pain, he hung up the phone. "Done."

"Don't go away, huh? This shouldn't take but—" Screws sibilated out of their spiral nests as the tech hummed off-key. Metal tapped plastic, ceramic, more metal. The tech grunted, switched tunes, and reversed the order of his sound effects. "Awright, try it now."

He lifted the phone, but it was still dead. "Uh-uh." He dropped it back on its hook.

"Dammit. Lemme try calling in to you—" Buttons clicked.

Feighan stared numbly at the instrument. Fever swept chills through his body. He was no longer certain that he could carry on a coherent conversation. Nor was he certain that he cared any more. It would be so pleasant just to lie down, curl into a ball, and drift off to sleep . . .

Through the intercom roared, "Dammit, dammit, dammit!"

"Huh?" He jerked his head up and almost vomited.

"The break's on your side of the wall."

"Tell me where the door is and I'll unlock it for you."

"No, I— oh, all right, you explain it."

F'taox's reptilian hiss of a voice slipped out of the intercom. "Unfortunately, Mr. Sv— Feighan, regulations prohibit permitting nonmedical personnel entry into an occupied Quarantine chamber."

"What?" It came out a wail. "What are you *talking* about?"

"There is a finite possibility that you might infect the technical specialist, who might then spread the disease through the world-city."

Ah, now, he could empathize with F'taox's reluctance to let an unknown plague run free through an unprotected, unsuspecting populace. "In that case— Hey! I've got a great idea. Why don't you wire the intercom into the telephone on your side—"

The tech himself replied to that one. "Sorry, buddy. No can do."

"Why not? It ought to be—"

"Just for starters, we're talking different optical frequencies here, so I'd have to wire in a converter, too. But the only place I can patch it in is after the translation circuitry—"

"That doesn't matter! Thurndriddle speaks English!"

"—which means it doesn't get digitized, which means the telephone at the other end is trying to convert into sound an analog signal that it thinks is digital. Which means even if your buddy speaks English, he ain't gonna understand a word you say 'cause all he's gonna hear is garbage."

"Can't you cook *something* up?"

"Maybe, if I didn't have thirty-eight repair calls waiting on me right this minute. Lissen, I'm a technical *specialist*, which means I fix it if it's broke. Whatchew want is a technical *developer*, you know?"

"How do I—"

"Futtocks here'll put in an R&D request for you; somebody'll get back to you."

"When?"

"I dunno, a couple days, I guess. Maybe a week."

"I can't wait that long!"

"Buddy, I'm real sorry about the jam you're in, but there's nothing I can do, it's worth my job if I get caught doing development. Lissen, I gotta go, here's the doc again."

"Mr. Sv— Feighan?"

"All right," he said desperately, "look, you've probably got this cubicle negatively pressurized, right?"

It asked a question of its colleague before replying, "Of course we have, Mr. Feighan."

"Well, pop the door open a crack and toss in a radio. Then make sure Thurndriddle has another radio and—"

"I am sorry, Mr. Feighan, but there is a great deal of

delicate electronic equipment in the immediate vicinity. To broadcast would almost certainly cause some of this equipment to fail. Wireless communications devices are, therefore, prohibited. Unless you can suggest something more feasible, we shall almost certainly have to wait for a technical developer to be assigned to your case."

"Wait a minute, wait a minute—what about just getting a second phone and passing it through the doorway?"

"Hmm. An interesting idea. It will take a few minutes to evaluate, though."

Once again, "a few" stretched into "many." Too damn many. *Filoso, you bastard, I swear I'll get you for this.* He lay groaning on the force field, wishing they would hurry up and let him talk to his old friend while he still could. Twice he had to hurry to the drain, but he had long since emptied his stomach, and shuddered instead through the agony of the dry heaves.

At last Dr. F'taox turned on the intercom and spoke. "Mr. Feighan?"

"Yes? Have you got the phone?"

"We're sorry to say that the wires would prevent a perfect seal, and thus increase the odds of the contagion spreading."

"Oh, God! Please! Don't you understand that the longer you keep me here, the more Rehmal are going to die?"

"Mr. Sven— Feighan, why are you so obsessed with the fate of the Rehmal? Your file clearly shows you have never visited their planet in your life, and have no Rehmal friends or acquaintances."

"That's not my file, don't you hear me? I'm being framed and I don't even know why!" Inspiration struck just when he needed it most. "I can prove I'm McGill Feighan. Get a Minder down here—"

"Oh, come. We are doing our best to humor you, but if you think we will bring a Minder within range of you, after what you did to that poor child in Tokyo—"

"What?" He could not remember the last time he had been in Tokyo. "What are you talking about?"

"It's all in your file."

"That's not my file!"

"We can understand why you might wish to deny being an Amplifier, and we have, I think, proven ourselves willing to address you by a name other than your own, but really! We will not permit you to overload the brain of another telepath."

To himself he mumbled, "This is a nightmare!"

"We quite agree. And as soon as your infection has run its course, we shall deal with your mental affliction, as well. Who knows? Perhaps the former actually caused the latter, in which event physical recovery will bring about psychological recovery. In the meantime, we are willing to indulge your obsession. We have, after all, coded your request for a system developer with the second highest possible priority."

"Only the second?"

"Priority One relates only to armed attack on the Hub or its companion satellites."

"One last try, huh? Please get Thurndriddle down here in person—"

"Mr. Feighan. The Senior Flinger has a pathological fear of disease and will not come within seven decks of the Hospital Region, not even for its semi-annual checkup. It will surely refuse to come down for a chat."

Feighan did not dare to give up. Too many lives depended on him. "Will you carry a note or a tape to it for me?"

"We would, but Thurndriddle will refuse to accept it on the grounds that it might carry germs."

His head was beginning to hurt as badly as his stomach. "How about recording my voice through the intercom and delivering the tape or bubble to the Senior Flinger's office?"

"Ah! Again, an excellent suggestion, Mr. Feighan. We actually have a recording device built into our console. Please, state your message any time you're ready."

He almost cried out his relief, his joy. *There's always a way around rules, always, and I found it again!* he thought. His head swam with dizziness. Leaning against the wall, needing its firm reality to hold himself in place, he began, "Thurndriddle, this is McGill Feighan, and I need your help in a real bad way..."

When he finished, he passed out.

"Mr. Svensson?"

He lifted his head from the impermeable tiles. The sterile white room's corners spun around him like the poles on a carousel. An asthmatic jackhammer beat away at the back of his skull. He wanted to die. He wondered why he had not.

"Mr. Svensson?"

"Who—" Jagged dry things clogged his throat; he coughed to clear them away and they tore harshly at his flesh. "Who is it?"

"Dr. F'taox, Mr. Svensson. Oh, I do apologize. You prefer the name Feighan. Do you know where you are?"

He moved his head slowly, very slowly, and blinked his sandpaper eyes. "Uh— huh."

"We regret to inform you—" The papery alien voice sounded genuinely distressed. "That our courier reports that as Senior Flinger Thurndriddle did not recognize your name, it refused to permit the tape into its office."

"What?"

"It also called for a decontamination team to sterilize its reception area. The Senior Flinger fears death greatly, Mr. Feighan."

"Oh my god, my god..." He pushed himself to his hands and knees, and paused there, head hanging. Was getting to his feet really worth it?

Yes, he decided, *as long as I can stand up long enough to collapse on the bed.*

"On the more optimistic side, our request for a development specialist has been approved, and the specialist will report here within—" It paused; keys clicked. "—sixty-seven of your hours."

The second voice murmured softly in the background.

The alien spoke again. "We are not certain, however, that you will survive for another sixty-seven of your hours, so we will leave the tape recorder running in the event you wish to make verbal arrangements of your affairs."

To hell with this! thought Feighan. He would give it one last try: he closed his eyes, concentrated on himself, visualized Walking Mule's office, felt his body slipping down into those soft pillows, knew how to move himself from tile to foam, and—

Four dark whirlpools sucked down his strength, spun him around, and left him at their exact mid-point.

Unconscious.

· Chapter XVIII ·

Thursday, 8 October 2105

Davis stared at Agent Red in disbelief. "You have him *where?*"

The Timili stretched his long legs casually. "In the infirmary."

He could hardly believe his ears. His stomach hurt. "On the *Hub?*"

"Hub Quarantine is the most escape-proof enclosure in the Network."

"Perhaps." Sweat ran down his neck. Gryll would *flay* him. "But—"

"Listen to me, Schoolteacher. Only the Anchors and the physicians know of his presence, and they believe him to be Carl Josef Svensson, a Terran Flinger with a fever that has induced homicidal schizophrenia. He may say whatever he likes, but they will not take him seriously, nor will they permit him to gain his freedom. He is well and truly caged, in the one place in the Network where his friends will not think to search."

"You'd better be right."

"Of course I am." Agent Red threw back his head and laughed.

Davis toyed with a pen. "As long as you realize it's your life if he gets away." To himself, he added, *And mine. And mine.*

· Chapter XIX ·

Thursday, 8 October 2105
—Monday, 12 October 2105

Before this trip to the Hub, Feighan had never even encountered a concealed four-Anchor square. Now he had to escape from one. If he did not, a billion Rehmal would surely die. And so, probably, would one McGill Feighan. All because of a treacherous assistant *(why does he have it in for me?)*, a paranoid old fool, and that damn Subsection 82, paragraph 46C. What was wrong with these people, that they followed their rules and regulations so blindly?

Fever magnified fear, rippled waves of it through him, making his teeth chatter, his heart race.

Aliens. When you met your first two or three, all you could think was how *weird* they were. But you worked with them for a while, and you lived with them on their planets, and you got used to them. You started seeing them almost as humans in costume. Then they did something like this, and you could not for the life of you understand their values. How could a rule, a few words on paper, a damn guideline when you came right down to it, mean more to them than a billion lives?

Whether they were officially on his side or not no longer mattered. They had imprisoned him. Filoso had provided false information about him. The longer they held him, the more certain the extinction of his— yes, of his friends. He could not permit that, even if it meant harming FNC people or property as he broke free.

If he could only see the anti-teleports! Then, ah, then it would be a different story. His Talent had freed him from that sort of hold several times. All he had to do was impart a high, aptly aimed velocity to any nearby object: pebbles or coins or—his hand dropped to his waist—the gems embedded in his belt. Energized, the object became a bullet. *Or a battering ram*, he thought, remembering the furniture he had hurled on Delurc.

But here! His captors hid behind at least one wall and maybe more. He could blast an emerald through the first wall without even trying, but even if it still carried enough momentum to inflict real damage, what should he aim at?

No, he could not shoot his way free this time. Nor could he Fling a speeding topaz and let their powers suck it in their direction. Since they were four, anything he teleported would re-materialize at the intersection of the square's diagonals: i.e., right in the middle of the force-bed.

Gina, he thought wryly, *for once I'd trade my Talent for yours and think I got the better end of the deal.* God, it was aggravating. If *she* were pinned down like this, she could mindscream for help, and he would hear her from the far side of the Network. But he could burn his brain out trying to call her, and never come close to getting through, because he was no Minder, and she was much too far away to monitor him.

But just in case: Gina, help! I love you. HELP!

If only he knew more about Anchors than their effect on Flingers. He closed his eyes, rubbed his hot forehead, and tried to delve into memory. Anchors had trapped him before. Was there anything he had seen, anything he might have heard . . . No, just faces, surprised or dead or both . . . Some textbook information, from a course back at the Academy, claiming that they could turn their power on or off voluntarily, but not otherwise control it consciously. The book also said . . . oh, yeah. Maintaining the attractive field did take real psychic energy.

His sole hope, it seemed, would be to wear them out.

GINA!

He took a very deep breath. He undid his belt, ran it through the plastic handle of the vaccine case, buckled it up again, and slung it over his shoulder. Then he lay back on the bed to stare at the featureless ceiling. He imagined New York; and the pillows in Walking Mule's office; *no,* he thought, *make it Gina's office,* for the homey clutter of that small room pulled his emotions more strongly; and the familiar smell of the Flinger Building all around him, and . . .

He closed his eyes. Concentrating, visualizing, he felt the path open up and knew how to follow the path and—

PING

He lay on his back, the mathematical center of his body atop the mathematical center of the bed.

And he groaned, because he suddenly realized that to maximize his chances of wearing the Anchors out, he should start as far from the intersection of their powers as possible. The greater the distance they had to shift his mass, the more energy they would expend.

Trembling, he pushed himself up from the bed and walked to the corner. And tried—

PING

He stood, for a second, at the center of the force field's upper surface. Then his knees collapsed and he fell onto the resilience that urged him not to struggle, to lie back and conserve his strength for the sixty-seven-hour wait till the technical developer arrived.

The hard lump of the carving in his pocket urged him to take a different, more dangerous tack.

He swung his legs off the bed and staggered to a different corner. He would have to exhaust all four Anchors as equally as possible.

PING

His legs buckled immediately. He dropped to a kneeling position on the bed. His head hurt so much . . . Grunting, he went to a third corner.

PING

How could anyone possibly expect him to get up again? Had he not just proven that the Anchors had him cold? Struggle was useless. Th'hweet would understand. Sure he would. He was a doctor. Any good doctor would tell Feighan to just relax, let his eyelids tumble, let himself drift into sleep . . . Th'hweet would realize that the Flinger could do nothing different. He could not even stand up.

So he crawled to the fourth corner on hands and knees, the case banging on the tiles with each motion.

PING

GINA! Oh God, it hurts! Sobbing, he clutched his temples. His pulse beat fast and heavy, like tribal drums the night before war. His skull could take no more. Ten more seconds of that throbbing would split the bone in half, and his brain would force its way out through the fissure. He was in Quarantine. Shouldn't the doctors give him something for the pain?

Hanging the case behind his shoulder, he dragged himself back to the corner.

PING

He fell face-down on the bed's stream of flickering colors. So cool to the cheek, so soft. If he had to move again he would puke.

Therefore he hauled his aching body to the corner with the force-drain and retched through more dry heaves before—

PING

Stupid, stupid, stupid. He was sick, they were healthy; he was one, they were four; he—

Was Rehma's only hope.

He gasped and panted and made it to the corner an eternity later and—

PING

—needed no time at all to bounce on the force field.

Good force field. Friendly force field. Satin texture, foam-rubber consistency, just what a Flinger consumed by raging fever needed to recover on. Some medication, a few days' sleep . . .

And a billion intelligent beings would be rotting where they fell.

His knees hit the tiled floor with a painful thwack. He gripped the porcelain with the pads of his fingers, gritted his teeth, and pulled himself toward the corner.

PING

Surely they had to be weakening. Another try, he was capable of that, though not of two more, just one more try—

PING

Well, maybe just one more, even if a pulsating heat burned inside every joint of his body and peaked with every thud of the blood surging through his overstressed under-strength skull.

PING

No good, no good, and it was getting harder to drag himself along the floor, the toes of his scuffed black boots kept slipping, they offered no purchase, so what he would have to do, he decided, was yank the boots off and use his toenails as pitons.

PING

The colors of his energy tunic faded as his strength ebbed but he could not let that distract him, he had to force himself back to the corner, sweeping the boots angrily to one side for they were in his way—

He rocked back onto his haunches. God, thought had to *fight* its way through the pain and the nausea but the boots loomed a large blur in his vision and hefted heavy in his hand . . . Just how much damage could a pair of boots do to a Quarantine cubicle wall when shot into it at the highest velocity a sick, bedraggled Flinger named Feighan could muster? And how much distraction would that damage do?

Only one way to find that out.

Since he needed both hands for propulsion, he seized the boots with his teeth and struggled to the corner. A delicate problem of timing presented itself. How long should he wait after battering the boots into the wall before he tried to Fling home?

Accepted wisdom among Flingers said that it took five minutes to get back to full strength after a Fling.

Clearly, once he had—he hefted the boots again, thoughtfully; yes—once he had blown a hole clear through the opposite wall, he could not afford to wait five minutes. Not only would the dust have settled, and the Anchors have recovered from the distraction, but someone in a position of authority might well have decided by then that an anesthetic grenade was just the thing for a troublesome quarantinee.

But if he moved out any faster, he risked a sudden and disastrous loss of Talent. Right in the middle of his Fling.

And when you lose it halfway out, you can re-enter the Universe through the heart of a star—although statistical probabilities favor the intergalactic vacuum. Galaxies are, after all, spread rather far apart.

Oh, God, Gina.

He sat up in the corner, moved the case around to his chest, pressed his shoulders against the walls. No, wrong angle. From there the force bed blocked the path the boots would take. He would have to stand.

Sure. Easiest thing in the world, right? In the course of his twenty-three years he must have pushed himself to his feet, oh, twenty, thirty times a day, call it ten thousand times a year, probably worked out to over a quarter million times in his life. Absolute minimum. So how come he stayed put? Why did his legs refuse to thrust?

He could not make them work. He put his hands on the floor, palms down, and lent his legs the strength of his arms—but that, too, was depleted. He did not budge.

He could have cried. He probably would have, but he

suspected that his captors were watching him through closed-circuit. He would not give them the satisfaction of reducing him, McGill Feighan, to tears. But his vision blurred even more, and he had to blink quickly, repeatedly, to clear it.

There was another way.

He took a breath. A deep one, all the way to the bottom of his aching lungs. Another. Then, before he let himself realize the full danger of what he was about to do, he pointed himself at the ceiling and gave himself a small *jolt* of momentum.

He rose like a rocket, quick and hard, but he had doled velocity out carefully. Gravity caught him just as his toes left the floor. *Brace!* he told his knees, and settled back onto his heels. His knees locked first, then his hips. The corner caught his shoulders and held them. Success. Now all he had to do was knock down the far wall with a pair of boots . . . oh, yeah, and Fling halfway across the Network a second or two later.

Sweat from his upper arms slicked the white tiles and cut to almost nothing the friction that was holding him in place. He slipped down two inches. His legs began to shake.

He had no time, none at all. He held the boots at eye level, and focused on them the worn remnants of a Talent that, in its prime, could alter the momentum of 918 kilograms by two kilometers per second in any direction whatsoever.

The boots leaped away. Leather scorched his fingertips. As he should have expected of something moving nearly three hundred kilometers a second.

The wonder was that he had any fingers at all.

A shockingly loud sonic boom slapped Feighan hard. Air resistance torched the boots on take-off. Heat licked his cheeks till impact with the wall quenched the flame.

It almost quenched Feighan, too.

The Builders of the Hub built well. Behind the perfect white tiles with their multilingual message shimmered a force field. This was, after all, Quarantine—and if the Builders had anything to say about it, nothing would leave a Quarantine cubicle without permission.

But the Builders had not reckoned on megajoules of kinetic energy smashing into the force field in a microsecond.

Feighan tasted lightning. His hair crackled and rose from his skull. The far wall glowed brilliant, blinding; he had to turn his head and shade his eyes. In the movement he lost his balance. He began to fall. He tried to Fling—

The force field shorted out with a bang and a sizzle.

The room went dark.

Oh, Gina, Th'hweet, I blew it, I'm sorry. Feighan lost consciousness a second after he hit the floor.

"—another couple seconds he'll come around, but why in the name of God—" A cool, wet cloth swept relief across Feighan's forehead. "—you won't let the poor guy sleep, which is about the only damn thing that's going to pull him through, if anything does—"

Feighan opened his eyes. "Where—"

"Well, how do, partner." The Director of the North American Consortium reached out to pat Feighan's shoulder. "Good to have you with us again."

"He shouldn't be with us." The staff physician pressed the cloth against Feighan's cheek. "Your behavior is disgraceful, and I'm telling you now, the Board will hear of it. Drugging this young man awake is cruel and inhuman treatment, and there is no excuse—"

"Somewhere out there, ma'am, is a three-year-old child who just might need our help real quick like. The kid ought to be with McGill here, but he ain't, which means he is probably stranded on a planet where he can't speak the language and don't dare eat the food 'cause it'll kill him. I'm sure McGill here'll be the first to say we did the right thing. Hey boy?"

"Sam's okay, Walking Mule. But there's a lot more—

oh, God." Abruptly convulsed with dry heaves, he rolled his head to one side and retched helplessly.

The doctor swabbed his neck and temples. She stroked his head with her hand. Fury raged in her voice. "This man is seriously ill, Director! He needs—"

"I need to report, first!" He tried to sit up, but could not. "Help me, please, just prop me up—"

"No!" She stepped back and folded her arms.

Walking Mule gave her a disgusted glance. He pressed a button; the bed hummed. The top third of the mattress swung Feighan up into a sitting position. "That better?"

Feighan tried to look around the room, but everything swam and danced in his vision. The doctor's round brown face floated upside down before him, then spun in wide woozy spirals. He clutched his stomach. "Is this the Infirmary?"

"Yes," said the doctor.

"Did I hang on to the samples?"

Walking Mule hoisted the case Feighan had brought from Rehma. "This what you're talking about?"

"Thank God. Look." He gasped as sharp pain stabbed his abdomen. "There's a plague on Rehma."

"We know," said the Director grimly.

"I got it—I caught it."

"That's impossible!" said the doctor.

He had to laugh, but not for long. "It's not native to Rehma. It's imported. Mutated avian flu. From Earth. Courtesy of The Organization, we think. In there— go ahead, open it. There's a vaccine, and medicine."

Walking Mule handed the bag to the doctor, who said, "Well, that's going to make things easier." Drawing out a vial, she held it up to the light to read its label.

"No!" For a moment he was terrified that he would pass out and she would inject him with all the medicine. "No, you've got to use that to make more, that's all there is in the whole Network, vaccine, too, and—"

"Whoah!" Walking Mule held up a hand. "What do you

mean that's all there is?"

Haltingly, his narrative punctuated by spasmodic vomiting, he explained the situation on Rehma and the mad bureaucrats at the Hub. "We've got to do something, Walking Mule, quick, or else—" He shuddered. "There's so little time before they all die!"

The staff physician raised the two vials tentatively. "I can have these analyzed in thirty minutes, Director. If the disease actually does derive from a terrestrial influenza virus, we can have vaccine and medication in production by the end of the afternoon."

Walking Mule looked at Feighan. "Well?"

"The analysis doesn't destroy it, does it? I mean, in case you can't manufacture them, if the samples are destroyed—"

"Don't worry about that. We can manufacture *anything*— we're very good at that, you know—but some of the more exotic vaccines take longer, that's all. The samples will survive, I guarantee it."

"Okay." He let her take them. She hurried for the door, but stopped on the threshold. "Oh, Director Walking Mule?"

"Yes, ma'am?"

"Ah—with all due respect, sir—just in case, would you please consider yourself quarantined until further notice?"

The older man's dark eyes widened in astonishment. "Say what?"

"If what Mr. Feighan says is accurate, the disease he's carrying could have the same effect on Earth as it's been having on Rehma. I think it might be best if we limited exposure to it now, while it's still relatively easy to identify everyone who's come in contact with Mr. Feighan."

Walking Mule put his hands on his hips. "Well, now, ma'am, just how long you plan to keep us penned up in here?"

"Perhaps forty-eight hours, although I certainly can't guarantee that. If, as I suspect, I can obtain a prototype of the anti-viral medication by early this evening, I might be able to release us all tomorrow afternoon. Only careful monitoring of contagiousness will let me determine the exact time."

"So you're including yourself in this party?"

She gave a rueful smile. "I've had as much contact with him as anyone. There's no way I'm going home to my kids till I know I'm clean." With a nod, she disappeared through the door.

"Now what?" he asked Walking Mule.

"I guess we wait around to hear what she says," said the Director. "And I'll tell you the truth, McGill, you sure do look like you could use some just plain waiting around."

"But what about the Rehmal? They're running out of time. And then there's Filoso and those fanatic idiots at the Hub, I—"

"Whoah! There's nothing we can do about the Rehmal till the stuff gets into production. As for those idiots at the Hub, y'all want to slow down and think this thing through, McGill. 'Those idiots' just happen to be the folks we work for. It'd be pure-D foolishness for us to rush in without planning everything out in advance. Besides which, you're in no shape to go rushing anywhere."

"Hey, Walking Mule, I can—"

"Maybe lose it in the middle of a Fling and take all of us with you? See, you're gonna have to get us there, McGill, because you are the only one who's been to where it all happened, and I will be damned if I let somebody who's so woozy with fever that he didn't see his girlfriend come into the room move me an inch, even if you are a good buddy." He winked at Feighan. "Gina, you want to take over as nurse to this bull-headed Irishman while I commandeer the next ward so I can push some paper?"

"Sure." Gina Maccari came to the edge of the bed, sat, and kissed Feighan on the forehead. "Hi, McGill."

Relief and pure joy at seeing her again, when he had thought he would die without another glimpse of her, overwhelmed any embarrassment he might have felt at missing her entrance. "I have gone to heaven."

"From the little I heard, it sounds more like you escaped from hell." She took his hot, dry hand in hers. "I think I can keep him under control till you get back, Walking Mule."

"Use a whip. McGill, soon as I hear from the doctor I'll be back. Try to get yourself some rest now, hear? You're no good to us sick."

"Okay." He nodded, gulped at the dizziness, and held himself very still. "And thanks, Walking Mule."

"Right. I'll see you after a while." He closed the door on his way out.

Feighan looked up into the eyes of the woman he was certain he loved. "Hello, beautiful. You shouldn't be here. I'm probably contagious. And besides, don't you have, uh—"

"Cancer? Not anymore." She bent her head and parted her hair. A patch of fine black stubble surrounded a spot of redness no wider than a fingertip. "Didn't they do a nice job?"

"Yes, but—"

"Don't worry. The flu isn't going to affect this one way or the other. Worst case, they'll give me a shot, and everything will be fine." Her cool fingers touched his temple. "McGill, I can't tell you how glad I am that you made it back alive."

"For a while there, I thought I wouldn't."

"Where's Sam?"

"Still on Rehma, providing early warning service to Th'hweet and Lu'reeng. He should be all right, if you haven't been Minded about him." He told her about the state of affairs there, of Sree?sree?sree?'s fate and the burning of the factory. "You're sure nobody's tried to get through to you about Sam?"

"Nobody at all. And I know what you're going to ask next, and the answer is no, there is no way a Rehmal Minder could try to reach me without my knowing about it. First of all, I've been in contact with them twice a day, remember?

And second, at that level, telepathy isn't a power we can turn on and off. It's like . . ." She screwed up her face in thought. "Imagine you're all alone in a library, a reading room, hey? And everything's very quiet, very peaceful, until somebody shouts your name—right in your ear. Could you possibly fail to hear that?"

"No." One of the fears twisting within him relaxed at her words. Sam might be in trouble, but he had not yet called for help. Then his eyes widened as a new thought occurred to him.

"Stop that," said Maccari sharply. "Of *course* there are still Minders alive on Rehma. Stop tormenting yourself. Rest. Recover."

"Okay." He laced his fingers through hers. "As long as you promise not to leave, okay?"

"They couldn't pry me out of here with a crowbar, McGill Feighan." She kissed the tip of his nose. "Now go to sleep."

It was surprisingly easy to obey.

He awoke to soft music and cool air. Maccari's gentle hand still lay in his. He squeezed it. "Hi." Yawning and stretching, he suddenly realized, with an emotion bordering on wonder, that he did not hurt at all. And his stomach felt . . . ravenous! "Hey!"

Maccari flashed him her widest smile, and tousled his hair affectionately. "Feeling better today?"

"It's tomorrow already? I mean—"

"I know what you mean, McGill." She tapped her temple with a forefinger. "Although it's usually easier to figure out what you mean when your tongue doesn't contradict your mind."

"Give me a break, I just woke up. And as for— let me rephrase it. How long have I been asleep?"

"Twenty-one hours, Mr. Feighan." The staff physician hove into view behind Maccari's shoulder. Her round brown face bore new lines, but satisfaction glowed warm in her eyes. "The latest monitor readings say you're absolute flu-free, and your little nap should have refreshed you, so I'm willing to discharge you at your convenience."

"So the stuff worked?"

"Stuff?"

"The samples I brought from Rehma."

"Oh." She shook her head briskly. "They were species-specific, though the disease itself will attack either Rehmal or Terran hosts. But it only took a few minutes to tailor something that would be effective in a human being." She shrugged. "The machines do it all, anyway; I just make sure they're plugged in."

"What about the drugs for Rehma, then? Can we—"

"Commencing production already, at facilities donated by two major American pharmaceutical houses. You can thank the director for that." She raised her eyebrows. "I'm not sure just what pressures he brought to bear on the companies, but I did happen to hear his conversation with the FDA about regulatory approval of the drug." She shook a finger at Walking Mule in mock reprimand. "Tsk-tsk-tsk. Frankly, sir, I'm quite certain you can go to prison for threatening a government agency like that."

Walking Mule grunted, but smiled at her. "It's like the way the mule trainer explains how he uses his two-by-four: He says, first you get their attention . . ."

"At any rate, Mr. Feighan," said the doctor, "you should be able to teleport the first shipment of drugs to Rehma early tomorrow morning. The director has all the details. If you'll excuse me—" She nodded to the three. "—I think I'd best get home and make sure my teenagers eat something other than pizza for dinner tonight."

"Thank you, doctor."

"My pleasure, Mr. Feighan, believe me, it was my pleasure." She headed out the door.

Walking Mule cleared his throat. "McGill, I played back the tape of your report once I'd done a little digging, and you know, this Filoso you ran into was lying through his teeth from word one."

"None of it was true?"

Maccari leaned forward. "I got in touch with one of the Minders in Hub Admin last night, and they talked to Thurndriddle, and Thurndriddle says it never knew you were attempting to contact it."

"But—"

"Number one, Thurny's been on vacation for a week," said Walking Mule. "And number two, this Rogue Flinger never existed at all. They figure they've got a major mess, and asked us to come help them clean out the stables. You ready to put the finger on this Filoso character?"

"Well, sure, but—"

Maccari said, "Hush." She closed her eyes; she frowned; the veins in her temples stood out like cables. Then she relaxed. Exhaling, she opened her eyes again. "They said to give them ten minutes to get in position, and then go."

"Go where?" said Feighan.

"To Senior Flinger Thurndriddle's reception room." Walking Mule loosened a predatory grin. "We're gonna take Mr. Filoso by surprise."

"In that case—" Feighan got ready to throw back the covers, then manually checked that he still wore his underwear. "—I think I'd better brush my teeth and splash some water on my face."

Ten minutes later, clad in shirt and pants that Walking Mule had picked up from Feighan's penthouse in the interim, Feighan wiped a last sleep crumb from his eye. "All set."

Maccari took his hand. "Then let's go."

He looked at her in surprise. "You're—"

"Going with you." She patted his cheek. "You're really not going to argue about it, are you?"

He thought about it for a moment, then put his arm around her shoulders. "Nope. You're in better shape than I am, and I sure wish I'd had a Minder along last time. But what's the plan?"

Walking Mule answered that one. "We go in—you identify Filoso as the one who put you through the wringer, if he is the one—and we grill him."

"And just how do we plan to hang on to him?"

"Same way he did to you—those were Staff Anchors he used."

Feighan nodded slowly. "It sounds good. Let's go!"

PING

Filoso looked up from his desk as Feighan's use of his Talent triggered the Timili's own. His huge eyes grew even larger as he recognized the Flinger who had escaped him. "You!" He glanced from Walking Mule to Maccari. He seemed to come to a decision.

Something tugged at the back of Feighan's mind.

"No!" he shouted, leaning forward, reaching for Filoso's shoulder—

But the Timili no longer sat behind the desk.

He stood in the far corner, his Talent negated by a concealed four-Anchor square.

"Mighty excitable today, aren't you, McGill?" said Walking Mule. "I take it this *is* our man."

"That's him," he said grimly.

Filoso straightened to his full two meters. "I demand to know the meaning of this."

Maccari gasped. "He works for The Organization!"

"Gina, how come that still surprises you?" Walking Mule eyed the Timili with weary resignation. "I should have thought you'd be used to it by now. You've exposed enough of these snakes."

"I should be," she said slowly, "but somehow, every time is just as disgusting as the first time...Oh, geez. The Organization is definitely behind the whole plot."

Filoso pulled on dignity like a cloak. "I do not know what you are talking about."

Balling his fists, Feighan moved closer to the Timili. "Keep probing him, Gina. I want to know everything."

In a distant, distracted voice, she said, "The Organization

started the plague. Filoso knows all about it. He helped plan it. Ernest Williams and Celeste Quandala—do you know those names?"

"Yes," said Feighan, not taking his eyes off the other Flinger. "They're missionaries."

"More like The Organization's agents-in-place. They brought the bug to Rehma."

"Why?"

"Do you mean why are missionaries working for The Organization?"

"No. What does The Organization think it's going to get by wiping out an entire species?"

"It wants the whole planet for . . . wait a minute." Furrowing her brow, she concentrated harder. "Something to do with a luxury resort and, and . . . a staging/training area for operations."

Walking Mule snorted. "You ride with some real bastards, don't you, Filoso?"

The Timili said, "I don't know what—"

"Damn you!" said Maccari. "You sick pig!"

Feighan watched their captive closely. "What's the matter, Gina?"

"It was *his* idea to time the epidemic to peak during Festival so as to kill as many Rehmal as possible. And he's laughing. Festival is already under way. Their plan will still work!"

· Chapter XX ·

The voice emerged from the speaker with dangerous softness. "Have attempted to conceal bad news, Davis. Unwise policy. Hazardous to health."

Nathaniel Davis had dreaded this moment. Hands shaking, he gulped. "As you can understand, sir, Filoso was, er, less than eager to tell me that Feighan had escaped in the first place, and of course I had to confirm—"

"First telepathic report of escape touched your Minder twenty-two hours thirteen minutes ago. First confirmation of safe arrival in New York came eighteen hours forty-seven minutes ago." The blue and gold gases suddenly churned, like water reaching a furious boil. "Waited patiently to be informed, Davis. Was not informed. Am . . . disappointed in you."

Please, I don't want to die. "I can't blame you, sir, but—"

"Yet even so, still try to hide fact of Filoso's capture, eh, Davis?"

He could not disguise his astonishment. "Fi— Filoso? Captured?"

"Ah, is news?" The speaker clucked. "Make miracle, Davis. Or . . . ?"

He steadied himself. "I planned well, sir. One miracle coming up."

▪ Chapter XXI ▪

Monday, 12 October 2105

Security was on its way. Standing shoulder to shoulder before the great wall-holo of the Ylsslypn seashore, the three Terrans watched Filoso for hostile moves.

Feighan felt dazed. Things were happening just a bit faster than he could react to them. He wondered— Maccari touched him; he turned his head. "What is it, Gina?"

"I have to talk to you." Worry creased her sun-tanned forehead. "Walking Mule, keep an eye on him?"

"You bet."

"Over there, McGill." She led Feighan to the corner, cast a wary glance at their captive, and pitched her voice low. He had to lean close in order to hear her. Not that he minded. "There's something wrong with Filoso's thoughts."

He could accept that. "He's an alien and a spy, Gina, you—"

"No. His thoughts, not his values! Their texture. His mood. I can't quite define it but . . ." Her worry disappeared beneath frustration. "He's *confident*. And serene, not tense, and in this situation, he ought to be all knotted up. I can't squint out any details, but everything feels odd, out-of-kilter. And ominous, too. I thought you ought to know."

Oh, boy, what's Filoso up to now? He stared at their prisoner in dismay. "You can't get anything more?"

"It's all drowned out by his mood. And that's so good it scares me."

"Don't let it." Feighan tried to sound casual. No veneer of unconcern could fool a telepath like Maccari, but it might help him to deceive himself, given the way his mind was running. Or, more accurately, wandering. Could the drugs have befuddled him? From the moment of awakening in the Infirmary, he had felt out-of-step with the rest of the world, as though he perceived all events one tenth of a second after everybody else. "If you keep Minding him, we'll have nothing to worry about."

"Sure, I—" She raised her left hand to her forehead and half-shielded her brown eyes. Her head bobbed slowly, once, twice—

"Oh, no!"

Startled, he reached for her. "Gina, what is it?"

She dropped her hand. "McGill, Walking Mule, they—they—"

"Who?" said Feighan. "Who is they?"

"The FDA."

Bewildered, he stepped back. He really was out-of-synch. "The FDA?"

Impatience pursed her lips. "I just got a message from New York. Two messages. First, the FDA reconsidered, and got a court to issue a temporary injunction against any manufacture of the drugs, pending testing and hearings."

Walking Mule tugged at one of his braids. "What kind of testing?"

She spread her hands. "It wasn't in the message. I can call back and find out, if you want."

"Not yet, but it's an important point. Full-scale testing can run seven years, easy."

Feighan's jaw dropped. "They can't do that!"

"They think they can," said Maccari. "And there's worse." Brushing back her silken black hair, she took a deep breath.

"The unions at the pharmaceutical houses have gone on strike. They say they won't manufacture alien plague drugs no matter what the FDA decides."

Filoso, still standing casually in the corner, chuckled aloud.

Feighan whirled. "What's so funny?"

"Your unending entrapment in rules and regulations, Mr. Feighan." The Timili's flawless English rang mockingly in the room.

Lowering his voice, Feighan said, "Gina, is this what you sensed at the back of his mind?"

"No . . . it isn't." She sounded more concerned than ever. "That was totally different." She frowned at Filoso. Then, eyes widening, she took a step away. "McGill! He—"

The world went suddenly crazy. Feighan's head spun as his Talent, twanging in response to Filoso's, kicked open the door on a place where time did not exist. At once everything slowed to a crawl. Even him. He continued to lag a beat behind. But still he wondered *What the hell's Filoso doing?*

Walking Mule shuddered as if struck.

Maccari rose to her toes, yelped, bounced into the air.

A hurricane caught Feighan and hurled him off his feet.

Walking Mule grunted, crouched, and set his jaw.

A meter above the floor and flying fast, Maccari gasped.

Feighan rushed head first at the wall. Wind snatched his breath away.

Omigod, that's *what he's doing.* His instincts surged awake.

There came the soft *thud* of a body falling.

If she's dead, so is he. He did not need to determine his velocity. His Talent *knew* it, coldly, exactly, and instantaneously. The wall loomed immense, unyielding.

An alien laugh burst out—

Get 'im! With one precise, immediate touch, his Talent adjusted his velocity. G-forces pulled at his cheeks. His arms flew apart.

—the laugh died in a huge-eyed gape—

His feet slammed into the Timili's belly, folding the alien Flinger in half across Feighan's legs. Not waiting to see if Filoso were alive or dead, he kicked loose of the limp form and scrambled to his feet. "Gina!"

Walking Mule knelt by her side. "She's okay, McGill. Guess I yanked her back a tad too hard, 'cause she sat down real quick like. I think the main damage is to her dignity." He winked at Feighan. "Although for the next couple of days, she just might prefer setting her force chair to super-soft."

Maccari let loose a wry smile. "Nice reflexes, Walking Mule. Thank you. Thank you very much."

"My pleasure, Gina." He took her arm. "Let me give you a hand up."

She accepted his assistance. "McGill, are you all right?"

He hugged her hard. "Still shaky, but otherwise okay. Except real embarrassed he caught me off-guard like that."

Walking Mule strode over to inspect the prostrate alien. "He's alive."

"What a shame," said Feighan.

"Enough of that," said the older man. "Toss me your belt—and Gina, could I have your scarf for a while?"

"You planning on tying him up?" Feighan slipped his belt out of the pant loops; as an afterthought, he detached the jewel-encrusted buckle. He did not want that potential weapon anywhere near Filoso.

"Gonna blindfold him, too." The Director fit his actions to the words. "The Anchors will keep him in one place, and the scarf will keep him from seeing anything else he might care to toss around the room." Walking Mule rolled Filoso onto his stomach in order to lash his wrists behind his back. The Timili groaned heavily. "Although this just might be overkill—I suspect you caused him some serious internal damage, McGill."

Feighan snorted. "I find it difficult to care a whole lot, Walking Mule."

"Well, yeah, I reckon I can understand your point of view, but let me say this, McGill—" He panted as he tightened the bindings. "One of the ways I tell myself from Organization skunks like Filoso is that I just can't see how it'd help a whole lot if I did unto my enemies as my enemies would do unto me, given half a chance. By which I mean to say that if I absolutely have to hurt 'em, I will, and I won't lose any sleep over doing what I have to do, but if I don't have to, I'm going to treat 'em as much like human beings as I can afford."

"You're more charitable than I am, Walking Mule."

He rocked back onto his heels. "Could be I've had more time to think about it."

"Could be." He lowered himself into a chair. "So now what?"

"Well—" Standing, Walking Mule dusted off his hands. "We wait till the security types show up to take charge of the poltergeist, here, then we do some talking to Thurndriddle."

They spent five minutes waiting, ten minutes answering questions, and forty-five minutes reviewing transcripts of their statements. When the Head of Security finally thanked them and told them they had given her all she needed, they followed the Senior Flinger's Acting Deputy into Thurndriddle's presence.

The ancient Ylsslypn clung to the acrylic-covered wall two meters off the ground. Its wrinkled grey skin hung in loose, limp folds. A showerhead jutting from the ceiling hissed out a spray that kept the Senior Flinger—and the more forward of its visitors—bathed in a fine salt mist. Water ran down the wall in thin sheets, and disappeared into a white tiled trough at the bottom.

"How do, Thurny?" Walking Mule stopped just outside the cloud of spray.

The goggle-lensed box on its desk studied the colors that played across its damp skin till they faded, then angled a mini-speaker at the Terrans. "Walking Mule, how good to see you. And little McGill, as well—it has been too many years since the night you saved my life, and in all that time you have never visited my estuary, child."

Feighan's bow hid his sigh. Would he ever live long enough to convince the three-thousand-year-old being of his adulthood? "Hello, Thurndriddle. It is good to see your words again. Your palette glows as full and bright as ever."

"Thank you." It paused. "I have only just learned that your channel had been barred. My sincerest apologies, old friends, and please accept my assurance that Filoso will learn how to treasure his own rock, and how not to envy others theirs."

"Sure do hope you mean that literally, Thurny."

"Our Psychiatric Section is famed for its skill."

"Yup, yup, that it is . . ." Walking Mule shifted his weight from one foot to the other. "Uh, I hate to be rude, but I'd sort of like to get right to the heart of the matter, which is that we need your help bad. Although it's not us, exactly, it's the planet Rehma. See, The Organization set this plague loose, and it looks like Filoso's job was to keep you from finding out about it . . ." He outlined the situation, asking Feighan and Maccari to fill in places where they knew more detail than he did. He finished by saying, "So what we need is a couple emergency medical teams, and a whole lot of medicine for them to pass around once they get there."

The desktop translator said, "Of course. All the medical teams do, truly, swim in troubled waters elsewhere, but our drug manufacture plants have more than enough capacity to produce what you need. Their excess capacity alone will suffice. Take the samples to them at once; the paperwork will be completed by the time you reach them."

"Thanks, Thurny. I knew we could count on you." Walking Mule sketched a salute.

"Must you ride the first tide?"

"I'm afraid so. When this is all over we'll get together, all right?"

"Of course. Good-bye. Come visit my bay, little Mc-Gill."

"As soon as I can, Thurndriddle. Shine bright and clean until we meet again."

When they left the office, Walking Mule put his arm around Feighan. "I'm going to zip back to New York for the samples. Why don't you make yourself comfortable out here—wouldn't hurt you none to doze off, either—and wait for me."

"I thought I'd go pick up Sam."

The Director shook his head; his black braids swung from side to side. "I want you where I can find you. You're still recuperating, remember? We'll all of us head off to Rehma when I get back."

"If you say so, Walking Mule."

"I do."

"All right." He set the controls of the nearest piece of force furniture to "chair, terrestrial," and plopped into it. "See you in a while."

Walking Mule moved a few meters away so the sudden use of his Talent would not affect Feighan's, and disappeared.

Feighan yawned behind his hand. "Want a chair, Gina?"

"No, I'm fine." She gestured to the paintings on the wall. "These are Rii—edsch, and I've never had the chance to see so many this close before."

"You mean no one ever asked you if you wanted to come up and see his Rii—edschings?"

Maccari groaned. "McGill, that's the—" Horror washed across her face. Her mouth opened and closed but no words escaped.

Feighan leaped to his feet. "Gina! What—"

"They're dying!"

He wrapped his arms around her. "Who?"

"Them. Guards. At the—"

Sirens shrieked to life, wailing so loudly that he could not hear her next words. Far down the corridor something exploded. The sirens cut off.

Maccari had calmed down a little. "It's an attack. The Organization is attacking the Hub!"

The Director of Security came loping by and Feighan called out, "Is there anything we can do to help?"

She waved a paw dismissively. "There are only five hundred of them. My forces can handle them easily. Just lie doggo until everything's quieted down."

Maccari said, "Would you rather we went back to New York and got out of your way?"

"Why, yes, that— on second thought, no." She gave them a quick, careful scrutiny. "You've both had a number of encounters with The Organization. There's a chance one of you might recognize some of the prisoners we take. If you would not mind waiting around—?"

"Not in the least," said Feighan.

"Fine. I'll talk to you later, then." She dropped back onto all fours and dashed off.

"Looks like we get to cool our heels a little longer," said Feighan.

"It's a good room for it." She looked puzzled. "You know, there's something not quite . . ." Standing in the middle of the reception room, she spun slowly on one heel. "I can't quite put my finger on it, but . . ." She went to the door and looked out into the hallway. "Yes. I think, just maybe . . ."

He followed her. "What is it?"

"I'm not sure." She moved tentatively down the corridor. "Something about . . . I don't know, like *déjà vu,* only . . ." She drew up short in front of a plain, unmarked door. "Yes!"

"What?"

She touched the baked enamel finish of the metal door. "This is what he was thinking about with such glee."

"Who?"

"Filoso. Remember, just before he tried to escape?"

"Oh, yeah. His serenity." He seized the doorknob, but it was locked. He thought a moment. "Hmm."

"McGill, you can't—"

"Can too. Now stand back."

She obeyed. "It's FNC property."

Ignoring her protests, he closed his eyes, concentrated—
"Is the hallway clear?"

"Yes, but—"

He accelerated the lock out of its setting; it smashed into the wall across the way. "I don't think they'll mind too much—and if they do, they can always dock my pay." He pushed the door open.

A moment of fumbling against the wall found a touch-plate. Overbright light fell on a large assembly of boxes, tubes, and spheres. On the front panel LED's read 67.

Maccari snapped her fingers. *"Hydrogen fusion!* That's what he was thinking. This is a bomb, McGill."

From the doorway Walking Mule said, "What?"

Feighan said, "Hush." Closing his eyes, he concentrated on the bomb, visualized the lonely star around which the Hub orbited, felt how to slip the former neatly into the heart of the latter, and—

"Oh sweet Jesus!" he said. "It's too heavy to Fling!"

The LED's flickered down to *33*.

And counting.

· Chapter XXII ·

Monday, 12 October 2105

Nathaniel Davis touched a square on the blueprints of the Hub his Executive Assistant had brought in. "It's located right here, sir. With the strike force diverting all Hub Security personnel away from the area, the odds against its being found and disarmed in time are staggering. According to the latest word from our Minder on the Hub, the only people in the vicinity of the device are Feighan and his girlfriend. When it goes off, which it will in a short time, they will almost certainly die." He paused thoughtfully. "Unless, of course, they stumble over it by accident."

Gryll whirlpooled; the speaker hissed. "Feighan is Flinger, Davis!"

He permitted himself a small, self-congratulatory smile. "It masses fifty percent more than the maximum anyone in the Network can Fling, sir. And it's all one unit, so he can't teleport the components separately. Oh, no, sir. If McGill Feighan finds our little surprise, the only thing he can do is get the hell out before it blows."

And if I'm wrong, I'd better be ready to do the same . . .

· Chapter XXIII ·

**Monday, 12 October 2105
—Friday, 16 October 2105**

McGill Feighan stared at the bomb. Icy sweat coated his forehead. The LED's blinked again: *29.* He took a huge breath; his stomach cramped in fear. He tried to keep his voice level. "Give me a hand, Walking Mule."

The Director reached Feighan's shoulder in a single stride. "The sun?"

"Yeah. This one, though. It's closest. On the count of three."

24.

"Who sights it?"

Feighan paused a beat. "You. I'm dead. Give it all you've got. I'll push."

19.

"Okay." The AmerIndian nodded grimly. "You count."

"Right."

16.

"But for God's sake, McGill, don't slip."

"I won't. One!"

12.

"Two!"

11.

"Three!"

Walking Mule stiffened.

Half-tamed energies flared in Feighan's mind. He drew from them an image: a seething hot ball of furious hydrogen. The storm of light rang with sound, as well—the music of "right-placedness," an atonal melody of spatial relationships that Feighan's kinesthetic sense could decipher. He knew *exactly* where those fires raged, and how to move himself and his cargo from *here* to *there,* and when he should hurl his strength at the chill resisting metal, and as the moment of unleashing drew closer in nanosecond ticks he ached he trembled he *needed* to Fling and the instant and the moment and the now is NOW!

*PI—

He slipped.

ohmigod!

For McGill Feighan, time literally stopped. He had blown it. To him, with his sensitivity, it felt as though he had hurled himself over a precipice.

He was outbound for the Hub's sun, riding a fusion bomb that would add its minute flash of light and heat to the star's steady outroar.

His reflexes had betrayed him.

He had trained those reflexes, those marvelous patterns of ingrained responses, by following another teleport, or occasionally pursuing one, and in those cases he had wanted to Fling in lock-step with the other. In those cases he had learned to surrender control, to let his instincts chase the other's glimmering Talent-tracks as though they were the tail lights of a car. In those cases, as it developed, he had weakened his defenses against this very fate.

In no time at all the Hub's sun would crisp him.

He had never boomeranged a Fling before, but he would have to, now. At most he had dodged: swerved a meter or so just before materializing, to avoid the mass he sensed occupying his goal. Even that small change in direction called for frantic readjustment of the forces at his command, so this, this mad lunge for his last chance, might well be beyond his control.

Then it struck him: If he did not maintain his share of the Fling carrying the fusion bomb to its pyre, that Fling would abort, and no matter where Feighan himself wound up, a nuclear blast would consume his two best friends in exactly eleven seconds. Walking Mule would not have recovered enough strength to teleport out of the room, much less off the Hub. Not in a lousy eleven seconds.

He had to Fling himself back with pinpoint precision while continuing to muscle the bomb in the opposite direction.

A two-end Fling.

Impossible.

But he had to try.

Anguished, he screamed into the void forever.

And before any time had passed he triggered his Talent.

His reflexes—his fickle, unreliable instincts—took over.

Instinct seized the reins knowing—not numerically, but with an accuracy equivalent to eighteen decimal places nonetheless—mass, location, velocity, and residual angular momentum for both Feighan and the bomb. It knew the precise spacial position of the little room where Walking Mule and Maccari would soon notice that the bomb—and someone else!—had vanished. It ignored the sun: Walking Mule knew its location; it did not need to.

Talent gazed into the hazy globe of its inner reality and searched out a glittering helix half a system long: the path and play of the desperate joint Fling.

Reflex stepped into the flow, diverting energy first this way, then that; gushing forward, looping back; plunging on, peeling off; gauging; rationing; flicking back and forth a billion times a nanosecond like a mad binary counter.

Instinct measured momenti. It borrowed the bomb's, adjusted Feighan's, checked the Hub's. It sped the spin, trued the line, dropped the arc a hair.

Talent turned itself inside out—and tore in half.

Even at the best of times, to Fling was to suffer. Now the teleporting was shredding him, was stretching him to unimaginable sizes while ripping off great elongated strips of his essence. And simultaneously it compacted him, reaching inside to squeeze out the spaces between the atoms of his being. It was like dying, only worse, because it did not end, ever, for where Feighan was, time was not.

And since time was not, it ended instantly.

—NG*

He shot across the room a meter off the ground and slammed into the wall. It hurt. It hurt a whole lot.

But he fell unconscious with a smile on his lips anyway.

The light disturbed him. The low-voiced conversation in the corner frustrated him because he could not make out the words. He thought about rolling over but the pounding in his head warned him not to move. Instead he cracked one eye open, blinked his vision clear, and stared at the IV rack floating next to his bed. He cleared his throat. "I seem to keep waking up in hospitals."

"Y'all seem to keep needing to." Walking Mule got to his feet and ambled over to Feighan's side. Gina Maccari followed half a step behind. "What went wrong?"

"I slipped." He groaned at the memory, then took Maccari's hand as she sat down next to him. "I was halfway there before I could recover."

"Impressive."

"Embarrassing."

"I meant getting back alive was impressive, not almost killing yourself in the first place." The older man grinned. "Gonna have to enroll you at the Academy for a refresher course on how to keep your footing, McGill."

He snorted. "And to *teach* a course on joint Flinging, right?"

Walking Mule looked thoughtful. "Think you could?"

"Teach that?" He closed his eyes and tried to recall the meshing of their Talents. "Walking Mule, I'm not sure I could *do* it again." He paused. "In fact, I still don't believe we *did* it."

"I know exactly what you mean, but the evidence is irrefutable—we ain't been blown to Kingdom Come."

Maccari combed his hair with gentle fingers. "And as an outside if very partial observer, McGill, I can testify that the bomb disappeared at precisely the same moment you imitated a blind bird."

"*That* was unavoidable."

Walking Mule laughed. "You didn't have to escort the bomb."

"All right, all right, given what I'd already done, it was unavoidable. There, you happy? Or you want to rub it in some more?"

The Director's gaze softened. "I'm sorry, McGill, I didn't mean to make you feel worse. We're just so happy you made it we've been sorta giddy, if you know what I mean."

He scowled, but lost it to a giggle. "I suppose I did look pretty silly there, didn't I?"

"Not at all." Maccari tucked the sheets neatly around his neck. Then she turned her head. Her shoulders twitched.

"Is she laughing?" he demanded of Walking Mule.

The older man studied Maccari, then shook his head judiciously. "Tryin' not to's more like it. Doing a pretty good job of it, too."

Feighan sighed. "With friends like you two . . . How long was I out this time?"

Maccari was dabbing her eyes with the corner of his sheet. "Just a couple of hours."

"Are we still on the Hub?" When they nodded, he said, "Well, what about the attack?"

"Over and done with." Walking Mule pointed to the ceiling. "Got a couple hundred prisoners upstairs—amazing how quick a space-suited guy in vacuum surrenders when one of those razor-clawed little guard 'bots latches on to him. The Hub took some heavy hits, too, but it's a big place, so we didn't lose much air at all."

"I can't believe they thought they could get away with it."

"With what?"

Puzzled, Feighan cocked his head and looked at Walking Mule. "What do you mean?"

"What were they trying to get away with?"

"Well, they—" Catching himself, he stopped short. He frowned. "Come to think of it, I'm not sure. I just assumed that, uh, they'd declared war or something."

"Uh-huh, and why were they attacking?"

"To take the Hub—to seize Flinger Network Control. I mean, that's what you do in war, right? You grab your enemy's territory and occupy it?"

"With five hundred troopers?"

"You're right." In retrospect, not even The Organization at its most megalomaniac could have hoped that five hundred soldiers would conquer an artificial planetoid with a population of over a billion. "So why were they throwing their people away like that?"

"Their commander says their mission was to take the Medical Sector and hold it for as long as possible."

"Were they crazy? The bomb would have wiped them out."

"Think again. You know how many force fields there are in here."

"But they would have overloaded, shorted out the whole Sector and probably a few more besides."

"Yup, yup, they would have—but they'd have dampened the nuke enough to keep from harming the attackers. Their purpose wasn't to control the Hub, McGill. It was just to stop the pharmaceutical production lines long enough to make sure Rehma died."

"They came awfully close, didn't they?" he said slowly.

"But not close enough." Walking Mule winked. "Now, your next assignment—"

"Already?"

The director let loose a mock scowl. "Is to lie there in

bed and recuperate until the first batches of flu drugs roll off the production lines."

"I'll help," said Maccari.

As Th'hweet had predicted, teleporting all the vaccine and all the anti-virals that Rehma could conceivably require took but two full Flings and one partial one. Feighan did them all, and carried Maccari and Walking Mule with him on the third.

PING

They materialized in the wicker-walled Flop Booth. Walking Mule nodded approvingly. "Looks like you got your touch back, McGill—real smooth set-down, there."

"Thank you." He looked around, awaiting the customary greeting and immigration procedure instructions from the Booth's operator.

Walking Mule sniffed the air. "Is that smell—"

"Yeah." God, he hated that slaughterhouse stench. "The whole planet smells that way."

The doors opened. Warehouse mechanisms—automated pallets, mobile winches, self-programming robots—scuttled in, and hustled the medicines out of the Flop Booth into storage areas.

"Seems a little deserted," said Feighan uneasily.

Maccari half closed her eyes. "It is. Oh, not completely, but there isn't a fraction of the mental noise there should be."

Walking Mule raised an eyebrow. "Trouble?"

Maccari listened inside her head for a moment. "No, but everybody went . . . south?"

Feighan's heart sank. "Festival must have started." Had they gone to these great lengths to save the planet's population, only to have arrived too late? "Let's see if there's a message for us at the lab."

Walking Mule bowed. "Fling away."

PING

A blur of tail and scales raced around his feet. "McGill!

You're back! An' Gina an' Walking Mule, too!" Sam bounded into Feighan's arms. "I was *worried!* The Minder said you were in the hospital again."

"And it also told you I was okay, didn't it?" He hugged his ward tightly, then upended him to slither down to the floor. "You should have more faith in me, kiddo. Hey, have you been keeping out of trouble?"

"I've been good, McGill, and it's been real quiet, and Doctor Th'hweet and Lu'reeng are next door, safe and sound."

"Where's Drudru?"

"She went south with her family." He made a face. "Just in time, too, 'cause I was sort of restless with you gone, and I didn't do too good in silence or self-control class, so I wasn't getting any snacks! But she said she'd bring me a souvenir."

Feighan chuckled. "Well, maybe that's taught you something. Let's go see Th'hweet and Lu'reeng." He let Sam lead the way.

The epidemiologist and his nephew perched in glum silence. Th'hweet stared at the pieces arranged on a chess board; Lu'reeng, at the console, was scrolling through a novel. They barely looked over when Sam entered the room. Th'hweet said, "Have you finished your lessons?"

"McGill's here, doctor!"

Th'hweet's crimson crest lifted a centimeter as he craned his neck around. "Mr. Feighan, how good to see you healthy again. And to meet your friends," he added pointedly.

Feighan performed the introductions. "And we've got a couple shipments for you over in the Flinger Building."

Th'hweet brightened at once. "Vaccines and anti-virals?"

"A billion doses of each."

Crest fully upraised, and rippling now, the epidemiologist said, "When I did not hear from you, I abandoned hope. A second message announced your triumph; I exulted. Then they told us you had been hospitalized, and despair crept upon me once again. But now—" He trilled a song of joy;

Lu'reeng warbled in counterpoint. "During my, shall we say, manic phase, I devised a plan for distribution. If we put it into effect immediately, we might still save my people. Come, come!" With anxious sweeps of his wings he shepherded them into his office, where he laid a large map flat on his desk. He jabbed at a point at the south end of Rehma's main continent. "We go here—"

"Can you show it on the console?" asked Feighan.

"Of course, of course. Lu'reeng—" He whistled a few bars at his assistant, who banked his novel with visible reluctance and brought up the geographic display. "Forgive me, Mr. Feighan, I'm so excited by the prospect of success that I've forgotten how you work."

Lu'reeng drew their attention with a chirp and pointed to the screen. "Sticky wicket, what?"

Sunlight glistened off the sheet of ice covering the lower half of the picture; small streams leaped from the glacier into the barren, rock-strewn valley to the north. Th'hweet tapped the console with a claw. "This is the southernmost point of The Cliffs and of The River. This is where and when our civilization renews itself every year. Even now, the strongest and the quickest of our fliers are reaching this point and turning northward to soar back home along the banks of The River."

Sam pushed his face close to the console. "When'll Drudru and her family get there?"

"Not for several days, Sam," said Th'hweet softly.

Walking Mule squinted at the televised image. "Do all of you overfly this here spot, or just the strongest?"

"All of us, Mr. ah, Director, from the youngest to the oldest."

"So you figure to set up a distribution point here?"

"Precisely."

The older man chewed one of his braids thoughtfully as he studied the picture. "Reckon the best thing to do is go there right now, get acquainted with the way it feels, wouldn't you say, McGill?"

"Sounds good."

"We'll be back in a flash, folks," said Walking Mule.

PING

The wind whipped straight off the glacier at a good thirty knots, immediately sending Feighan into uncontrollable shivers. Two hundred meters above his head, a pair of Rehmal banked into a one-hundred-eighty-degree turn and headed north. He stamped his feet. He was not likely to forget how that place felt. "Seen enough?"

The Director's teeth were busy chattering, so he merely nodded.

PING

Th'hweet looked down at them from his perch. "Well?"

Walking Mule blew on his hands. "Wouldn't happen to be another spot just like 'un, only a few some degrees warmer, would there?"

"Alas, there would not."

He nodded glumly. "I was afraid of that. My blood's too old and thin to enjoy teleporting into a deep-freeze."

Th'hweet had them go first to the Flinger Building, and send down the medicines. Then he guided them to a warehouse on the north side of Stonehills City. The hangarlike building nearly bulged with the additional material the epidemiologist and his nephew had requisitioned during Feighan's absence—tents, and portable heaters, and telescoped perching racks, and tons and tons of grain.

Feighan looked at a ten-meter-high stack of equipment in dismay. "It's going to take forever to get all this down there, doctor."

"We can commence operations with a small fraction of it, Mr. Feighan, but we will, in effect, be erecting a huge field hospital to care for those too enfeebled by disease to continue their flights."

Walking Mule narrowed his eyes. "Aren't you talking *millions* of people?"

"Yes, but recall the essential three-dimensionality of Rehmal life, and you will see that in certain respects, it will be more like caring for tens of thousands of your people."

Feighan was not sure what that meant, and decided not to pursue it. Instead, he leaned forward to read the stenciling on the nearest crate. "Weather balloons? You don't need these, do you? You've got a satellite system."

"We do need them, Mr. Feighan, but not, as you've deduced, for meteorology."

"For what, then?"

"You shall see, and in a very few moments, as well. Now, as your limit is 918 kilograms per Fling, I've ordered the pallets loaded to a maximum mass of 916—lest some of the resident vermin prevent a successful Fling by ah, hitching a ride, so to speak." He looked over his shoulder to Lu'reeng, who was turning the focus on the console's screen. "He will stay here with you, indicating which pallet is to go next, and centering, as nearly as possible, its intended destination on the screen."

"Neat trick," said Walking Mule.

"We worked this out in great detail, Mr. Director, and before we surrendered to despair, Lu'reeng spent a considerable amount of time practicing with the console. I believe you'll find him more than competent."

Lu'reeng lifted his beak. "Forsooth!"

In a low voice, Th'hweet said, "Before I go, Mr. Feighan, I would like to speak to you privately."

"Sure. Over there in the corner?"

"That would be fine."

They walked over in silence. When Th'hweet stopped, he twisted his neck all the way around to look back at the group clustered at the console. He nodded, and clacked his beak. "Mr. Feighan, as you may know, Drudru has flown south with her family."

"Sam told me." He frowned. Th'hweet seemed uncomfortable, almost abashed. "What's wrong?"

"Sam expects her to return."

"And she won't?"

"I do not believe she will survive the trip."

Feighan winced. "She caught it, then?"

"Yes. And I did not know how to tell Sam." He flared his wings half a meter. "One should never lie to a child about death, but I could not bring myself to tell him the truth. I realize that I was acting *in loco parentis,* as it were, and that I have evaded my responsibilities, but..." He trailed off.

Feighan gazed across the warehouse. Sam was swinging his tail from side to side as Maccari scratched his skullplate. Walking Mule was smiling at them both. "Sam's pretty mature... but I sympathize with you. I'm not going to enjoy breaking the news to him." He closed his eyes, and gently rubbed them with his fingertips. "Let's wait. Maybe she'll reach your operation in time."

"As you wish." Th'hweet bowed his head.

They walked back in sadness.

Th'hweet popped his wings for attention. "Let us begin, yes?" He touched the screen. "As you can see, the first and hardiest of the southerners is already reaching the site."

Feighan Flung Th'hweet and the appropriate pallet first, then watched the epidemiologist on the console as Lu'reeng pointed out the second shipment to Walking Mule and centered its destination on the screen.

The video image of Th'hweet bustled about the stack, peering at the sides of crates, jabbing here and twisting there. In his wake, the crates opened to disgorge a squadron of robots, each apparently programmed to perform a sequence of tasks.

One trotted to the cartons of vaccine. Another began to inflate a weather balloon. A third toted a tent perhaps a kilometer due south, where it quickly popped it open and staked it down.

His Talent thrummed softly. Walking Mule had just sent his load on its way. It appeared on the screen. "My turn?"

"Yup."

Lu'reeng touched the next heaped pallet in line with the tip of his wing, then showed Feighan where it belonged.

He concentrated, visualized, felt, knew—
PING

So it went, all day long. The image of the windswept rocks so filled him that the warehouse itself faded from his consciousness. At one point he looked up and realized that Maccari and Sam were missing. "Lu'reeng!"

"Sirrah?"

"Where are Gina and Sam?"

"Hotel. Eat."

He sank lower in his chair. "God, I didn't even hear them leave."

"Me either," said Walking Mule.

On screen, a tent city slowly arose; perch racks and heaters and sacks of grain disappeared inside the plastic structures. A kilometer north of the city, weather balloons bounced into the sky. Each bore on its side a large message in native script; each held up a thousand meters of monomer filament. At two-meter intervals, the cord, an impossible grape vine, sprouted great bunches of small bags. Now and then a Rehmal would fly up and take a bag.

Feighan rubbed his weary eyes. Already it had been a long day, and he was barely halfway through it. Nodding to the image on screen, he said, "What do you figure's going on there?"

"Could be individually wrapped doses of vaccine." Walking Mule stretched, and began to rub the small of his back. "A shame your buddy here can't explain."

"Fiddlesticks!" Lu'reeng bobbed his head, and half hopped, half flew to the next load of cargo.

Feighan sighed. "We'd better get back to it." Not that he wanted to. Under normal conditions, he would Fling once every five minutes for four hours, rest for four hours, then return for another forty-eight Flings. But these were not normal conditions. He and Walking Mule had been teleporting on three minutes rest for over five hours, now, and if the Director felt anything like he did, they were both ready to drop. "God, this is a big warehouse."

"Try not t' think about it."

"Will that help?"

"Nah, but it'll give you something else to do."

"Oh, thanks."

As the hours passed, their banter faltered, then faded into silence. Feighan had never pushed himself like that in his life. Fling, shiver with illusory chill, breathe, don't open the burning eyes because maybe if you don't, Lu'reeng will give you an extra couple of seconds, then groan and glance and nod your understanding, before concentrating, forcing the image to take shape in the exhausted grey matter, begging the Talent to find the way one more time, twitching and stifling moans of pain as yet another laden pallet disappeared *here* and reappeared *there*.

"Hi, guys."

A hand touched his shoulder. He started, then reached out to Gina Maccari. "What's up?"

"I realized I'm no use to anyone here, McGill. I figured that if you could send me down there, I could help out at the hospital. So Sam and I went to the hotel shopping mall and bought some camping gear. See?" She pulled a fleece-lined parka out of a light wicker box, then giggled. "Poor Sam. They had nothing for Rhanghans, so we had to find a tailor to alter what they did have."

"I'm afraid to ask."

"Look for yourself."

He turned his head as Sam rustled up to them. The child wore three down parkas stitched together, one for his arms and one for each pair of his legs. Two long scarves knitted together created a woolen tube for his tail. He wore boots on his feet and stamped them happily. "Whaddaya think, McGill?"

"I think somebody forgot the effect Arctic winds are going to have on a cold-blooded kid, that's what I think."

Maccari slapped her forehead in dismay. "You're right! I just never thought—" She gave a wry smile. "Well, at least he's got his coat for school this winter."

Sam looked from one to the other in confusion. "What's the matter?"

"What happens when you get cold, Sam?" asked Feighan.

"I go inside where it's warm."

"And if there's no warm inside to go into?"

"You mean like last year when the power went off for two days and it got really cold?"

"Right."

"I get sleepy."

"Precisely."

"You mean if I go with Gina—"

"You're going to fall asleep as soon as you get there, and you won't wake up till you're back here. Or till spring comes, I'm not sure which."

"Oh." Disappointed, he began to unzip his string of parkas. Then he lifted his snout and grinned. "That's okay, McGill. I'll stay here and help *you!*"

"What day is it, Walking Mule?"

"I think it's Friday, but I coulda lost track."

"Friday?" Had they really spent forty-eight hours inside the warehouse? "Sam, is today Friday?"

He put down his crayons. "Uh-huh. October 16. Have you seen Drudru?"

"I couldn't pick her out of the crowd if I did." Feighan hoped that would satisfy the child. "It's the windows."

Walking Mule raised a busy eyebrow. "Case you hadn't noticed, boy, there aren't any windows here."

"That's what I mean. That's what disoriented me. I couldn't see if it was day or night, so I didn't know what day it was."

"You sound about as punchy as I feel."

"Yeah. But we're getting the stuff down there."

"Forsooth." Lu'reeng waggled the levers on one of the control boards, and the next pallet floated up the aisle. Tiredly, the Rehmal pointed to the screen. "Gad."

"You can say that again."

"Gad."

"No, that's not— never mind." He rubbed his burning eyes and tried to focus on the monitor. Activity swirled at a hundred different altitudes above the encampment. Hundreds of flyers hovered to read the messages and to snatch medication from the dispenser lines. Robots winched bare-wired weather balloons down to earth for reattachment to fully laden filaments. Healthy Rehmal soared lazily around and began to fly north along The River. The weak, sick, and dying glided down to the hospital tent, where Maccari, Th'hweet, and singers from the Flock of True Lore waited to assist them.

A meter of feathers covered the ground between the tents, and puffed up into the air when the robot litter-bearers carried another corpse to the tent serving as the new morgue.

The first morgue had reached capacity long ago.

In a few days, things would get *really* busy.

Feighan eyed the pallet with a complete lack of enthusiasm. He did not know if he could Fling it. By rights, he should already have drawn his Talent down to zero balance. If not well into negative numbers. But every time he thought he had utterly depleted his strength, five simple words floated through his mind: *If I don't, they die.*

PING

The pallet materialized on target. He exhaled in relief. Something disturbed the steady flow of flocks at the bottom of the screen. Exhausted, he ignored it. He leaned back in his chair. He closed his eyes. *Oh, to sleep, perchance to dream—*

He sat up straight. "Walking Mule, isn't that a helijet?"

The Director squinted at the console. "Sure looks like one."

Feighan turned to the Rehmal. "Lu'reeng, can you increase the magnification just a little?"

"At once, milord." He touched the keyboard, then raised his hands in triumph. "Sirrah!"

The lens zoomed; the image swelled larger and larger

until the helijet filled the screen. It landed a hundred meters from the perimeter of the hospital camp. A gull-wing hatch swung up and out; a ladder dropped. Booted feet came down the ladder, but the hatch hid the visitor's upper body. Another pair of feet followed the first.

Then Ernest Williams and Celeste Quandala stepped away from the helijet, hands on their hips, scowls on their faces, and automatic pistols in their shoulder holsters.

· Chapter XXIV ·

Friday, 16 October 2105

It was all over. Oh, Williams and Quandala would manage to destroy that silly bird's drug dispensary, but the damage had been done. Tens of thousands of Rehmal had already been vaccinated. They would survive. And Flinger Network Control, along with its pestiferous allied planets, would forbid anyone to take control of the planet so long as any of the miserable natives lived. Operation PlayGround had failed. As had Nathaniel Davis.

He hoped the survivors enjoyed living in a world-sized charnel house.

Quickly, he reviewed his plan. His bags were packed. The Flinger waited in its own cabin two minutes away. Davis would hand it the stuffed envelope; it would teleport Davis to Canberra, Australia; the larger of the two suitcases would underwrite a most luxurious life.

He went to the door. Which would not open, no matter how he pulled, pushed, twisted, scratched, banged, kicked, battered, rammed, cried—

The cabin speaker crackled into life. "Am ... disappointed, Davis."

He knew what was coming next. And wished he didn't.

· Chapter XXV ·

Friday, 16 October 2105
—Sunday, 18 October 2105

Feighan, Walking Mule, and Lu'reeng stared at the screen.
The Director chewed the tip of his right braid pensively.
"Looks like Th'hweet's got a problem down there, don't
it?"

"Take another look. He's got about ten thousand prob-
lems." He tapped the lower half of the picture, where dense
flocks swirled above and around the "missionaries" helijet.
"They brought their congregation. And those are the same
ones who burned the factory."

"You reckon they're going to try it again?"

"Uh-huh." Damn, but it was unfair. They had come so
close to saving this world. Against all odds, they had found
the virus, cooked up both a vaccine and an effective anti-
viral medication, pressured entire governments to ensure
the medicines' mass production, devised an ingeniously ef-
ficient means of distribution—and for what? So an Organization goon posing as a preacher could incite a religious
rabble into ruining everything? And maybe killing Gina
Maccari in the process? No. No, he could not allow that.
Not without a fight. The fight of his life, it would be: one
angry Flinger against ten thousand outraged crackpots. Not

good odds—for the crackpots. He stood up. "Sam, get my coat."

As the child scampered off to obey, Walking Mule grabbed Feighan's wrist. "McGill, you're not—"

"I've got to. Gina's down there."

The older man's brown eyes widened in dismayed surprise. "I'm so frazzled I plumb forgot. Go. Get her—and Th'hweet, too—then get your ass back here quick."

"I'll send her back first thing." Sam handed him his coat. "Thanks, kiddo." He rubbed his ward's skullbone. "Take care of Gina for me, huh?"

"Sure thing, McGill!"

Walking Mule would not release Feighan's wrist. "It's suicide, McGill. What good can you do against that mob?"

"More than you think." He bared his teeth in a savage grin. "And a helluva lot more than *they* think. I still owe 'em for Sree?sree?sree?."

"You're too worn out!" Angry, now, he stood nose to nose with Feighan and punctuated his objections with sharp finger jabs to Feighan's chest. "If you were fresh, yeah, maybe. *Maybe* you could keep Flingin' 'em away before they slashed you to ribbons, till they finally got tired and went home. Maybe. But—"

He grabbed the Director's burly shoulders and held the man at arms' length. "Walking Mule, I haven't got time for this. Williams is trying to whip up a riot, and if I get there too late, Gina—" He flinched from the thought. "Trust me. I know what I'm doing."

Walking Mule nodded slowly. "All right. You're a big boy, you're supposed to be able to take care of yourself. But get Gina out of there before you try anything heroic."

"Right. Lu'reeng, a clear spot near the hospital?" He stepped back, so the use of his Talent would not trigger Walking Mule's. "Believe it or not, I have a plan."

The plan did not call for sinking waist deep in a pile of cold feathers immediately upon materialization. *God, am I tired*.

I thought it was dirty snow. Worse, he had completely blown the angle: The hospital tent blocked his view of Williams and Quandala. And what he could not see, he could not Fling.

Mobs break up easily when their leaders fall silent, and Feighan had planned to snatch Williams and Quandala away before the impostor could whip his congregation into full frenzy. It would be only fitting to drop them right into the hands of Hub Security.

But now— He struggled through the feathers. Down at foot level they were warm, and in some places hot. Even in this outdoor icebox, bacterial processes continued. McGill Feighan was wading in a giant compost pile. The awareness nauseated him.

The stink of death and corruption welled up from underneath, and wafted to him on the frigid winds blowing past the morgue. He paused, wrapped a handkerchief around his face to screen out dust and feathers, and breathed through his mouth. He hoped he could keep from getting sick.

Gusts caught the feathers he stirred up and tossed them high. It was like trudging through a blizzard. *Hell, this isn't a pile, it's a pool!* It crossed his mind that he was so tired he might not be able to fight his way to clear ground. He forced down panic.

Ernest Williams' voice bawled through a bullhorn: "Not only does this violate the teachings, it is an abomination in the sight of the Lord! It is a repudiation of God's Will! It is a denial of the benevolence of the Great Winged Retz-glaran!"

Even as he worked his way to freedom, Feighan had time to ponder the oddness of Williams' delivering his call to battle in English. Who was going to understand him?

Another bullhorn crackled; Rehmal song at a hundred decibels or better filled the air for miles around. Glumly, Feighan assumed that Williams had brought a translator. He could only hope that he had not had time to incite the mob to total madness. He sneezed, and pushed on.

Birdsong blared from a third bullhorn, this one nearer by.

Feighan began to revise his plan. He would find Maccari and get her to safety first, before he attempted to deal with Williams and Quandala. If the mob decided to attack, it would reach the tent in seconds.

The feathers sloped away to bare ground. He moved more easily, now, hurried around the corner of the tent—and stopped dead. Antarctic gales clawed at his coat.

Th'hweet stood ten meters away, holding the third bullhorn. At his side stood a bedraggled female. Three ice-blue feathers made up her entire crest. Great patches had fallen from her pumpkin-orange plumage. She shivered in the wind.

Drudru! Ignoring, for an instant, the mob he was about to confront, Feighan grinned with relief. *She got here in time!*

At a chirp from Th'hweet, Drudru spread her wings wide before the crowd. New feathers had already begun to fill in the bare patches.

As she pirouetted, tail high, a murmur ran through the massed Rehmal. And Feighan caught sight of Maccari. "Gina!"

The Minder came over to him, arms extended. "Isn't it wonderful?"

"Wonderful?" Feighan caught her hands and squeezed them. "I'm going to Fling you back to the warehouse—"

"No, there's no danger here, not now."

"Gina, there's a mob—"

"Hush." She tapped her temple knowingly. "I'm sensing their mood right now. And I tell you, McGill, they're not working themselves up for an attack on Th'hweet, they're—" From the midst of the winged horde came a shrill screech. Maccari gasped; her eyelids popped all the way open.

"What?" he said urgently.

"Anger!" She put her hand on her throat. "All of a sudden, like somebody lit a match, this hot flame of *anger* just raced through them."

"See?" He slid his arm around her shoulders. "Come on, grab your coat and I'll Fling you back."

"No, no, the anger's at *them.*" She bowed her head and covered her eyes with her hand. "I think— I'm not sure, I don't know Rehmal mental idioms well enough, but I think Th'hweet just convinced them that Williams has been lying to them all along." She took a frightened breath. "And they're *mad,* McGill. All of them."

"At us?"

"No, no, at—" A scream ripped from human lungs to rise above Th'hweet's song. Maccari held up a hand. She paled, and swayed as she stood. For a few seconds she seemed paralyzed. "Save them!"

He spun, and raced toward the source of the commotion.

An automatic pistol chattered madly. Dust kicked up just behind his right foot. Rehmal shrieked in anguish. He caught a brief glimpse of a bloody-faced Williams lashing out with one hand while trying to push Quandala up the ladder with the other. Before he could Fling them to safety, dozens— then hundreds—then thousands of angry Rehmal dropped on them from the sky.

He stopped. He visualized a ball of air nine meters in diameter, floating perhaps a meter off the ground. Concentrating, he triggered his Talent—reached into the Energy Dimension to spin the globe on its vertical axis with an angular momentum of two hundred kilometers an hour— aimed it at the heart of the mob—and let it rip.

It struck like a cyclone. A storm of feathers burst into the air. Then followed the Rehmal, too light, too weak, to resist such a mighty wind. They hurtled outward like shrapnel from a bomb, squawking their outrage, tumbling head over tail while they spread their wings and fought for balance. The helijet rocked back and forth, then steadied.

Feighan ran to the base of the ladder.

Ringed by dead Rehmal, Williams and Quandala lay in

a gory huddle. Talons had torn away their clothing, sliced through every square centimeter of skin.

Clenching his jaw, he lifted Williams off Quandala as gently as he could, and rolled the man on his back. Two bloody, eyeless sockets stared up at him.

"Oh sweet Jesus!" He turned his head, but not quickly enough. Impelled by horror, his gaze had run up and down both corpses.

The bodies had no fingers. Or ears. Or noses. Or throats.

He staggered away.

"McGill—"

He raised his encarmined hands to keep Maccari from coming any closer. "Don't look—they're dead."

Maccari wrapped her arms around his waist and buried her face in his shoulder. "I know," she whispered.

He looked down. She was crying. "But they were Williams' people!" he said. "What happened?"

"They made a mistake. A bad one." Maccari's voice nearly broke. She sniffed, and went on. "Williams, Quandala, they thought they could fool the Rehmal forever. But these aren't primitives—they're intellectually sophisticated. They can see Th'hweet is curing the sick. They *like* people who cure the sick." Tears spilled down her cheeks; she sobbed.

"Hey, easy." He took her into his arms.

"McGill, they were so *mad* when they discovered they'd been lied to. They'd trusted Williams and Quandala, and when they found out that those two had actually spread the plague, they—" She buried her face in his jacket.

He hugged her hard. "It's okay, Gina. It's okay."

"McGill—" She trembled uncontrollably. "At the end, oh god, at the end, McGill, I could feel everything Celeste Quandala felt—and it hurt so bad . . ."

Tenderly, silently, he held her close.

No one else objected to Th'hweet's operations. In the following days, hundreds of millions of Rehmal swooped by to pick up their medication and wheel north.

The flocks filled the entire sky. Two flight paths led south, one over the western Cliffs, the other over the eastern. At the glacier's edge they banked, the western group to the left and the eastern to the right, and merged into one solid stream over the very source of The River. Completing their loops, they headed north to follow the bed of The River through the twelve hundred kilometers of rock-walled twists and turns they called The Gorges.

So many made the journey that they flew at a dozen different altitudes, each spaced a safe ten meters from the layer above or below it.

So many celebrated Festival that The Cliffs, The Gorges, and The River lay in twilight shadow for days.

And of all those who passed, not one was very large, and golden. Not one proclaimed itself Great Winged Retzglaran. Not one came to find McGill Feighan, and thank him.

Heart heavy, he turned to Th'hweet. "I guess you're set now."

"I would presume so. The epidemic is checked; The Organization, thwarted." The epidemiologist stood on one leg and preened the feathers of its other thigh. "My people have survived, and a great deal of the credit belongs to you, Mr. Feighan." He cocked his head, and eyed Feighan closely. "But you seem somehow disappointed. Why?"

"Well, I'm not, really, but—"

"He thought he was gonna get to meet the Far Being," said Sam.

Drudru clacked her beak warningly. "Sam!"

He hung his head. "I'm sorry."

Th'hweet splayed his talons and admired them. "You truly thought so?"

Feighan shrugged to conceal his embarrassment. A certain big-mouthed little kid was going to discover that other people could use Drudru's teaching methods...

"Hey. I'd heard the legends, and . . . and I didn't *expect* to meet the Far Being, but you know, it would have been nice, I mean if It had visited this year, that is, I . . ." He shrugged again. "It just would have been nice, that's all."

Th'hweet clacked its beak, then extended a violet wing and stroked Feighan's shoulder with its tip. "I *thought* you lacked understanding."

The Flinger bristled. "What's that supposed to mean, huh?"

"Oh, I am sorry. No insult intended, I assure you, Mr. Feighan. I merely meant to say that it was perfectly clear, to me at least, that you never did realize the reason for your specific presence."

"To Fling for you, of course," he said in confusion.

"No, Mr. Feighan. Any Flinger could have done that. But you, sir, you were here precisely because the Great Winged Retzglaran could not be. It needed a trusted associate. Now, if you'll excuse me—" It bowed to the four of them, then flapped its wings and leaped into the air.

Feighan stood open-mouthed for a long moment. "Did Th'hweet say what I thought he said?"

Maccari took his hand. "Yes, McGill. We all heard him."

"That's right, boy," said Walking Mule. "Seems like you've just been promoted from 'hapless pawn' to 'trusted associate.'"

Sam tugged his sleeve. "Now can we go home, McGill?"

He nodded. A warm glow spread through every part of him. "Sure. Yeah. Let's go."

Home in their New York penthouse, exhausted, they collapsed into bed scant seconds before they fell asleep.

And Feighan dreamed again. Again a familiar, long-lost voice echoed through his mind. This time, though, a small Rehmal spoke. "Thank you," it said. Dingy grey, half its feathers lost to the disease, it looked the most insignificant representative of its race possible.

But it wasn't.